MOUNTAINS OF LOVE

Donna Winters

Bigwater Publishing LLC

GreatLakesRomances.com

New Mexico

To all the women who served as Harvey Girls,
thank you for inspiring me to write this story!

Acknowledgments

I would like to thank Mary Hahn and Pat Carter for reading the first draft and making valuable suggestions.

CONTENTS

CHAPTER 1

Fayette, Upper Michigan
Saturday, July 1, 1893

"Uncle James, I can hardly believe it! We're on our way to the World's Fair! We're *really* on our way!" Cedena Rossier stood at the rail of the pleasure yacht Uncle James and Aunt Nancy had chartered for their trip from Chicago and back. Fayette's Snail Shell Harbor, lined with nine hundred feet of mostly empty docks since the iron furnaces had shut down two years ago, receded behind her in the grayness of early morning. A cool breeze wafted across the water, delivering the comforting scent of Uncle James's cherry pipe tobacco. Below, the humming steam engine sent vibrations through her feet and up her calves.

For years, Cedena had dreamed of escaping Michigan's Upper Peninsula, whether temporarily or permanently, until twenty-three years of her life had passed into history. Today, she was making one small step toward her quest for a measure of independence.

Yes, she would be surrounded by relatives on this trip, including her overbearing widowed mother, but at least this was a start.

Too bad Father and her twin brother, David, weren't alive. They would have loved to see the Fair. Why'd they have to disappear on the lake in a storm two years ago? And why hadn't the wreckage of their fishing boat or their bodies ever washed up on shore? They simply vanished during one of the worst storms of 1891. The funeral held months later had offered no closure. Cedena often had dreams of David, her best friend, confidant, and supporter, especially when Mother became difficult. Last night, Cedena had dreamed that David was going on this trip to the Fair. And then she awoke to the disappointment that it had only been a dream.

Uncle James stepped closer, wrapped his arm about Cedena's waist, and gave a squeeze. "Tell me, Cedena. What do you want to see first at the Fair?"

She gazed up into his mustached face, which was lit by the sparkle in his blue eyes. Thanks to some bullying, he and Aunt Nancy had convinced Mother to accept their invitation to come to the World's Columbian Exposition as their guests.

"What I want to see first is your display. Paxton Pharmaceuticals sounds so important."

"And after that?"

She leaned close. "Don't tell Mother, but I really want to see the Midway Plaisance from one end to the other— the Ferris wheel, Cairo Street with the camel rides, the tethered balloon ascensions, and all the villages built by different countries."

"Now *that* will be a challenge, but there's always hope, don't you think?" said Uncle James, grinning.

Cedena leaned back, catching a glimpse of the straw boater Uncle James was wearing. There, tucked behind the black grosgrain hatband was the green feather he'd put there years ago to distinguish his hat from similar ones. She'd have thought he'd have refurbished the hat with a new band or at the very least replaced the old green feather with a fresh one for this trip, but no. Some things never change. And on such a big venture without Father or David, that brought comfort.

CHAPTER 2

The Fair, Chicago
Monday, July 3, 1893

Matthew Waren stepped back from the display of Paxton Pharmaceuticals at the World's Columbian Exposition and studied it with a critical eye. The small brown bottles of essential oils contrasted nicely with the yellow satin covering the round turntable, but the even distance between them had been disturbed by visitors who had picked them up and carelessly replaced them. Oh, well. At least none had disappeared yet this morning. Matthew quickly positioned the bottles equidistant from one another and moved on to the next section.

The elixir bottles on stepped shelves of baby blue velvet had fared a little better with only a few adjustments necessary. But the powders and pills on the tiered round stands covered in burgundy satin appeared a bit spare. He quickly restored the missing items from the inventory kept beneath the display.

Matthew moved on to his favorite products—costly perfumes, colognes, toilet waters, and bath powders. The various items, inaccessible to casual passersby, maintained their neat arrangement. Cut crystal bottles of perfumes—pieces of art, really—were the showpieces. Yet the display seemed a bit hard edged. Perhaps a narrow length of pastel silk draped among the various scents would do wonders. Such an item might be available from the silk textile display only a short distance away. Perhaps he'd go there later.

To the right of the glass cabinet, a gold tray of business cards and a silver caddy of fliers offered potential customers necessary contact and product information, but both needed replenishing. Matthew grabbed a handful of each from boxes beneath the display. While resupplying the fliers and cards, he remembered that he needed to get out the perfume testers and set them atop the glass cabinet. As he did, he caught sight of his boss approaching with his wife. Another lady and a young woman were with them. They had to be Mrs. Rossier and her daughter Cedena. He'd heard about the family for years. Too bad Mrs. Rossier's husband and son had been lost on Lake Michigan two years back. Mrs. Paxton had made no secret of the hardship it had caused and how Mr. Paxton sent Mrs. Rossier money for rent each month.

Matthew focused on Cedena. Mr. Paxton had said this would be her first trip away from Upper Michigan, her first time in Chicago. She was twenty-three, unmarried. He'd said that with a wink.

Beneath a white straw hat, Cedena's face beamed. She was evidently caught up in "Fair Fever" as many first-day fair-goers were. But more than a look of excitement was on her attractive face. Her full lips curved in a smile bordering on mischievous, her wide-set eyes echoed the honey brown of her upswept hair, and the pink in her cheeks matched the silk ribbon about her neck.

Matthew chided himself for staring, stepped around from behind the display, and shifted his focus to his employer. Mr. Paxton's bushy silver mustache was perfectly trimmed, as usual, but his blue eyes, which had formerly appeared tired, had a renewed liveliness. The trip north must have done him good.

Mrs. Paxton looked rested, too. The normally pinched look to her mouth had broadened into a friendly smile, and the casual middy-style outfit she wore made her look younger than her fifty-one years.

"Welcome back, Mr. and Mrs. Paxton! How was your trip?"

"Wonderful!" Mr. Paxton gave a cursory inspection of the perfume case and shifted his gaze back to Matthew. "And how was your week? Get some new leads, did you?"

"I have several new leads, and they look promising, sir."

"Excellent! Fill me in on the details later, won't you? Right now, I'd like you to meet my wife's family."

As his boss rattled off the names, Cedena offered her hand. For a moment, Matthew was tempted to kiss it, but instead, he grasped it firmly and shook it rapidly as her white lilac perfume wafted up. "Pleased to meet you, Miss Rossier. I pray you'll enjoy your days at the Fair."

She offered a grin that produced the most alluring dimples he'd ever seen. "I plan to, Mr. Waren. But first, you'll have to stop working my arm as if it were the handle to a well pump badly in need of priming, eh?"

"Great Scott! So sorry!" Matthew released her as heat surged to his cheeks.

Mr. Paxton rested his hand on Matthew's shoulder. "Now that you've met Nancy's kin, tell them about our products, won't you?"

"Yes, sir." Matthew drew a quick breath and stepped behind the counter. His description of the essential oils' potency, the powders and pills' purity, and the elixirs' effectiveness rolled off his tongue. All the while, his mental focus remained on Cedena. Conscious not to stare at her, he nevertheless delivered his pitch as if she were his only audience. Suddenly, it was important to make a good enough impression for her to see him as more than just her uncle's employee.

Matthew moved on to the perfume case. "Only the finest fragrances are distributed by Paxton Pharmaceuticals. Many of them are imported from France where the climate produces an abundance of flower petals in a wide variety of scents. Rose perfume, cologne, and toilet water are among the most costly to manufacture, requiring sixty roses to produce one tiny drop of rose oil." He picked up a tester and spritzed the air with rose perfume.

Cedena sniffed. "Isn't that heavenly, Mother?"

Mrs. Rossier smiled, producing dimples that matched her daughter's. The effect softened the severe manner in which her coffee hair, tinged with silver, was pulled back by a tortoise shell comb and twisted into a tight bun. "I'd liken this scent to a rose garden in a bottle, and a fancy one, at that." Her gaze shifted to take in her sister and brother-in-law. "We came past some beautiful yard goods on our way here. I'd like to go back there."

The group began to move off.

Matthew quickly stepped from behind the toiletries case and tapped Cedena on the shoulder. "Before you go, I simply must ask your opinion on something."

She offered a guarded smile. "I have to warn you that it will be completely honest and perhaps a waste of your time."

He grinned. "I'll risk it. I'm wondering about this display." He indicated the glass cabinet. "Do you think a narrow length of pastel silk woven among the products would improve its appearance? Make it more appealing to the ladies?"

Cedena rested her chin in her hand as she studied the arrangement. A moment later, her gaze met his. "There's only one way to find out." In a flash, she untied her ribbon, stepped behind the glass case, and began carefully laying the fabric between the bottles and powders.

When she had finished, she came around front and assessed the change. "I'm not sure it's any improvement. My ribbon is wrinkled where it was tied in a bow, and that ruins the effect." She focused on Matthew. "I have an idea, though. Get some silk that is nicely pressed and work it among the items like I did. Then add some silk flowers to match the scents—violets, roses, crab apple, and heliotrope."

"Great Scott! You've come up with a brilliant plan! Thank you so much for your help!"

Cedena gave a nod and gazed off in the distance. "Now where have my folks gone? I'd better catch up with them or risk being separated from them for the entire day."

Matthew rocked up on his toes. "I can see them at the textile display. Go straight down this aisle. And if you ever get lost, come back here."

"Thanks!" Cedena stepped off.

"Wait! Don't forget your ribbon!"

She hurried back, tied it about her neck, and headed briskly toward the textile display.

When she disappeared into the crowd, Matthew drew a deep breath. But that wasn't enough to help him clear thoughts of Cedena Rossier from his mind and focus again on the display. This was dangerous. His history with the gentler sex was anything but successful. His last attempt at wooing had ended when Lydia Schuster had publicly spurned him at the Firemen's Ball. In the year since, he'd resigned himself to a life of celibacy. Now that decision was being tested.

A few minutes later, Cedena, her face aglow, returned with her uncle.

"If you want to go in search of a length of silk, Uncle James says he'll tend to the display. The lady at the textiles booth up yonder says they have nothing they can loan or sell, but she highly recommended the bazaar at the Chinese Village on the Midway Plaisance. You and I should go there now, eh?"

Mr. Paxton stepped behind the display and nudged Matthew toward his niece. "You and Cedena have a good time. And here…." He reached into his pocket, coming up with several coins that he pressed into Matthew's palm. "Won't you treat Cedena to lunch? And have her back here by two o'clock so she can tour the Transportation Building with her mother and my wife."

"Yes, sir. And thank you, sir."

His boss's bushy silver mustache couldn't hide his grin.

Matthew pulled his straw boater from a box beneath the display. Cedena had already headed at a brisk clip out the north exit a few feet away. Matthew followed her out the door. Though he was a foot taller than her height of a little over five feet, he had difficulty keeping her white straw hat in sight as her slim form slipped past groups of tourists. He opened his stride, but she disappeared from view. His heart raced. Great Scott, he couldn't lose her. He just *couldn't*. What would his boss say? He broke into a jog, finding her just before the footbridge to Wooded Island. With a firm hand on her elbow, he turned her toward him.

"Miss Rossier, I'm getting the impression you don't like me. In fact, I think you're trying to run away from me."

She gazed up at him with an impish smile. "I'm sorry, Mr. Waren. I guess my feet just have a mind of their own, and they are thinking that time's a-wasting. I've got but two weeks to see the Fair, and we both know that is hardly enough. So I would like you a whole lot more if you would pick up the pace." She released his grip and stepped onto the footbridge.

Matthew grasped Cedena's hand and placed it in the crook of his elbow, locking it there with his hand over hers. When she tried to pull free, he tightened his grasp, stopped dead, and turned to face her. Her topaz eyes sparked.

He bent close, his nose a mere two inches from her small, pert one. "Miss Rossier, I will like *you* a whole lot more if you stay close. Otherwise, I will toss you over my shoulder, carry you back to your mother, and go alone to find the silk."

She sniggered. "You wouldn't dare!"

He narrowed his brows. "Try me."

She drew a quick breath and let it out slowly, its sweetness belying her stubbornness. "I believe the Midway Plaisance is down that-a-way." She jerked her head to the east. "Would you be so kind as to escort me there?"

"It would be my pleasure." He prayed the words would prove true.

CHAPTER 3

Cedena tried to hurry Matthew along, but it was like dragging an anchor. Why couldn't a man with such long, skinny legs, move faster? If only her twin brother David were alive, they would be setting a much brisker pace. He had loved new adventures and would have been fascinated by the Fair.

Without a word, Cedena and Matthew stepped off the footbridge onto Wooded Island. Structures topped with graceful tile roofs lined their path.

"What are those buildings for?" Cedena pointed with her free hand. "I've never seen beams carved on the ends with lion heads. You sure don't see that on the log cabins in the Upper Peninsula."

"Nor in Kansas City. They are copies of the Japanese temples and palaces. I hear they are very beautiful inside. Would you like to see?"

Cedena shook her head. "We'd better keep going. The Chinese Village is almost a mile away—down at the far end of the Midway, from what the textile lady said. It will take us the better part of a half-hour just to get there, let alone come back—if you don't dawdle."

"Dawdle?" Matthew's dark brows met above his dove gray eyes.

"No offense, Mr. Waren, but your pace hasn't exactly been brisk. If you didn't have me tethered to your right arm, I guarantee I'd make it to the other end of the Midway ahead of you in a walking race."

"Not possible."

"Let go of me, and I'll prove it." She tried to free her hand, but he tightened his grip.

"Nothing doing, Miss Rossier. I'm responsible to get you safely back to the Manufactures Building by two o'clock. I'm not going to risk losing you in the crowd. Besides, you'd never beat me in a walking race. I'm a competitive wheelman, the fastest in the Fairmount Cycling Club. My legs are in better shape, and my stride is much longer than yours. I'd beat you by half a mile. But we're not going to race, and that's final."

Cedena sighed. Maybe Matthew *was* in good shape, but he certainly wasn't any fun.

He led her off the other side of the island between the Woman's Building and the Children's Building. She promised herself to check those out later.

The sunshine dimmed. Cedena gazed skyward. A wall of clouds was moving in, the kind that said rain would arrive sometime in the next several hours. Hopefully, it would hold off until they were back in the Manufactures Building.

Now that they were entering the Midway, the Chinese Village was only about twenty minutes away. Both sides of the walkway were lined with shrubs, trees, and gardens abundant with poppies, jasmine, roses, and violets. The unavoidable fragrance of so many blossoms made Cedena sneeze.

"Gesundheit, Miss Rossier."

Cedena pulled her hanky out and held it to her nose until the urge to sneeze again had passed. "Sorry, Mr. Waren. Guess I'm not used to so many flowers all in one place. We're lucky to get our roses to bloom by July in the Upper Peninsula."

Matthew picked his pace up a tad until they were past the nursery.

In the far distance, a giant wheel rose toward the gray heavens. "Have you ridden the Ferris wheel yet, Mr. Waren?"

"Not yet."

"Aunt Nancy and Uncle James rode it before they came north. Said it was the most marvelous trick of engineering on earth and the view was indescribable. Want to go up?"

He glanced her way. "I thought you were in a hurry to get to the Chinese Village."

"Maybe after we do that, we can ride the wheel."

"I'd prefer to go up in the tethered balloon, myself, but it costs two dollars. I haven't decided whether it's worth the money."

"How much money did my uncle give you?"

Matthew cast a dark look her way.

"You're scowling at me as if it's none of my business about the money, but it *is* my business. I only asked because if he gave you enough to buy the silk and lunch, you might have enough for a balloon ticket. We could buy the silk, skip lunch, and go up in the balloon instead. I have money to pay my own way."

"But *should* you? You haven't been at the Fair for even one hour yet, and already you're eager to spend a small fortune. Shouldn't you hang on to your money for a while? There is so much else to see, so many other things you may wish to spend your money on."

Cedena grinned. "You have a good point, but I'm not convinced. As I said, this place is too big to see everything in two weeks, *unless* I go up in a balloon. Then I could see it all in just a few minutes."

"If a cursory view would satisfy, I'd agree with your way of thinking, but the real Fair experience is on the ground, inside the various buildings with all their exhibits. Let's take it one thing at a time. Chinese silk and lunch today, and the afternoon with your folks at the Transportation Building. A ride on the Ferris wheel or up in a balloon must wait until later."

"If I may ask, Mr. Waren, how much of the Fair have you seen since you arrived to take charge of my uncle's display?"

"Not much, I'm sorry to say. I got here just a day before your uncle left for Upper Michigan, and I've been tending his display every day and evening since."

"Then you deserve a chance to look around . . . from a balloon, maybe?" She gazed up at him with the most charming smile she could muster.

He chuckled. "You are incorrigible, Miss Rossier. But I'm not going to change my mind."

She pressed her lower lip forward in a pout. "You're no fun, Mr. Waren, but you do have a penchant for good judgment, I'll grant you that. So as you say, Chinese silk, lunch, then back to meet up with my relatives for a tour of the Transportation Building. Now, do you think you could let go of me? I'm feeling a crick in my arm."

"Will you promise not to run off?"

"On a stack of Bibles, if you had one."

He gave her a steely look and then removed his hand from atop hers.

She slipped her hand free from his elbow and shook her arm as if to loosen the muscles, though they were not at all tight. At least she was no longer tethered. And just to her right was Cairo Street, the most interesting place on the Midway Plaisance, according to Uncle James. He'd said the camel rides were quite entertaining, and a woman was trying to mount a kneeling camel at this very moment.

Matthew be dashed. Cedena wasn't about to miss this. Her feet made double time toward the camel.

In a flash Matthew's hand grabbed hers and again jailed it inside his elbow as he led her away. When they had returned to the center of the Midway, he paused to face her, his cool gray eyes sparking. "Miss Rossier, I am about at my wit's end with you." He spoke through clenched teeth. "You promised not to run off. You even said you'd swear on a stack of Bibles. Yet less than a minute later, off you went. What do you have to say for yourself?"

"Naughty, naughty, naughty. I'm sorry, Mr. Waren. Can you forgive me?"

Thunder roared. The smell of rain was in the air. Cedena gazed off to the west. A black line of clouds stretched across the heavens, producing a narrow tail as it approached. A fierce gust of wind whipped at Cedena's hat and skirt, and tore Matthew's boater off his head. He took off after it like a shot.

CHAPTER 4

Matthew caught up with his hat several yards away. With one hand on her hat, and the other lifting her skirt, Cedena hurried toward him.

Holding his hat on his head, Matthew wrapped his arm firmly about her waist. "Let's find shelter."

He guided her past the Algerian and Tunisian camps toward a wooden awning in front of the Hawaiian volcano exhibit. Several others joined them there as rain pelted down, driven by a ferocious wind. Anything not tied down took flight. Glass crashed to the ground. Hats, scatter rugs, small potted plants, and loose paper flew in drunken paths down the walkway. The boards overhead creaked. The iron poles supporting them began to bend.

Cedena's heart raced. *God, help us!*

A roar like a train approached. Wind lifted the wooden awning from its bent poles and sent it tumbling and crashing to the ground, splinters flying. Women screamed. Men shouted epithets.

Matthew crushed Cedena against his rock solid chest, his hand against the back of her head as she buried her face in his jacket. Buckets of rainwater poured down. Within a few moments, Cedena was soaked to the skin. The scent of Matthew's wet linen suit mingled with that of her saturated cotton shirtwaist. A shiver ran through her.

The rain ceased and suddenly all was calm. Cedena peeked out at the sky. No longer was the black cloud visible. An eerie green color dominated the heavens. Water dripped from the roof of the Hawaiian building and splashed into puddles.

Matthew tipped her chin toward him, his gaze steady, confident. "It's all right, Miss Rossier. The storm is over."

Cedena took a deep breath. "I've seen many a storm roll in off Lake Michigan at the upper end, but nothing like this. Thanks for keeping me safe." She stepped free of Matthew's embrace and assessed her costume. "This is really something, eh? I'm wetter than a drowned rat."

The sun began to shine. Matthew's wet pants stuck to his legs, revealing an outline of muscular thighs and calves. Cedena could imagine him riding in a cycle race and easily wheeling past his opponents. He tried to shake water from his slacks with little success and then offered her a hint of a smile.

"I guess we'll just have to wait for the sunshine to dry us out."

Cedena nodded. Her thoughts skipping ahead, she gazed down the Midway to the west. "I wonder if the Chinese bazaar is in operation, or if they got blown apart and flooded."

Matthew held out his arm. "Let's go see."

As they approached the Chinese Village, their attention was drawn to the Captive Balloon Park next door. The gate to the park stood wide open, no one collecting the twenty-five cents admission as stated on their sign. Inside, decorative fountains and rustic benches had been overturned, flowerbeds were decimated, and the huge, colorful silk balloon rested in shambles on the ground, its cable and miles of thick cords heaped in a tangled mess. Half-a-dozen men were trying to make order out of the chaos. One of them was calling out instructions.

Cedena pointed. "Looks to me like they could use some help."

"I agree." Matthew led her toward the man who appeared to be in charge. "Sir, would you like some extra hands to help you untangle?"

The stocky fellow turned, his gaze taking in Matthew and then Cedena. "You two volunteerin'?"

Cedena offered a quick smile. "Won't cost you a cent."

"Great! First, we got to get the balloon free of her lines. Go on over there," he pointed to the west side of the disaster, "and be gentle with the silk. It's not as strong when it's wet."

"Yes, sir!"

Matthew shed his pinstriped chestnut jacket, laid it over a bench to dry in the sun, and rolled up his shirtsleeves. Cedena pushed up the sleeves of her shirtwaist and worked side by side with him to cautiously free the silk from the coils and cables. One of the workmen made his way toward them as he coiled a line—a short, fleshy fellow wearing a flat cap. When he was about a yard away, he spoke to Cedena in a low, gravelly tone.

"This ain't no work for a female. What's the matter with that man o' yours, anyway? He's acting the maggot, lettin' ye tend to this mess!"

Matthew dropped what he was doing and stepped face to face with the man, their noses inches apart. "Did you call me a maggot?"

Before the workman could answer, Cedena sandwiched herself between the men. The insulting fellow's foul odor assaulted her as she pinned her gaze on him. "Sir, Mr. Waren is no maggot. He's intelligent enough to know that where I come from in the Upper Peninsula, this is exactly the kind of work we women do, helping our fishermen untangle their nets. Now let's get back to work, eh? Before your boss comes over here."

No sooner had she spoken those words than the boss man called out from his position several yards away. "What's going on over there? You got a problem, Paddy?"

"No, sir. No problem." The disagreeable man backed away.

Cedena and Matthew returned to their task. As Cedena carefully folded the fabric, she couldn't help thinking how beautiful a piece of this silk would be in her uncle's display case once it was washed and pressed. She prayed the Chinese bazaar would have what was needed.

The process of salvaging the balloon was slower and more tedious than Cedena had anticipated. She wasn't sure how long they'd been working when they finally finished rolling the balloon into a wet, muddy pile. At least the sun had been shining the whole time and had dried her clothing.

The boss man came over. "Thanks, you two. Now, you'd better go and get lunch. But first, I've got something for you." He reached into his pocket and pulled out two tickets. "When we get back up and running, you are each entitled to a free ride." He placed a ticket in each of their hands.

Cedena's heart leaped for joy and then plummeted to her feet. "Thank you, sir. But when will you be able to fly the balloon again? I'm only staying until the end of next week."

"Don't you worry, miss. We'll be back in the air tomorrow with our smaller balloon. Or you can hold off a few days to see if the bigger one is flying before you leave for home."

Cedena turned to Matthew, who was grinning at her. "Now we've got no reason not to go up in the balloon, eh?"

"Right! Are you hungry? I could do with some lunch. I'll fetch my jacket," he said, motioning to where he had left it on a bench, "and then we'll go and find something to eat."

Cedena lowered her gaze. Her shirtwaist and skirt were streaked with mud, as were Matthew's white shirt and pinstriped pants. "I don't think any restaurant will let us in the way we look."

Matthew assessed their soiled clothing and then offered an encouraging smile. "I saw some washrooms near the Ferris wheel. We'll go there first and do what we can to clean up. Then we'll find a café. We'll take seats before anyone notices the dirt."

When he'd retrieved his jacket from the bench where he'd left it, Matthew offered his arm. "I hear the Chinese café is quite good. Both American and Chinese food is served, and better yet, it's close by. Are you willing to try it?"

Cedena nodded and placed her hand in his arm. Her first day at the Fair had turned into a much bigger adventure than she had expected, and it was only half over.

CHAPTER 5

As Matthew escorted Cedena toward the Manufactures Building a little before two o'clock that afternoon, he prayed her folks would not be terribly upset about the stains on her clothing. Their stop at the washrooms had helped with the worst of the dirt, but many smudges remained. Mr. Paxton would understand, but would his wife and Cedena's mother?

Matthew prayed, too, that the package of silk he carried under his arm would please his boss. It certainly was beautiful, but Mr. Paxton could be extremely particular where his displays were concerned.

Matthew opened the door and ushered Cedena inside. Her mother and Mrs. Paxton were chatting in front of the pharmaceutical display. His boss stood behind the counter.

Cedena slipped her hand from Matthew's arm and hurried toward her mother. "You wouldn't believe what happened to Mr. Waren and me! We got caught in that gale this morning."

Mrs. Rossier studied her daughter. "You look like a child who played in a mud puddle, I reckon."

"Like I said, we got caught in that gale. You should have seen us. We ran under the awning at the Hawaiian Volcano with a passel of other folks. Then the wind hit and tore it away from right over our heads! I was so scared that I thought we'd die! But Mr. Waren kept me safe. Where were you when the gale came through?"

"Right here in this building. We hardly knew about the storm."

Cedena continued. "So after the wind blew the roof away, buckets of rain came down and soaked us right through. When it was all over, we were going to go to the Chinese Village, but we noticed a mess at the Captive Balloon Park."

Mr. Paxton leaned across the counter. "The Captive Balloon Park is next door to the Chinese Village, isn't it?"

Cedena nodded to her uncle and focused again on her mother. "We asked them if they needed help. The huge silk balloon was in a soggy, muddy mess, all tangled up with the lines and cables that kept it tethered to the car and the ground. Good thing we helped them because look what I got." She reached into her pocket and held up her ticket. "A free ride in the Captive Balloon! It's worth two whole dollars! Mr. Waren got a ticket, too. We're going up tomorrow." She turned to Matthew. "Aren't we?"

Matthew nodded. For a young woman of twenty-three, Cedena Rossier had a delightfully childish enthusiasm about her.

Mrs. Paxton took a close look at Cedena's ticket and handed it back. "Where did you eat lunch?"

Mrs. Rossier scowled. "I reckon no reputable restaurant would seat you."

Matthew spoke up. "I thought the same, but we had no problem getting seating at the Chinese Café."

"I've heard the food there is quite good. What did you have?" Mrs. Paxton's gaze darted from Cedena to Matthew.

Matthew opened his mouth to reply, but Cedena answered before he could get a word out.

"I had ham and pineapple, and the best rice I've ever tasted. And afterward, I had *huamei*, a preserved plum that is one of their specialties. And Mr. Waren ate their corned beef, sliced tomatoes, and an éclair for dessert. But the best part was their Chinese tea. Mmm. It's the finest I've ever tasted." Her focus shifted from her aunt to her mother. "You'll have to buy some and take it home. Folks back in Fayette will really be impressed."

Mrs. Rossier shook her head. "I told you before we left home that I have no intention of stepping foot on the Midway Plaisance, let alone spending any of your uncle's hard-earned money there. And I wish you wouldn't go there, either. You should spend what time you have here in the fairgrounds proper, visiting the exhibits. But I reckon there's no stopping you, now that you have a free ticket for the balloon ascension."

"Think of it this way, Mother: I'll see the entire Fair from a new perspective."

"Speaking of a new perspective," Mr. Paxton gestured toward the perfume case, "what about this? You found what you were looking for, didn't you?"

Matthew held out the brown paper package he'd been carrying. "Right here, sir. Your niece picked out what she thought would look best. I hope you approve."

"May I see that, please?" Mrs. Paxton held out her hand and Matthew passed her the silk. She very carefully slid off the string and folded back the brown paper. "How gorgeous!" She held up the robin's egg blue silk in one hand and the crab apple blossom, heliotrope blossom, violet, and rose in the other. "With these, the perfume display will look twice as attractive to women, don't you think, James?"

"Yes, dear. You'll put them in the display case before you go off for the afternoon tour, won't you? If I do it, I know you'll come back and rearrange it later." He winked.

His wife grinned and carefully draped the delicate fabric among the merchandise, then added the flowers beside their matching perfumes.

Mrs. Rossier studied the new look. "I reckon that will please the womenfolk." Her focus switched abruptly to her sister. "Now, are we ready to tour the Transportation Building? We'd best get moving. Come along, Nancy, Cedena." She started down the aisle toward the west exit. Her sister followed.

As Cedena stepped away, she turned to Matthew. "See you tomorrow for that balloon ride, eh? And thanks for taking me to the Midway and buying lunch. It's an experience I'll never forget!"

"You're welcome. Now be sure and take a good look at the cycle display in the Transportation Building. I hear it's quite amazing."

She nodded and hurried after her mother and aunt.

Mr. Paxton nudged Matthew. "Son, take the afternoon off and tour the Transportation Building with the ladies. You're keen to see it, aren't you?"

"Yes, sir, but maybe *you* should go with them while I take the afternoon shift here."

His boss's gaze momentarily slipped down to Matthew's smudged pants and rose again. "Go. Have a good time. Come back here this evening and help me decorate for tomorrow's Fourth of July celebration."

"Great Scott! I'd forgotten that we need to decorate. I'll be back." As Matthew hurried to catch up with the others, he was fairly certain his boss had given him the time off because of his muddy appearance. Mr. Paxton, who always dressed impeccably, likely didn't want him representing Paxton Pharmaceuticals looking the way he did right now.

Muddiness aside, Matthew wondered which would hold more fascination this afternoon: the cycle display in the Transportation Building or Miss Cedena Rossier.

CHAPTER 6

That evening, Matthew worked long into the night to help his boss hang a red, white, and blue bunting on a frame they constructed above their display. Back in his room at the boarding house, Matthew was so tired he was tempted to drop onto his bed with his clothes on. The hard work had paid off, though. Mr. Paxton was quite satisfied with their Fourth of July preparation. And tomorrow was certain to see record crowds at the Fair.

As Matthew undressed and pulled on his nightshirt, thoughts of the patriotic display slipped from his mind, replaced by the memory of Miss Cedena Rossier's beaming smile and their delightful afternoon in the Transportation Building. Cedena had been remarkably obedient under the watchful eye of her mother, not one bit impulsive, and she'd even shown interest in the cycle display and asked intelligent questions. Or maybe she was just being polite. As Matthew drifted off to sleep, he couldn't help wondering, *Is she thinking of me tonight as I am of her?*

~*~*~

The following morning, Matthew arrived at the pharmaceutical display bright and early and dressed immaculately. Mr. Paxton was already there, pulling drapes off the display cases and storing them beneath the cabinets. It was impossible to beat him to work, though Matthew had tried on many occasions.

"Good morning, Matthew! Sleep well?"

"Yes, sir." Matthew stepped behind the display. The holders for business cards and promotional literature were empty. He pulled the needed items from boxes below the display.

Mr. Paxton worked alongside him, wiping fingerprints from the glass perfume case. He pulled out the testers and set them on top. With a twinkle in his eye, he squeezed the rose perfume's bulb and inhaled its delicate fragrance. "Mighty fine, don't you agree, Matthew?"

"Yes, sir, the best."

His boss set the tester alongside the others and turned to him. "I know you and Cedena are planning to take your balloon ride today. I'd suggest going as soon as Mrs. Paxton and the Rossiers arrive, while the wind is still calm. The weather might change by afternoon. Lake Michigan is rather unpredictable, don't you know? Aside from that, a huge crowd is expected later today for the Independence Day celebrations."

"Yes, sir. I'll work the display this afternoon and evening. It will give you some time with your relatives and the opportunity to watch the fireworks over the lake."

Mr. Paxton's mustache twitched. "Perhaps. We'll see what plans Mrs. Paxton and her sister come up with for this afternoon and tonight. I may ask you to act as their guide like you did yesterday in the Transportation Building. They very much appreciated your company and knowledge on the various displays. That's quite a compliment coming from Isabella—Cedena's mother—don't you know? She can be," he paused to look around and then lowered his voice, "difficult and domineering at the very least, and from what I've observed, she's gotten worse since she lost her husband and son. Small wonder Cedena escapes her clutches every chance she gets."

So, thought Matthew, *that's why Cedena sometimes acts like a puppy off its leash.* "Whatever you think best, sir."

Within the hour, Mrs. Paxton and the Rossier women had arrived. Cedena, dressed in a fresh white shirtwaist and dark blue skirt, offered Matthew a smile so wide he thought her lips would crack.

"Mr. Waren, are you ready for your ride on the Captive Balloon?"

"Most certainly." He came around from behind the display.

Isabella shook her finger at her daughter. "Remember to meet us back here promptly at eleven o'clock. Nancy and I are going to the Government Building while you're up in the balloon, and when you return, we three are going to the Art Galleries."

"Yes, Mother. We'll be here at eleven." She placed her hand on Matthew's arm. "We should go, eh?"

With a nod, Matthew started for the exit. Cedena was not short of conversation as they followed the same route they had the day before. Thankfully, today she made no effort to run away. When they entered the Midway and encountered the nursery exhibit, they agreed to walk past it as quickly as possible, Cedena holding her handkerchief to her nose and successfully avoiding a sneezing fit. With no efforts on her part to divert their route, they reached the Captive Balloon Park a quarter hour later. A large sign posted at the gate immediately brought them up short.

Cedena read the words in a tone of disbelief. "Captive Balloon Rides Permanently Shut Down. Acrobatic Performances to begin here July 10th." Ticket in hand, she waved it in front of Matthew. "Worthless."

"Miss! Sir!" a voice called to them.

They turned to find a man approaching from behind, the one who had given them the tickets yesterday. "I'm so sorry about this." He indicated the sign. "The stockholders met last night and made a decision not to restore the balloon. I feel so badly. You two were such a help to me yesterday." He reached into his pocket, pulled out a silver dollar, and offered it to Matthew. "I'll tell you what you can do. Take this over to the Ferris wheel and buy yourselves two tickets."

Cedena put her palm out. "Keep your money, sir, and tell those stockholders for me that I think they ought to have their heads examined!"

The man laughed, as did Matthew. Then the fellow forced the coin into Matthew's hand. "I'll feel much better about this if you'll go up on the wheel, my treat. Mr. Ferris's invention only ascends 264 feet, not 1,493 like the balloon did, but at least you'll get a pretty good view of the Fair. Go on now. Enjoy the ride." He jerked his head in the wheel's direction.

Matthew slipped the coin into his pants pocket and extended his hand. "Thank you, sir. I'm sure we'll enjoy the wheel."

The man gave a firm handshake. "Bless you, now. And you, too, miss."

As the man walked away, Matthew turned to Cedena. "There wasn't much of a line at the Ferris wheel when we came past there a few minutes ago. We shouldn't have a long wait to get on." He extended his arm.

Cedena shoved her worthless ticket into her skirt pocket and slid her hand inside his elbow. "That balloon ticket is one for my scrapbook. It was awfully nice of that fellow to give us a ride on the wheel. I'm sure it will be impressive." She chuckled. "Impressive? Downright awe inspiring! The highest I've ever been was a couple of hundred feet above Snail Shell Harbor, and that was with my feet on the ground at the bluff. The view is breathtaking there, but this will be really, *really* magnificent!"

In the very next moment, Cedena's expression changed from a bright smile to a downturned mouth and thoughtful look.

"Something wrong, Miss Rossier?"

She shook her head. "I was just thinking about my brother and father, and how much they would have enjoyed being here." With a slight shake of her head, her smile returned. "Life goes on, and today is going to be wonderful!"

A few minutes later, tickets in hand, Matthew followed Cedena up the stairs to the loading platform. A car waited there, its door open and a conductor standing by.

"Tickets, please." The uniformed fellow offered a smile as he took the pasteboards from Matthew. "Find a seat, folks. We'll be underway in a few moments."

Cedena preceded Matthew into the car and stopped abruptly, pointing to the passengers occupying the chairs on the opposite side. "Well, look who's here!"

CHAPTER 7

In the Ferris wheel car, Cedena barely noticed the twenty or so passengers to her left. Instead, her sights were set straight ahead. "Mother, Aunt Nancy, what are you doing here?"

Mother scowled. "The question is what are *you* doing here?"

"The balloon rides have been terminated. Why aren't you at the Government Building?"

Mother pointed to Aunt Nancy. "It's her fault, I reckon."

Aunt Nancy grinned broadly. "Guilty as charged."

Cedena laughed. Good for Aunt Nancy. She had insisted Mother come to the Fair, and now she had convinced her to take a ride on the wheel. Maybe Mother was losing her stubbornness.

A young couple entered the car and took seats opposite Cedena and Matthew. The conductor closed and locked the door, and the wheel began to move.

The conductor's gaze shifted to take in all the passengers as he spoke. "Welcome! Thank you for choosing to ride the Ferris wheel today. The wheel will make five more stops for passengers, and then it will make one revolution without stopping. I'll be glad to answer any questions you may have, so feel free to ask away!"

Cedena's attention reverted to the couple across from her. The young woman was probably seventeen or eighteen. Her blonde hair was pulled up into a Gibson Girl style and she was smartly dressed in an organdy pale pink gown with matching lace on the leg-o'-mutton sleeves and the bodice. Nobody, but *nobody* ever dressed that way in Fayette, at least not on a weekday.

How plain and unstylish Cedena felt by comparison. She smoothed her navy blue cotton skirt and fussed with the plain cuffs of her narrow-sleeved shirtwaist. Then she caught another glimpse of the young woman; her attractive costume and hair could not compensate for her very narrow face and slightly pointed chin.

The fellow beside her, however, was anything but homely. From his wide-set blue eyes beneath the brim of his white boater, to his casual smile and tidy seersucker suit, he could turn heads. He appeared to be about ten years older than the plain girl beside him. But why had he settled for *her*?

The pink-clad girl turned to the conductor. "Sir, will my brother and I be able to see Kenosha from the top of the wheel?"

So that explained it—they weren't a romantic couple.

The conductor took a step in their direction. "We might catch a glimpse of Kenosha if clouds don't get in the way."

"Are you from Kenosha?" Aunt Nancy asked.

The girl shifted her gaze to Aunt Nancy. "Yes. Our father owns a store there, Young's General Merchandise."

The fellow in seersucker spoke up. "Alice and I are usually there working in the store, but our father gave us a little money and time off to see the Fair. Where are you from?"

"I'm from Kansas City, Missouri. So is Mr. Waren here." Aunt Nancy nodded in Matthew's direction. "The others are my relatives from Fayette, in Michigan's Upper Peninsula."

Cedena spoke up. "Have you two been to the Manufactures Building yet?"

Alice shook her head. "Father said we should go there straightaway, but Orin insisted we go up in the Ferris wheel first." She smiled wryly.

"I can certainly understand your brother's choice." Cedena's gaze darted to Orin and then back to Alice. "But when you're done here, you two really ought to go to the Manufactures Building and look up the Paxton Pharmaceutical display on the first floor near the north exit. You'll find the most wonderful toiletries there, including the finest perfumes from France, and you can test them, too!" Cedena turned to Matthew. "Do you have a card?"

Matthew reached into his inside jacket pocket, pulled out a business card, and stepped across the car to hand it to Orin. He glanced briefly at it and passed it to Alice.

The car rose higher, then paused, and the conductor pointed to the east. "We're high enough here to get a good view of the Midway and beyond."

Cedena rose to get a better look out of one of the five east-facing windows.

The conductor continued. "On the left, close in, you'll see A Street in Cairo, the German Village, and the Javanese Village. Down the right side are the Moorish Palace, the Turkish Village, the Panorama of the Bernese Alps, the Natatorium, and farther along, Hagenbeck's Animal Show."

Alice and Orin left their chairs on the west side of the car to stand beside Cedena as the conductor's commentary continued. Mother and Aunt Nancy stood, too, for a better view out the windows.

The conductor pointed. "Farther down, you can see the elevated railroad. On the fairgrounds proper, the landmarks from left to right are the Fine Arts Building, the Illinois Building, the Fisheries, the U.S. Government Building, the Manufactures Building, the Horticulture Building, the Electricity Building, the Transportation Building, and the Administration Building."

It was more than Cedena could take in. She stared in awe and tried to remember the landmarks the conductor had just listed. But it was impossible. The Manufactures Building she knew, and the Transportation Building for certain. The others would be more memorable when she visited them.

As conversation and the wheel's revolution continued, Alice tried to draw Matthew out, studying his card and asking him questions about the pharmaceutical display. Perhaps Cedena was wrong, but the highly stylish Alice appeared to be all but flirting with stodgy Matthew, and he seemed oblivious.

Orin shifted his position, stepping back from between his sister and Matthew to stand near Cedena. She glanced his way, intending only to take a cursory look, and then she couldn't keep from staring. He was much shorter and sturdier than Matthew, but his extra-wide shoulders filled out his natty suit jacket and made up for his lack of height. The perpetual smile he wore didn't hurt, either. He seemed genuinely at ease, not anxious or controlling the way Matthew was much of the time. And with Orin came the delightful hint of lemon grass, one of the few scents that didn't make Cedena sneeze.

Orin pivoted his gaze from the view out the window to Cedena. "I'm afraid I didn't catch your name."

"I'm afraid I didn't drop it!" said Cedena, grinning broadly. "I'm Cedena Rossier." She extended her hand.

He clasped it in a firm handshake. "I'm Orin Young. Pleased to meet you, Miss Rossier."

"And I, you."

Mother's hawk-eye gaze settled on Cedena. "I reckon you're going with Aunt Nancy and me to the Government Building next. Isn't that right, Cedena?"

She withdrew her hand from Mr. Young's and dragged her focus from him to Mother. "I suppose so."

"Say, would anybody know about the Fourth of July celebration tonight?" Orin wanted to know. "When and where are the fireworks taking place?"

"I can tell you." The conductor spoke up. "The fireworks will go off from 8:30 to 10 o'clock over the lake. They'll be visible from the beach in front of the Manufactures Building. You'll want to get there plenty early.

Otherwise, you'll certainly be able to see them from the Ferris wheel."

Orin shook his head. "I'm sure you and your passengers will have the best view from up here, but this is our only ride on the wheel."

Aunt Nancy turned to the conductor. "I think I read in the paper that there will be some free concerts today. Isn't there one in Festival Hall at two o'clock?"

The conductor nodded. "That's the first concert today, but there are several others. At half-past five, the Machinery Hall chimes will ring out wartime and patriotic melodies, and at six o'clock there will be an orchestral concert in the new bandstand on the lakefront. The bands of Cincinnati, Chicago, and Iowa State are each giving separate performances."

Cedena turned to Mother. "Let's go to the six o'clock concert. That way we can tour the Fair all afternoon, and end with some lovely music and the fireworks over the lake."

"Good idea, Cedena." Mother turned to Aunt Nancy. "What do you say?"

"That's a good plan."

Orin faced his sister. "Alice, what do you think? Should we do the same?"

Alice offered a smile that softened her bony cheeks. "Absolutely!"

Cedena spoke up. "Why don't we go together? You two could meet us at the Paxton Pharmaceutical display at, say, a quarter till six."

Alice's smile broadened. "I'd like that if it's all right with Orin."

Orin fixed his gaze on Cedena. "We'll be there! A quarter till six at the Paxton Pharmaceutical display."

The conductor spoke again. "We are now starting our full revolution without any stops . . ." As the conductor named the landmarks, the others watched the view out the window, but Cedena's focus remained on Orin. He was someone she could look at for hours. Did he have a sweetheart back in Kenosha? No doubt he could take his pick of the available young ladies there. Why was she even thinking these things? She should be paying attention to the view of the Fair. Just as she tried to wrench her focus away from Orin, his gaze met hers and he grinned.

Cedena's cheeks warmed. She grinned back. She should watch the Chicago skyline, but Orin held her attention like a magnet. Her mind raced ahead. The concert and fireworks were going to be interesting, but not nearly as fascinating as Orin Young.

CHAPTER 8

By a quarter till six, when Cedena and her relatives left the Forest King Restaurant and headed north toward the Manufactures Building, crowds already jammed the area around the basin south of the building. The beach to the east where the concert and fireworks were to take place was packed with people, too. Cedena kept her eye on the green feather in the hatband of Uncle James's boater, trying not to lose sight of him as people came between them on the way to the south door. Once inside, she prayed that Orin and Alice were waiting at the north end. A couple of minutes later, as she approached the Paxton Pharmaceutical Display, Alice was clearly visible carrying on a conversation with Matthew. Uncle James was busy handing out cards to two businessmen. But Orin was nowhere in sight.

Cedena approached Alice. "Are you ready for the concert? Where's your brother? Is he joining us?"

Alice nodded. "Orin will be here. He's taking a second look at the German display." As she pointed toward the south, a rose fragrance wafted up. "Mmm. Smell that?" She turned her wrist toward Cedena. "Matthew has been introducing me to the delightful perfumes your uncle sells."

Matthew? She was already calling him by his first name? "That's wonderful."

"I've never smelled finer perfumes than these," Alice continued. She indicated the testers atop the glass case of perfumes and powders. "I'm going to tell my father that he simply must start ordering his toiletries from Paxton Pharmaceuticals; that's all there is to it!"

Matthew smiled. Was he pleased because of added business, or because Alice was gazing at him with a look that could easily be interpreted as adoring? Cedena hoped it was the latter.

Cedena turned to look for Orin and caught sight of him approaching. His extra-broad chest was a distinct advantage as he cleared a path past the visitors who clogged the main aisle. When he saw Cedena, he offered a smile that set her heart aflutter.

"Are we ready to go to the concert?" Orin shifted his gaze to the others.

Mother shook her head. "You young people go. There's no place to sit out there, and I reckon I'm just too worn out to stand for the concert."

Uncle James reached beneath the display, coming up with a fold-out camp stool. "You're welcome to take this, Isabella."

"Thank you, James, but no. I'd be ever so grateful, though, if you'd just set one up so I could sit back there for a while."

"Mother, are you sure you don't want to take a stool outside for the concert and fireworks?" Cedena had never seen her so exhausted this early in the evening.

"Sure as a rabbit has ears."

Uncle James set up a stool for Mother and then turned to Matthew. "Go with Cedena and the Youngs. Mrs. Paxton and I will handle the display, and it looks like we'll have good company tonight, too."

"Thank you, sir." Matthew stepped from behind the display, his focus on the Youngs. "The bandstand is in front of the east exit, but the crowd is so thick there that I suggest going out the north end of the building and working our way around." As he led off in that direction, Alice quickly snagged his elbow.

Orin offered his arm to Cedena. "Shall we go?"

She placed her hand on his thick forearm and they followed the others out the door. Cedena had never seen anything like the crowd on the plaza and on the beach. There must be tens of thousands of folks packed tightly together. Thank goodness Orin was a sturdy fellow. Nevertheless, perspiration moistened her face and her palms. She hoped she wouldn't leave dampness on his seersucker jacket.

Matthew led Alice in a northerly direction where the gathering wasn't as compact. He stopped near the Life-Saving Station. "I think this is the best we can do. I wish there was a place to sit down."

Cedena glanced up. A member of the Life-Saving Station was on a railed walkway on the roof. She pointed. "That person will get a perfect view of the fireworks tonight." She waved and he waved back.

"We certainly won't see anything from here." Orin looked around, and then released Cedena. "Stay right where you are. I've got an idea." He began to back away.

Alice scowled. "Where are you going, Orin? Don't cause any trouble, *please!*"

"Me? Trouble?" Orin laughed and quickly headed north. He threaded his way past a couple of dozen folks as in the distance the band began to play the "Washington Post March."

After a moment's hesitation, Cedena followed Orin.

"Miss Rossier, come back here!" Matthew's demand trailed after her.

She ignored him, catching up with Orin as he rounded the far end of the station. She slipped her hand onto his arm.

He turned to her, a gleam in his eye. "You certainly don't mind very well, do you, Miss Rossier?"

Cedena grinned. "From what your sister said, you don't either, eh?"

"I suppose not. But now that you're here, you might be of some help with my plan. Do you have any coins I could borrow? A silver dollar or even a half-dollar?"

Cedena shook her head even though several silver dollars were tucked deep inside her hidden skirt pocket, knotted into a handkerchief to prevent jingling. "Sorry, Mr. Young. Hard cash is difficult to come by in the Upper Peninsula. Most business is done by barter."

His brows narrowed. "So how did you find the money to come to the Fair? Have you got a hidden gold mine up there in those hills?"

Cedena laughed and then placed her finger to her lips. "Shh. Not a word to anyone of what I'm going to tell you. Promise?"

"Promise."

"My mother and I are only here because my Uncle James and Aunt Nancy paid our way." Cedena immediately regretted the admission. What was it about Orin that made her reveal family secrets?

Orin's blue eyes registered understanding. "It's good to have rich relatives. Now come with me." He led her around the building to the lake side of the Life-Saving Station and right up to the front door. He paused to pull coins from his pocket and then pounded furiously on the door.

The door opened partway and a uniformed crew member greeted them. "Good evening, folks. Tours have ended for today. Come back tomorrow." As he started to close the door, Orin placed his foot on the threshold.

"We aren't interested in a tour. We have another problem, a very serious one."

The crewman's focus shifted from Orin, to Cedena, and back again. "If you're in need of restrooms, there are none for the public here. You'll have to go next door to the Government Building." He tried to close the door again, but Orin's foot remained firm.

"Sir, I'm afraid you don't understand. My friends and I—there are four of us altogether—would like to volunteer to help you watch for trouble on the lake from your rooftop lookout starting about eight-thirty." He opened his hand, revealing several coins totaling about three dollars.

The crewman studied the coins and then Orin. "Let me see if I understand you correctly. Are you bribing me to let you watch the fireworks from our lookout?"

Orin smiled. "Bribe is a bit of an overstatement." He jingled the coins.

The crewman's cheeks colored. "I'll give you to the count of three to leave this property, or be arrested by the Columbian Guard. One . . . two . . . ."

CHAPTER 9

Cedena tugged at Orin's elbow. "Let's get out of here."

Orin reluctantly dragged his foot from the threshold of the Life-Saving Station and escorted Cedena to the back of the building where they rejoined Matthew and Alice.

"There you are!" Alice greeted them. "I was worried. Where have you two been?"

"Trying to get arrested," Orin teased.

Cedena explained the unsuccessful encounter with the Life-Saving crewman.

Matthew's brow furrowed. "We won't be the only ones in a bad place to see the fireworks tonight. More people are showing up every minute who are in the same boat, so to speak."

"A boat even the Life-Saving Service is unwilling to rescue," Orin joked.

Alice dismissed the comment with a wave of her hand. "Let's just enjoy the music. The concert is truly wonderful."

Cedena tapped her foot to the stirring beat of the march tunes. Too bad live performances had all but vanished at Fayette since the Jackson Iron Company had moved out. She hadn't realized how much she'd missed those Music Hall concerts by the Cornet Band and others until now. As darkness fell, the strains of "My Country 'Tis of Thee" drifted in. Cedena sang along, joined by Alice who had a voice as sweet as a songbird.

As the last note faded away, the crack of fireworks sounded. At that same moment, a farm wagon pulled in behind the Life-Saving Station. Perched on the driver's bench, a farmer wearing a wide-brimmed felt hat called out.

"See the fireworks from my wagon! Fifty cents per person! I'll get you a good view, guaranteed!" He scrambled to the back end of the wagon.

A middle-aged fellow and his wife approached the farmer. "We'll take ya up on that offer." He paid with a silver dollar.

The farmer dropped the coin into his pants pocket and assisted the man and his wife aboard at the back end.

The farmer's hawking repeated, bringing additional customers.

Orin reached for Cedena's hand. "Let's get on, before that wagon fills up. It's a sure thing we'll see nothing back here. I've got the money in my hand." He led Cedena to the back of the wagon, paid their fare, lifted her aboard, and climbed on beside her. Moments later, Alice and Matthew joined them.

"Get to the front. Make room for others," the farmer urged. A couple of minutes later, the wagon held at least twenty people. The farmer hopped off the back end and climbed aboard at the front. "Git on, now, Goliath!" The farmer slapped the reins. The horse plodded forward, made a tight turn around the Government Building, passed the Fire and Guard Station, headed toward the lagoon, and turned again to the south.

"Where ya takin' us?" the gentleman first to board called out.

"South o' the Manufactures Building. Got the perfect place for ya to see the fireworks."

Five minutes later, the farmer stopped short of the southwest corner of the Manufactures Building, drew a rifle from beneath his bench, and pointed it at his passengers. "Everybody out! Now!"

"What?" someone asked in disbelief.

"Take us to where we can see the show!" Orin demanded.

The farmer raised his rifle and pulled the trigger, letting a bullet fly over his passengers' heads.

Alice screamed.

"Git out, all of you, before somebody gets hurt!" The farmer lowered his rifle to eye level.

Cedena's heart raced. Was this to be the end of her? Shot in a farm wagon by some thieving lunatic? She grabbed Alice by the hand and headed for the back end. Matthew followed close behind, jumped off the wagon, and lifted Cedena and then Alice to the ground. Orin and a few others were still on the wagon near the farmer.

Cedena made her way toward the front end of the wagon as complaints rang out against the cheating farmer.

"I'll get you arrested!"

"Give us our money back!"

By now, Orin was the only passenger on the wagon. He stood facing the farmer, his hands on his hips. "I'm not leaving until you give everybody's money back."

The farmer poked his rifle barrel into Orin's chest. "Go on now, young fella. Don't be foolish. No amount of money is worth a hole in your chest."

In a flash, Orin swung his arm, lifting the rifle barrel skyward.

A shot rang out.

Alice screamed.

Matthew hopped onto the wagon and helped Orin subdue the farmer and confiscate his weapon. With the farmer held tightly between them, Matthew called out.

"Somebody fetch the Columbian Guard."

"I'll do it." One of the cheated men took off.

"Everybody come and get your money back," Orin invited.

A cheer went up.

Cedena drew a deep breath.

Orin finished handing out the last of the refunds as two Columbian Guards arrived, spiffy in their navy blue uniforms and caps.

"These two stole all my money!" the cheating farmer claimed.

"He stole from *us* at gunpoint!" someone countered.

"You all paid me willingly," the farmer returned.

"We paid to see the fireworks from your wagon and then you drove us back here where we can't see a thing and told us to get out at gunpoint!" a man explained.

"That's right!" a chorus of voices confirmed.

"Arrest this man!" Orin said. "He's a crook and a danger!"

The two guards mounted the wagon and took custody of the farmer, removing him and his rifle from the wagon.

"I need witnesses to come with us to our station and sign a complaint," said one of the guards. "You, and you." He pointed to Orin and Matthew.

Orin turned to Cedena and Alice. "Come along, ladies."

"What about my horse and wagon?" the farmer asked.

"They'll be fine right where they are until we finish with you," a guard said.

At the station five minutes later, a guard sat at the desk and wrote up the complaint as told to him by Orin and Matthew, with details interjected by Cedena and Alice. When the report was finished, the other guard emptied the rifle of its remaining ammunition and handed it to the farmer. "Come with me. I'll personally escort you off the grounds. You are never to drive in or step foot on these premises again. Understand?"

The farmer nodded and left under escort.

The other guard jogged the pages of the report together and smiled up at Cedena and her companions. "That's all, folks. Thank you for your assistance. You are free to go."

Fireworks boomed in the distance.

Orin placed his hands on the front of the desk and leaned forward. "Sir, would you have any suggestion as to where we might get a good look at the fireworks? We thought we'd be able to see them from that fellow's wagon, but—"

"That didn't work out so well, did it?" A smile crept onto the guard's mouth. "Come with me. I know just the place."

CHAPTER 10

Cedena, Orin, Matthew, and Alice followed the guard out of the station and into the north entrance of the Manufactures Building. As they rapidly passed by the Paxton Pharmaceutical display where the scent of heliotrope perfume hung in the air, Cedena called out to her relatives.

"We're on our way to get a good look at the fireworks. See you later!"

"Have fun!" Aunt Nancy replied.

The guard headed out the south exit and through the crowd into the Music Hall. Using his pass keys, he led Cedena and the others into a back hall, up a staircase, and onto the roof. Several people had already gathered there, but the roof wasn't at all crowded, stretching as it did from the Music Hall across the Peristyle to the Casino at the opposite end.

Within moments, a brilliant explosion lit the black sky. Goose bumps peppered Cedena's arms as a dazzling array of red and white stripes unfolded, revealing a sea of blue stars. As Old Glory faded, a giant searchlight stretched across the sky and the crowd below roared approval.

Cedena's jaw dropped. She turned to Orin. "How on earth, or rather in heaven, was such a magnificent display conceived?"

He grinned. "Bet you never saw such a wonder in the Upper Peninsula."

She shook her head. "Nor you in Wisconsin, eh?"

"Nothing could compare to this," Alice claimed as she turned to Matthew. "Don't you agree?"

"It's ten times better than any show Kansas City ever put on for the Fourth. And this is the best place to see it." Matthew turned to the guard. "Thank you, sir, for bringing us up here."

He nodded. "Glad you folks are enjoying yourselves. Wish I could stay and watch the rest of the show, but I'd better get back and file that report. When the fireworks are over, just follow the others and you'll find the way out. This area was reserved for a few privileged guests, but I think you all qualify after the help you've given the Columbian Guards tonight." He turned back the way he had come and disappeared into the darkness.

More booms and cracks rent the sky and the image of George Washington's face with crossed laurel branches beneath it unfolded. Silence reigned until the display faded. The approving roar of the crowd nearly drowned out dozens of whistles from boats anchored just offshore. As the joyous sounds rose on the gentle lake breeze, Cedena's mind spun. Never again would she witness such a marvel. Too bad Mother had been too tired to see it.

Rockets flamed, sparkles burst in blossoms of red, white, and blue, and thunderous cracks split the air for several minutes. Then the sky went dark and silent.

Orin slipped his arm about Cedena's waist, pulled her snuggly against him, and pressed a kiss against her cheek. Shivers ran through her. She should pull away, but she could muster no resistance to his embrace and the scent of lemon grass that held her captive.

"I'm so glad we saw the fireworks together," he whispered in her ear.

"So am I."

Others on the roof began making their way to the exit.

Cedena glanced at Orin. "We'd better head to Uncle James's display, eh?" She eased out of his embrace, linked her arm with his, and started back. Matthew and Alice followed.

Within minutes, they had exited the Music Hall, but the mass of people outside made progress difficult. Cedena held tightly to Orin's arm. Thank goodness for his broad chest and sturdy legs making it possible to find a path to the south entrance of the Manufactures Building. Once inside, she drew a deep breath. A couple of minutes later, they arrived at the Paxton Pharmaceutical display.

"How were the fireworks?" Uncle James asked.

"Glorious! Too wonderful for words!" Cedena answered. "But we had just a speck of trouble before we got to a place where we could actually see them."

"Oh?" Aunt Nancy's brow rose.

"We'll explain later." Matthew stepped behind the display. "Right now, I'd suggest we get closed up and find transportation home. It's going to be difficult with the number of people here tonight." He began putting away perfume testers.

Uncle James removed the business card and flier holders from the countertop. "I bought tickets earlier this evening for all of us, the Youngs included, to take a steamboat back to Van Buren Street."

Within ten minutes, all was stowed away, the cabinets were locked, and the drop cloths were in place. Uncle James distributed the steamboat tickets and, with Aunt Nancy on his arm, led the way out the south end of the building. The crowd remained nearly as tightly packed as before.

Mother stepped out the door and reached for Uncle James's other arm, clinging tightly. The lights surrounding the building revealed the wide-eyed, ashen look on her face. "I reckon this is the biggest crowd I've ever seen. How will we ever get through, James?" Her voice shook.

"This is no time to panic, Isabella. I know what I'm doing."

Cedena exchanged glances with Orin, who placed her hand firmly inside his elbow. She looked back to find Matthew, his arm protectively around Alice's tiny waist as they followed close behind.

The pier, hundreds of feet wide and about a half-mile long, held thousands of people waiting to board a steamer tied up near the far end. Uncle James tried to push through the throng with unwelcomed results.

"Where do ya think you're goin'?"

"Y'd best get in line, mister, b'fore somethin' nasty comes your way."

Uncle James turned to face the others. "We'll have to be patient. It seems everyone here has purchased a ticket."

"Certainly that steamer won't hold this crowd," Mother observed. "I wish you had your yacht here, the one you chartered to bring us from Fayette."

"Another steamer is probably ready to come in when this one departs," Aunt Nancy said.

"Probably?" Lines deepened on Mother's forehead. "What if there *isn't* another one?"

"We'll cross that bridge when we come to it, Isabella." Uncle James offered an encouraging smile and then shifted his gaze to Matthew. "While we're waiting, why don't you tell us what happened when you went to see the fireworks."

By turns, Matthew, Cedena, Orin, and Alice provided the details.

Mother shook her head in disbelief. "Thank the Lord no one got shot. I wish we were going home to Michigan tomorrow. I just knew this fair would be a horrible place."

Cedena's pulse raced. "Mother, how can you be so ungrateful? After all the trouble and expense Uncle James and Aunt Nancy went to, bringing us to the Fair, you want to go home after one day? You should be ashamed of yourself!" The moment the words left Cedena's mouth, she regretted them. Never in her life had she spoken to Mother so harshly.

"Ashamed of myself? You impertinent child! How dare you speak to me that way?"

"I'm sorry, Mother. I shouldn't have said what I did, but please remember that our time at the Fair is just beginning. This evening started bad, it's true, but the fireworks more than made up for it." Cedena described the glorious images that had unfolded as they watched from the roof of the Music Hall. "It was like a miracle painted by a giant artist's brush on fire in the sky! I wish you'd seen it."

Mother sighed. "It would be wonderful if God would just bestow on us another miracle to get us back to our room."

As they waited to get on a steamer, Matthew released his hold on Alice and moved closer to Uncle James for some business talk while Aunt Nancy tried to calm Mother's fears.

Eager to ignore those conversations, Cedena turned to Orin and Alice.

"How long will you two be at the Fair?"

"All week." Orin grinned.

Alice shook her head. "Orin wishes we could be here that long. The truth is, we only have room reservations and spending money for two more days. And you?"

"We'll be here a total of two weeks if Aunt Nancy can keep Mother's fretfulness under control."

"What do you plan to see tomorrow?" Alice asked.

"I'm not sure what Aunt Nancy and Mother have in mind, but I'd sure like to see the Woman's Building."

"Me, too!" Alice turned to her brother. "You'll take me there tomorrow morning, won't you, Orin?"

"If you promise to spend the afternoon with me in Machinery Hall."

"Promise!"

The conversation continued with descriptions of their families. It turned out Orin and Alice had a middle brother, Paul, back in Kenosha.

"Didn't Paul want to come to the Fair with you?" Cedena's gaze slid from Orin to Alice.

"There was only enough money for two of us to make the trip," Alice quickly explained. "Father had us draw straws and I got the shortest one, but Paul insisted that I take his place, so here I am!"

"Father and Paul dote on Alice so much, it's a wonder she's not spoiled rotten, but she isn't." Orin sent an admiring smile Alice's way, and in that moment, a knife sliced through Cedena's heart that her twin brother, David, was no longer around to be her best friend, confident, and at times, even her admirer.

The conversation continued. Cedena wasn't sure how long they'd been talking when a steamer drew up to the dock. Many passengers mounted the boarding ramp, but the boat cast off leaving about two-thirds of the crowd behind. A buzz went up from the hoards on the dock.

"Another steamer is on the way," Uncle James announced. "That's the word being passed along."

Cedena stifled a yawn. "What time is it, Uncle James?"

Her uncle pulled his watch from his vest pocket. "Half-past midnight. Sorry we're so late getting out of here. It won't be long once the next steamer comes in, I promise."

Sixteen hours had already passed since Cedena had entered the gate to the Fair this morning. No wonder her legs felt like rubber and her feet, evidently swollen from the heat, seemed a size too large for her high-top shoes. At least a breeze had picked up off the lake, sending cooler air filtering through the elbow-to-elbow crowd.

About a half hour later, the second steamer pulled up to the dock. Pushing and shoving threatened to send Cedena to the ground. Alice squealed when a heavy fellow stepped on her foot. Orin wrapped one arm tightly around Alice's waist and the other around Cedena's as the crowd moved them down the pier.

At the boarding ramp, a near stampede threatened to send eager passengers into the lake. Crewmen managed the crowd by allowing folks aboard in a line only two abreast. Over the next several minutes, a stream of human cargo flowed onboard. Finally, Uncle James, Matthew, Aunt Nancy, and Mother made it onto the boarding ramp. Cedena and the Youngs would be next.

A crewman wedged in between and put his palms out. "That's all we have room for. No more boats tonight." In an instant, he chained off the entrance.

Cedena couldn't believe what she had heard. "No more boats? You can't leave us here!"

The ramp retracted. Mother's voice, nearly hysterical, carried from onboard. "My daughter! My daughter! We can't leave her!"

Dock workers released lines and tossed them aboard the vessel, which began to move away from the pier.

Uncle James shouted from the rail of the deck. "Cedena, take the train!"

Tears formed in Cedena's eyes. Take the train, but where? She couldn't remember the address of the boarding house they were staying in, and even if she could, she had no idea how to find the right train to get there. If only David were here! Without him, she was surely lost. And because of that, the best night of her life had just turned into the worst nightmare possible.

CHAPTER 11

"Don't cry, Miss Rossier." Alice offered her a lace-edged handkerchief, exquisitely embroidered with her initials and scented with rosewater. "We'll make sure you get to your room, won't we, Orin?"

"Of course we will."

Cedena shook her head as she returned Alice's handkerchief and pulled out her own plain hanky. "It's impossible. I don't know the exact address, only the landlady's name, Mrs. O'Donnell, and the street, Elmwood, I think. Yes, Elmwood." She dried her tears.

"There must be a hundred O'Donnells in Chicago," said Orin. "And as for Elmwood, I have no idea where that might be. Our room is at 483 Washington Boulevard. That, I can find. So spend the night with us. You can double up with Alice in her room."

"Yes. Stay in my room. I have a double bed. It will be fine. Tomorrow we'll go back to your uncle's display at the Fair and I'd bet my life that your mother will be there waiting for you." Her gaze shifted to her brother. "Orin, there's one thing we hadn't counted on. Mrs. Monahan said we had to be in by eleven o'clock each night or be locked out, and that under no circumstances would she let anyone in after curfew. It's already *way* past eleven."

Orin grinned. "Don't fret, Alice. I can get us in, guaranteed, and old Mrs. Monahan will be none the wiser." Orin took both Cedena and Alice by the elbow and ushered them off the pier.

The gate to the Fair had already been locked, but the Columbian Guard opened it to let hundreds of people through to the railroad station on the west side. There, a long line formed to buy tickets. An hour and a half after the second steamer had left Cedena, Alice, and Orin stranded, they finally climbed aboard a train that would take them to the station downtown. Within fifteen minutes, they had stepped onto the platform. Orin arranged for a hack, which took them to Washington Boulevard.

When Cedena, Alice, and Orin arrived at the Youngs' boarding house, it was completely dark. Orin spoke quietly. "Step lightly onto the porch. Mrs. Monahan has left the front parlor window open. I'll pop off the screen, climb in, and unlock the door for you."

The first step to the porch creaked under Orin's weight. He quickly removed his foot, skipped that step, and helped Alice and Cedena to do the same. The screen, attached to the outside of the window, was soon freed from its fasteners. As Orin set it aside, a voice shouted from the sidewalk.

"Hey, you! What d' ya think yer doin'?"

Cedena turned to look. The light from the street lamp revealed a policeman. He came marching up the front walk and onto the porch.

Orin wasted no time making an explanation. "Good evening, officer. I'm assisting these two young ladies who have been locked out of this boarding house along with myself."

"Why don't ye try knocking on the door?"

"We didn't want to disturb Mrs. Monahan," said Alice. "We're way past curfew due to no fault of our own."

"I'm getting Mrs. Monahan down here. She's the only one can say whether you're tellin' the truth, or just tryin' to break in." His gaze shifted from Alice to Cedena. "Can't imagine what two nice young ladies are doin' with the likes o' him." He jabbed his thumb in Orin's direction.

Cedena opened her mouth to reply, but the policeman's banging on the door made a response impossible.

A voice called out from an upstairs window. "It's past curfew. I ain't comin' down."

"Mrs. Monahan, 'tis Officer Riley. Please come down here and tell me if these folks I found on your porch are roomin' with ya, or if they're burglars tryin' to get in y'r front window."

"Burglars? I'll be there in a minute."

Cedena couldn't believe the pickle she was in now. Mrs. Monahan didn't know her. Maybe she could explain. "Officer Riley, I'm not one of Mrs. Monahan's boarders. I'm staying with a Mrs. O'Donnell on Elmwood Avenue, but I got separated from my family after the fireworks at the Fair, and I don't have any idea how to find my way back to my room. Alice, here, said I could stay with her."

Officer Riley smiled. "Mrs. O'Donnell on Elmwood Avenue, ye say?"

"Yes, sir."

"Don't you worry. I know right where to take you, and it's no more than a block away. But first, I've got to make sure things are straight with Mrs. Monahan."

Orin was putting the screen back up when the woman opened her front door. She took a good look at the Youngs and shifted to focus on the policeman. "No problem, officer. These are my boarders." She turned to Orin. "But why was ya takin' my screen off?"

He explained about the trouble getting home from the Fair, his concern about curfew, and his desire not to disturb her at such a late hour. "I'm sorry about the way things turned out, Mrs. Monahan; truly, I am."

She offered a wry smile. "I've got a son about your age. He'd have done the same thing if he'd been in your shoes. Come on in. Let's all get some sleep."

"Good night, Orin, Alice," Cedena said.

"Will we see you tomorrow?" Orin asked. "Aren't we three going to the Woman's Building tomorrow morning?"

"Meet me at my uncle's display at ten."

Officer Riley offered Cedena his arm. "Come with me, now. Mrs. O'Donnell's place is but a couple of minutes' walk from here."

Mrs. O'Donnell's lights were still on and the door unlocked. Cedena thanked the officer, stepped into the front hallway, and headed for the familiar voices coming from the parlor.

CHAPTER 12

Matthew sprang to his feet the moment he saw Cedena standing in the parlor doorway. "Miss Rossier! You're back!" A ten-ton burden lifted from his shoulders. He wished he hadn't sounded so enthusiastic about seeing her again, but he'd been in a dark pit since she'd missed the steamer, worried sick that she might not be safe navigating Chicago's rails and streets with the likes of Orin Young.

Isabella's constant fretfulness had deepened Matthew's angst. Mr. and Mrs. Paxton had tried to reassure her, but she had remained extremely apprehensive. How he wished he hadn't stepped away from Cedena and the Youngs to talk to Mr. Paxton while they waited on the dock. She could have gotten on the steamer in his stead and avoided all the apprehension.

Isabella dried her tears and hurried to her daughter, wrapping her arms about her. "Thank goodness you're all right! I was beside myself with worry!"

"You needn't have worried, Mother. I had the best possible escort to the door."

"Mr. Young?"

Cedena shook her head. "Officer Riley. He walked me around the corner from where the Youngs are staying. Good thing he came along, too, because I couldn't remember the exact address, only Mrs. O'Donnell's place on Elmwood Avenue."

Mrs. Paxton rose. "Now that you're here, let's turn in. It's been a long day."

Everyone headed for the stairs. As Matthew followed the others, he overheard Cedena's plans.

"The Youngs are meeting me tomorrow at ten at Uncle James's display. We're going to the Woman's Building, and in the afternoon, Machinery Hall. Do you all want to join us?"

"So you've already made plans?" Isabella's tone implied her daughter had no right.

"You're welcome to join us," Cedena replied.

"Nancy is taking me to the Art Galleries. I assumed you'd be with us."

Mrs. Paxton sighed. "Diddle-de-dum. It was only a suggestion, Isabella. We can go with Cedena and the Youngs instead."

Isabella paused at the door to the room she shared with her daughter. "No, no, Nancy. Let Cedena go with her new friends. We'll visit the Woman's Building some other time." With a huff, she turned and disappeared into the room.

Cedena grinned and spoke in a low voice. "At least she didn't throw a fit over it."

Mr. Paxton's focus shifted from his niece, to Matthew, and back again. "Cedena, wouldn't it be good if Matthew joins you and the Youngs tomorrow? I'd bet my last dime Alice would be pleased to have him along."

"That would be wonderful! Good night, Uncle James, Aunt Nancy, Matthew." Cedena headed into her room.

Matthew bid good night to the Paxtons and made his way to his room at the end of the hall. The thought of Cedena with Orin made his stomach knot. He didn't trust that fellow. Orin was entirely too interested in Cedena and too deceitful when trying to get what he wanted. And his sister was far too interested in *him*. She was just a kid, a good ten years younger than he. But if a day with the Youngs was what it took to keep an eye on Cedena, he'd gladly suffer their company.

CHAPTER 13

A week later

With Mr. Paxton taking a rare afternoon and evening off to spend with his wife and the Rossiers, Matthew tended to the pharmaceutical display. At closing time, he put away testers and draped cloths over the cabinets. All the while, he burned with curiosity over the letter in his breast pocket. It had arrived this afternoon in care of Mr. Paxton for Cedena.

Matthew pulled the lilac-scented envelope out and stared at it again. In the upper left corner was the name and address of Alice Young in Kenosha. The Youngs had returned home several days ago and Matthew had hoped neither he nor Cedena would ever hear from them again. He supposed he should have known better. Alice had promised to write to Cedena, and evidently, the Young girl was not one to renege on a commitment, even a promise as casual as correspondence. He tucked the envelope back in his pocket and strode out of the Manufactures Building.

As Matthew made his way back to Mrs. O'Donnell's by train and hack, memories of his experiences with Cedena and the Youngs flooded his mind. Their day at the Woman's

Building and Machinery Hall had put Cedena and Orin on a first name basis. The following day had been spent entirely with the Youngs as they toured the State and Territorial Buildings and the Art Galleries.

The more Matthew got to know Orin, the more he disliked the fellow. He was charming. Too charming. And a rascal. His antics seemed more like those of an adolescent than a man in his late-twenties.

Matthew would have completely discounted the Wisconsinite except for one thing: He had fearlessly stood up to the thieving farmer at the fireworks display. He'd been foolhardy, risking death so a few dollars would be returned to their rightful owners. But it had been a righteous act, and for that he had earned Matthew's grudging respect.

Orin's little sister was his opposite in so many ways— obedient, guileless, and anything but brave. How did two siblings, so very different, come from the same parents? Alice was sweet and almost pretty, and had clung to Matthew like a bur. But he didn't see their friendship having any future beyond the Fair.

The hack pulled up in front of Mrs. O'Donnell's. Matthew paid the fare and a tip and hurried up the steps and into the house. Familiar voices, Cedena's among them, drew him to the parlor. At least he could deliver the letter that had been burning a hole in his breast pocket. He strode into the room to words of greeting and paused in front of Cedena, who was sitting on the sofa between her mother and aunt.

"I come bearing tidings from Kenosha." Matthew slid the letter from his pocket and offered it to Cedena. "This came in the afternoon mail. I think Alice wants to be your pen pal."

"Thank you, Matthew." Cedena studied the envelope and then turned it over and broke the seal.

"Have a seat, Matthew." Mrs. Paxton indicated the red velvet wingback chair across from the sofa. "Surely you want to hear what Alice has to say."

"It's really none of my business." Matthew protested weakly.

Cedena's gaze met his. "Sit, Matthew. Hear Alice's news."

He sat down to listen as Cedena read:

Dearest Cedena,

I hope this finds you well and enjoying your remaining days at the Fair. Orin and I made it home safely and are back to work at Father's mercantile. We both envy your long stay at the Fair. You must write and tell me of the experiences you have had since we left. If we can't be there with you, at least we can hear about it in your own words.

Please give my regards to Matthew and my appreciation for his fine company as Orin and I made our way through the various exhibits. I will never forget the marvelous hours the four of us spent together. I must say that at the forefront of my reminiscences will always be the eventful Fourth of July celebration.

Orin insists that I include his greetings before I close, and that I ask your permission for him to write to you directly. Please write to me at the return address on the envelope. I so wish to hear about your experiences, and I know Orin will be pestering me to find out if you have made a reply.

Most cordially,

Alice Young

P.S. Matthew has my permission to write to me, if he should feel so inclined. I would be honored to hear from him.

Cedena folded the letter and gazed up at Matthew. "Sounds to me like you have an admirer, eh?"

Matthew's face burned. An admirer, yes, but not the one he'd hoped for. He shrugged. "We'll never see them again. Alice is a nice girl, but I have no inclination to write to her." He rose. "Good night, everyone. It's been a long day." As Matthew climbed the stairs, shut the door to his room, and prepared for bed, he wished he knew how to make Cedena as interested in him as Alice was. Time was growing short. The Rossiers would be at the Fair only three more days. He needed a plan, and he needed it fast.

CHAPTER 14

Three days later

Sun sparkled off the ripples of the lagoon behind the Manufactures Building as a gondolier poled Cedena and Aunt
Nancy toward the landing. The breeze coming off Lake Michigan reminded Cedena how much warmer Chicago's summer
weather was than that of the Upper Peninsula. She could get
used to this, and to the way Aunt Nancy had indulged her at
every opportunity, even buying Cedena the middy outfit she
was wearing today. Their matching costumes made them look
almost like mother and daughter. Yes, these past two weeks at
the Fair had been like a dream.

Memories of the Ferris wheel, the Youngs, their Fourth of
July encounter with the cheating farmer, fireworks from the
rooftop, and tours through the exhibits flashed through Cedena's mind. She wished this adventure would never end. But
tomorrow, she would return north with Mother. The thought of
it was utterly depressing.

What was there to return to? Her nothing life with a nothing future. At least that's what it seemed like now that she'd
escaped the wilds of Upper Michigan to experience the hustle

and bustle of a truly big city and its magnificent fair. Even the newspaper articles she'd read before coming, as overstated as they had seemed, hadn't captured the true picture. And there was a reason why they hadn't. Words alone couldn't convey the excitement of the Fair.

The gondolier slid the boat alongside the landing, made fast, and helped her and Aunt Nancy onto the dock.

Aunt Nancy tipped the gondolier and turned to Cedena. "We still have time before we meet your mother. I can't believe Isabella decided to go to the Midway with your Uncle James on her last afternoon here, but I'm glad she did. It's good that I have a little time alone with you before you go home. So what is your pleasure? Lemonade?"

"Lemonade sounds like an excellent idea." Cedena forced a smile and reminded herself to enjoy what little time she had left with Aunt Nancy.

"Let's go to the Marine Café." Aunt Nancy indicated the restaurant next to the Fisheries Building just east of them.

The café's architecture always took Cedena's breath away. No less than ten towers, each topped by a tall finial flying a colorful banner, reached for the sky. Alternating dark and light vertical stripes below each tower distinguished this building's exterior from the all-white structures that predominated at the Fair. It was truly a feast for the eyes like nothing she had seen in the Upper Peninsula. Yet soon she would be hundreds of miles away from here with nothing but defunct limestone company buildings and simple clapboard houses to break up the stump-riddled landscape.

A few minutes later, Cedena sat across from Aunt Nancy at a small, round table on the café's balcony with a view of the lagoon and Wooded Island. The waiter delivered lemonade in tall glasses rimmed with sugar and cooled by fish-shaped ice cubes that encased paper-thin lemon slices. Cedena took a sip. The sweetness of the sugared rim contrasted nicely with the lemonade's sourness. How well the beverage paralleled her life. The sweetness of spending two weeks at the Fair with Aunt Nancy and Uncle James; the sourness of knowing it was about to come to an end, returning Cedena to her inconsequential existence in a faraway town on the edge of nowhere.

Aunt Nancy sipped her drink and set it aside. "It's been a lovely two weeks. Not too much rain. I think your mother enjoyed herself after that first day, don't you?"

Cedena mustered a weak smile. "Mother adjusted rather well, thank goodness. As for me, this has been the most wonderful two weeks of my entire life! It's been so delightful I hate to leave." She lowered her gaze to the condensation dripping down her glass to the table, as if her very own life were dribbling into a meaningless puddle.

"Then stay."

Cedena's focus shot upward, riveted on Aunt Nancy. "Pardon?"

Aunt Nancy offered a smile. "You heard me. Stay. You can move into our suite. There's extra room for a cot. You and I could have a great time scouring every inch of the Fair, the Midway, and downtown Chicago. If you want, I'm sure your Uncle James could use your help at his display. He'd teach you all you need to know to fill in for him while he makes trips back to Kansas City to check on company business there. You'd be earning your keep."

Cedena's heart pitter-pattered. Then dark thoughts sent it plummeting to the soles of her feet. "Mother would never understand."

"Diddle-de-dum. Your decision should be your own, not the one you think will please your mother, which we both know is just about impossible."

"But . . ."

"But you don't want to face her wrath. I understand. She's used to getting her own way. And employing any means to do it—tongue-lashing, guilt-laying, and if they don't work, outright underhandedness. How well I know. But if you ever want a life that is truly your own, you're going to have to break away. And when better to do it than now, with your Uncle James and me here to lean on?"

How perfectly Aunt Nancy had summed up Cedena's predicament. "You're sure Uncle James would want me to stay?"

Aunt Nancy waved her hand dismissively. "We've talked about it more than once. He'd love to have you stay with us as much as I would."

Hope rose within Cedena. But could she stand up to Mother's objections? "Let me think it over. If I decide to stay with you and Uncle James, I need to come up with a way to put it to Mother so she won't have a conniption fit."

Aunt Nancy sighed. "Even the best diplomat in the world might have trouble with that. But you do what you must. And remember, you haven't much time."

A scene flashed through Cedena's mind. The four of them were eating dinner together at a restaurant that night. Talk of leaving for Fayette came up. Uncle James invited Cedena to stay and work for him. Aunt Nancy chimed in with the plan for Cedena to stay in their suite. Cedena accepted.

She shared the plan with Aunt Nancy.

"There's only one thing amiss. *You* must be the one to inform your mother of your plans. Your Uncle James and I will back you up all the way, but you must make it clear to Isabella that the decision to remain with us and to work for James is yours. Perhaps after dinner James and I should help you move into our suite. I'm afraid if we leave you alone with your mother overnight, she will shame you into going home with her."

"Would you do that?"

"Of course we would!" Aunt Nancy grinned and patted Cedena's hand. "But here's a thought. Wait until we've finished dessert. Perhaps over a final cup of coffee you can broach the subject. No point in spoiling a perfectly good dinner with what is sure to turn into a disagreement over your future."

Cedena nodded. But did she really have the gumption to part ways with Mother? She needed to pray for guidance and strength.

With their lemonade glasses empty, Aunt Nancy laid her napkin on the table. "It's nearly time to meet James and Isabella. We'd better head back to the Manufactures Building."

As Cedena accompanied Aunt Nancy along the walkway toward the Fisheries Building's west pavilion, her aunt suddenly stopped and pointed. "Cedena, look at those two fellows coming our way. Who do they remind you of?"

Cedena's gaze landed on a man of about fifty, and a young man near her own age. The resemblance to her father and brother was absolutely amazing. When they were no more than ten feet away, Cedena struggled to make sense of what she was seeing. Father and David, presumed dead two years ago, were about to walk right past her. They were so engrossed in their own conversation that they didn't even know she was there.

Cedena's heart raced. "Father! David!"

Immediately, they went silent and looked straight at her, their faces draining of color.

Cedena hugged her father and brother at the same time. Their arms wrapped about her, offering her the affection she had desperately coveted for the past two years. "I've missed you two so much!" She choked back tears.

"We've missed you, too." They spoke almost in unison.

When they released Cedena, she looked straight at Father. His acorn-brown hair had grayed more at the temples, but his honey-brown eyes still held warmth. Her gaze shifted to David. His blue eyes remained clear as northern Lake Michigan waters; his coffee-brown hair was still wavy, tousled, and fringing the tops of his ears, and he'd filled out some.

The most obvious question blurted from Cedena's mouth. "Where have you two been these last couple of years?"

Aunt Nancy spoke up. "Yes, where have you been? And don't you dare say 'gone fishing.' That's simply not explanation enough for a two-year absence that had everyone believing you were dead."

Father lowered his gaze and his voice. "I had to get away. Just couldn't take living with Isabella anymore."

Somehow, Father's words came as no surprise to Cedena. "I know Mother can be difficult, but you disappeared without any explanation. Everyone assumed you had been lost in a storm."

David reached for Cedena's hand. "We figured you were better off believing we were dead. You won't tell Mother you saw us, will you?"

"No." Cedena withdrew her hand. Had she just become as bad a traitor as Father and David had been?

When bells chimed the two o'clock hour in the distance, Aunt Nancy rested her hand on Cedena's shoulder. "We have to go. We'll be late to meet your mother, and you know how upset she gets when someone isn't punctual."

Cedena's focus pivoted to Father. "When will I see you again? Can we meet somewhere tomorrow?"

Father's brow furrowed. "You're not planning to bring Mother, are you?"

"I said I wouldn't tell her, and I meant it. Besides, she's leaving for home early tomorrow."

Lines formed between David's eyes. "And you're staying on at the Fair without her?"

"I'll be working for Uncle James. Mother doesn't know yet. Can we meet tomorrow?"

David jerked his head toward the Fisheries Building. "We work nights starting at seven, cleaning fish tanks."

Aunt Nancy spoke up. "Meet us right here at six tomorrow evening. We'll treat you both to supper before your shift."

After nods of consent from Father and David, Cedena started toward the Manufactures Building with Aunt Nancy and then turned back around. "Father, David, don't you dare disappoint me! I'll be looking for you!"

They waved and smiled, and then Cedena hurried to catch up with Aunt Nancy. Mother wouldn't be happy that they'd kept her waiting. As Cedena drew near the north entrance to the Manufactures Building, one question troubled her. Could she really manage to keep her secret from the most inquisitive, intuitive person she'd ever known, even if it was only until tomorrow morning?

CHAPTER 15

All through dinner, Cedena was on edge. She hadn't realized how hard it would be to keep her secret about Father and David. Every other minute, she felt an urge to blurt out that she had seen them and that they were right here, at the Fair. She kept pushing those thoughts aside and reminding herself that tonight, her most important responsibility was to tell Mother about her decision to accept Aunt Nancy's offer to stay on at the Fair. It was the perfect opportunity to gain independence, her great goal in life, and now, it came with the added benefit of spending time with Father and David. Her decision would come with a price, though, the least of which would surely be a war of words with Mother.

Dessert plates were removed and coffee cups refilled. Cedena clutched the napkin in her lap as she glimpsed Mother, seated beside her, from the corner of her eye. She was busy stirring sugar and cream into her cup. On the other side of her, Uncle James was sipping the hot brew. With a silent prayer, a deep breath, and a rapidly beating heart, Cedena began to speak, her focus on Mother.

"I have something to say to you, Mother. I'm not going back to Fayette with you tomorrow. Uncle James has offered me a position assisting him at the Fair, and I have accepted. I will be moving in with Uncle James and Aunt Nancy tonight, and staying with them until the Fair closes."

Mother's spoon clanked to her saucer. Her wide-eyed gaze pinned Cedena. "You *what*?"

Cedena offered a weak smile and swallowed hard. "I'm staying here. With Aunt Nancy and Uncle James."

"Nancy and James have put you up to this." Mother's focus swung to Aunt Nancy. "I reckon this all came about because you never had a daughter of your own. Now, you are stealing *my* daughter. You even bought her a middy outfit so she could look just like you!"

Aunt Nancy laughed shrilly and shook her head. "You have such an imagination, Isabella."

Heat coursed through Cedena. "Mother, no one is stealing me. I am staying of my own accord."

Mother flicked her wrist. "I knew nothing good could come of this trip." She turned to pin her gaze on Uncle James. "I reckon this is mostly your fault, James. *You're* the one who wanted us to come to the Fair."

Uncle James chuckled. "That's right, Isabella; blame it on me. I've got shoulders enough to bear the burden, haven't I?"

Mother swung her gaze to Cedena. "This is no place for you. Not for the long term, anyway. The Fair is fine for a short visit, but it's dangerous for an innocent young lady like you, day after day, week after week, month after month, mingling with all these strangers, foreigners, thieves, and worse. Just read the paper. There are stories daily about the crime here."

"I'm not afraid. Uncle James will see to my safety."

"Stay then." Mother's lip curled. "And when the Fair is over, don't bother coming back to Fayette. You no longer have a home there."

"But—"

"You heard me. It's your choice. Go home with me tomorrow, or don't come home at all."

Cedena's stomach soured. Was this really the end? No going home, ever? Could she give up her relationship with her mother for a job at the Fair? Perhaps not, but with Father and David working only two buildings away, Cedena would gain something to offset the loss. Why did life work that way? Why couldn't she have it all—Mother and Father and David the way it had been two years ago? It was a useless exercise, looking back. Her situation had irrevocably changed the day Father and David had disappeared. She'd had to deal with that loss, and now she had to deal with their reappearance.

Cedena sipped her coffee, more bitter than she had ever tasted, then returned her cup to its saucer. When she glanced up again, Mother's jaw was set in the hardest line Cedena had ever seen.

Lord, help me. A rod of velvet-coated steel straightened Cedena's spine. "I'm sorry you feel that way, Mother. Truly. But my mind is made up. This is a once-in-a-lifetime opportunity, so I won't turn it down. Aunt Nancy and Uncle James have generously offered me shelter and a job to pay my own way. I'm extremely grateful for their support, and it is my most fervent desire to have your support also."

Mother drew a deep breath. "Well, if you think you are going to gain my approval for this foolish escapade, you are utterly mistaken. I reckon it's time for me to go. I no longer have a daughter." She laid her napkin on the table and began to rise.

Heat rushed through Cedena. She wanted to strangle Mother. Reaching up, she grabbed Mother's shoulder and yanked her back into her chair.

Mother, her face pale, turned to Cedena. Never had such fear shown in Mother's eyes. Through clenched teeth, Cedena addressed her.

"Whether you like it or not, I'll always be your daughter, but you are no longer going to control me. Do you understand?"

For once, Mother seemed too surprised to speak.

Cedena gazed past her to Uncle James. "Shouldn't we go now? We've got some moving to do."

Uncle James gave a nod and tossed money on the table. A minute later, outside the Palmer House, he signaled to a driver and the four of them shared a silent ride to Mrs. O'Donnell's.

When they reached their rooms, Cedena began packing her belongings. All the while, Mother sat mute at a writing desk with her back to the room. When Cedena had finished, Uncle James carried her bag and chest to the suite across the hall. Cedena paused in the center of her mother's room, looked back, and tried to think of something to say, something other than revealing her secret about Father and David. With a heart heavier than a cannonball, Cedena stepped into the hallway where Uncle James and Aunt Nancy were talking.

Tears slid down Cedena's cheeks. Would she ever see Mother again?

Aunt Nancy wrapped her arm around Cedena's waist and guided her to her new home. Life was starting over. Although she now had to face it without the person who had been most influential in her life, she held tight the promise of a revived relationship with her beloved father and brother.

As she settled into her aunt and uncle's suite, she couldn't help wondering what Matthew would think now that Uncle James had hired her to help with his display. And what would Matthew make of her father and brother suddenly turning up alive?

CHAPTER 16

By the end of the following day, Cedena's head was spinning. Matthew had spent hours teaching her about Paxton
Pharmaceutical's products, and now she was in front of the
display handing out fliers and business cards to passersby. It
was all for the best, this flurry of activity. She hadn't had time
to think about the lost relationship with Mother or the dinner
meeting with Father and David, which was now only a few
minutes away. At least Matthew hadn't reacted badly when
she'd told him first thing this morning that they were alive and
that she and Aunt Nancy and Uncle James were meeting with
them for dinner tonight while he tended the display.

Aunt Nancy came around from behind the display. "It's
time to go to dinner."

Cedena set her fliers and business cards in the holders atop
the display case. Flanked by Aunt Nancy and Uncle James,
she headed to the meeting spot near the Fisheries Building.
Her pulse quickened. What if Father and David weren't there?
A knife sliced her heart for the second time since they'd disappeared.

Then she saw them. It was all she could do to keep from
lifting her skirts and hurrying to meet them. She tempered her

runaway emotions with a dose of propriety and remained firmly between her aunt and uncle.

Approaching Father and David, Uncle James opened the
conversation. "Didn't I attend a funeral for you two a couple
of years ago? And yet, here you are, alive and well. Hungry,
too, I presume. Where would you like to go for supper? On
me, of course, although I must say this is the first time I've
treated two Lazaruses to a meal."

Father wasn't smiling. This was the first time Cedena had
seen the two men come together without a handshake. "Nice
to see you again, too, James. As for dinner, the Marine Café is
close by, and you know how we Rossiers love fish."

"The Marine Café it is, then."

As everyone started toward the restaurant, Cedena slipped
free of her aunt and uncle, came alongside David, and placed
her hand on his arm. "So what were you and Father doing before the Fair opened and you got work cleaning the
aquariums?"

He shrugged. "Nothing too interesting. We repainted and
renamed the boat and fished our way down to Chicago. Then
we sold the boat, rented an apartment, and got construction
jobs on the Fisheries Building. When it was finished, we
helped set up the displays. Now, we clean them every night.
What about you?"

There was so much to tell, but having arrived at the Marine
Café, Cedena shook her head. "I'll tell you later."

As the waiter showed them to a table, Cedena's stomach
tightened. Dinner last night with Mother had turned into a
heart-wrenching affair. Tension was already evident between
Father and Uncle James. Could she possibly find a way to dif-
fuse it?

On the opposite side of the table from Father and David, Uncle James held a chair for Aunt Nancy, and then pulled out the one next to it. "Sit here, Cedena."

Though Cedena longed to sit between Father and David, she settled onto the chair across from them and Uncle James sat beside her. Talk about Paxton Pharmaceuticals and other exhibits at the Fair passed the time from appetizer to dessert. With dishes cleared and coffee cups refilled, Aunt Nancy took a sharp turn in the conversation.

"Charles, I know you did what seemed best in leaving Isabella. But did you ever think of the consequences to your daughter?"

Father gave a slight nod. "I did. I thought it best she believed me dead."

Aunt Nancy clicked her tongue. "Charles, Charles, Charles. The problem now is that you've been caught in your lie."

Uncle James set his coffee cup down with a clack. "And that is just the emotional consequence of your decision. Tell me, did you consider the economic difficulties your wife and daughter would face when you sailed away?"

Lines marred Father's forehead. "Sakes alive! I left a considerable sum in the cookie jar. They were far from penniless."

Aunt Nancy chuckled. "You couldn't take the cookie jar money with you if you were to be presumed dead. Taking it would have been a clear sign that you had simply deserted your wife and daughter. I suspect you thought of *that*. And I wouldn't be one bit surprised if you had been planning for some time to leave, and had been salting away a secret stash of cash no one knew about."

Father's cheeks reddened. David lowered his gaze. Cedena's pulse quickened. Had Father done what Aunt Nancy suggested?

Uncle James turned to Cedena. "Tell your father and brother what your life was like after they left, after the savings ran out."

Cedena tried to speak, but a lump in her throat choked off words. A tear trickled down her cheek.

Uncle James offered her his handkerchief and swung his gaze back to Father. "When Nancy and I went up to Fayette for the 'funeral' that was held a few months after you 'died,' Isabella and Cedena were struggling to put food on the table. They had no hope of paying their rent. The General Store had cut off their credit. They were about to be evicted from their home. I paid their bills and rent and bought enough supplies for the next month. I've been sending monthly support ever since."

Aunt Nancy scowled at Father. "Isabella and Cedena were thin as rails. They both had dark circles under their eyes. I'm sure they hadn't slept well in months. They had been doing odd jobs—watching over the neighbors' children, taking in sewing and laundry—altogether adding up to but a small pittance compared to their needs."

Cedena's worst nightmares sprang back to life. Going to bed so cold and hungry sleep would not come. Afraid that any moment they would be tossed out on the street for missing rent payments. Their pain and suffering had seemed a natural but unfortunate result of Father and David's deaths at the time. But now? How could they have been so selfish? Anger wrestled with joy that they were alive.

Uncle James sighed. "I used to feel sorry for you, Charles, dying before your fiftieth birthday." His focus moved to David. "And for you, gone over Jordan before you'd had a chance to really live. But now I'm sorry Nancy and Cedena ran into the two of you yesterday. I've lost all my respect for you now that I know the truth."

Cedena cleared the lump from her throat and drew a deep breath. "Forgive me, Uncle James, but I'm not sorry. I feel a little like the father in the story of the prodigal son. My father and brother were lost, but now they're found and I want to celebrate. But part of me feels like the older brother in the story." Her gaze met Father's. "I'm angry with you. I can't understand why you would cause so much hardship for me and Mother."

Father's amber eyes darkened. "I'm sorry, Cedena. Truly. I'm not worthy to be called your father. I wouldn't blame you if you never wanted to see me again."

"Never wanted to see you again?" The words shot out of Cedena's mouth at a volume far louder than intended. She cringed at the number of customers staring at her, and then she continued in a subdued voice. "Of course I want to see you again. I'll be working only two buildings away, at Uncle James's display near the north door of the Manufactures Building. Promise me we'll see each other often. Promise me!"

Aunt Nancy turned to Cedena, her lips forming a thin line as she fiddled with her napkin. There would be no approval from that quarter.

Uncle James's shoulders slumped as he stared off into the distance. Maybe he begrudgingly accepted Cedena's desire to see more of Father and David.

Father gave a tight nod. "We'll see you again, if that's what you want, daughter."

"Tomorrow," Cedena suggested. "I'll be waiting for you at the same place ten minutes before your shift. We'll have a few minutes to talk."

David pushed back his chair. "See you then, Cedena. Now, we'd better go or we'll be late for our shift. Much obliged for the dinner, Uncle James."

Father rose. "Yes, much obliged. Good evening."

Cedena fought the urge to get up and walk with them to the Fisheries Building. But for now, she must temper that desire with the necessity for smooth sailing with Aunt Nancy and Uncle James.

As Father and David disappeared from the room, Uncle James pulled out his money clip and slapped some bills on the table. "Those scoundrels!" He rose and pulled back Cedena's chair for her. "If I never see your father or brother again, it won't be too soon, but you do what you want. Just don't bring them near me."

Aunt Nancy stood. "It's been a long day. Let's head home."

CHAPTER 17

Three months later
Friday night, October 13

On the ride from the Fair to Mrs. O'Donnell's, Cedena was almost too tired to think. It had been a week of long days, attending to the pharmaceutical display with Matthew while Uncle James and Aunt Nancy returned to Kansas City to check on business and domestic matters. She'd never admit to anyone that working twelve hours, day after day, was much harder than she had anticipated.

Even though work days had been long, Cedena had still managed time for visits with Father and David. She had seen them for a few minutes before they started their shift tonight, as she had done several times each week since discovering they were working at the Fair.

The hack rolled to a stop. Matthew got out and helped Cedena down. When she stepped inside Mrs. O'Donnell's front hallway, a glance at the empty silver tray kept for incoming mail told her no letter had come from home. Her heart sank. She'd written to Mother three weeks ago, asking to be allowed to come home after the Fair ended. She should have heard back by now.

Mrs. O'Donnell came from the parlor. "Miss Rossier, you're back. Your aunt and uncle came in about an hour ago. They've taken your mail upstairs."

"Thank you." Hope rose anew in Cedena's heart as she dragged herself up the stairs. She could think of nothing more inviting than a comfortable chair, a pan of warm water and Epsom salts, and a good, long, foot soak while she read her mail.

Matthew climbed the stairs one step behind her. "You're tired. You should take tomorrow off. You've been working almost non-stop since your Mother left three months ago."

Cedena waited until they reached the hallway outside Uncle James and Aunt Nancy's door to face Matthew and reply. His amber-brown eyes were pinched together, rimmed above by lines. "You needn't look at me with such worry on your face. A solid night's sleep will surely restore my energy, and tomorrow, I'll be ready to put in another long day. Good night, Matthew." She turned and opened the door, but when she had stepped through and tried to close it, Matthew prevented her.

"I need to speak with your uncle."

He entered the suite and Uncle James greeted them both with a welcoming smile.

"Cedena, Matthew, how did your week go?"

Aunt Nancy gestured toward a pair of green jacquard chairs. "Sit down, you two. You look tired."

Uncle James took a seat on the small black leather sofa facing them and loosened his tie.

Matthew leaned forward, focused on Uncle James. "How was your trip?"

"Fine, just fine. Trains ran on time. All is well at the home office and at the house. Right, Nancy?"

Aunt Nancy joined Uncle James on the sofa. "Yes, all is in order. I began to wonder why we had even made the trip back. Now, how about you two? Have the crowds thinned out? Or were you as busy as usual?"

"Busier." Cedena reached down, tempted to untie her high top shoes, but she decided to wait until Matthew left.

Matthew leaned back. "You just wouldn't have believed the crowd on Monday. It was Chicago Day. Over 700,000 people came through the gates."

"Good, good." Uncle James removed his tie.

"The crowd has thinned considerably since then." Matthew glanced Cedena's way and then pivoted back to Uncle James. "Even so, Cedena is tired out. I think she should take tomorrow off." When he turned her way again, she was tempted to scowl at him, but didn't.

"I can arrange that easily enough, don't you know?" Uncle James pinned his gaze on Cedena. "You take the day off tomorrow, boss's orders." His attention turned to Matthew. "I'm giving *you* the day off, also, Matthew. Nancy and I will tend to the display. There's no need for either of you to step foot on the fairgrounds, if you don't want to."

"But I want to!" Cedena edged forward. "At five o'clock, the dromedaries, donkeys, and Arabian horses are racing on the Midway Plaisance. It will be the only chance in my life to see camels race!"

"Then surely you must go." Aunt Nancy turned to Uncle James. "You'll go with her, won't you, James?"

"I'll take Cedena," Matthew replied, "if that's all right with her." He gave Cedena a questioning look.

Cedena offered a slight nod. "That would be fine. But I also want to see the Grand Court Illumination at seven and the fireworks on the lake front a half-hour later. Are you interested?"

"Sure. I'll come by for you at four o'clock. That will give us plenty of time to get to the races at five." Matthew rose. "I'd better go. Good night."

When Uncle James saw Matthew out, he stepped into the hallway to speak with him in hushed tones. Cedena was too tired to wonder what they might be discussing. Moments later, Uncle James returned and approached Aunt Nancy. "I'm going to turn in now, dear." He leaned down and kissed her forehead.

"I'll be along soon." Aunt Nancy reached for an envelope on the end table by the sofa and brought it to Cedena. "Mrs. O'Donnell gave me this for you."

Cedena took the envelope and studied the address on the front. This was the very same envelope she had sent to Mother three weeks ago, only now, Mother's address had been overwritten with the word "REFUSED" and an arrow pointed to Cedena's return address in the upper left corner. Cedena's heart plummeted and her eyes filled with tears. Mother really *had* disowned her.

Aunt Nancy moved to the chair Matthew had vacated earlier. "I'm sorry. I know what it's like to be on the receiving end of Isabella's disapproval."

Tears trickled down Cedena's face. Aunt Nancy offered her a hanky.

As Cedena patted her cheeks dry, her stomach churned. "Why? Why does Mother have to be so difficult?"

"I don't know. She's been bossy and controlling for as long as I can remember." Aunt Nancy reached for Cedena's hand and gave it a squeeze. "You're welcome to live in Kansas City with James and me after the Fair closes. It would be best."

"But you've already done so much for me. I don't want to be a burden. Maybe Father and David—"

Aunt Nancy shook her head. "They abandoned you two years ago. Remember? Now listen to me, and listen well. You could never be a burden. You're the light in the lives of your Uncle James and me! We love having you with us. It's Isabella's loss. I can't believe she's turned her back on you much like Charles and David did. Maybe someday she'll see how wrong she is. Until then, please know you are welcome in our home and *very* much loved and wanted."

The lump in Cedena's throat about choked her. She somehow managed to swallow past it and eke out a reply. "I don't know how to thank you."

Aunt Nancy grinned. "Diddle-de-dum! That's easy as pie. Be yourself now that you are out from under Isabella's roof. Enjoy life." She rose. "I'm going to turn in now. It's been a long trip back. Good night."

"Good night, Aunt Nancy. And thanks."

As her aunt disappeared, questions flooded Cedena's mind. Was it really such a bad idea to ask Father and David to take her in? Didn't they owe her something? She would talk to them, but no point worrying about it tonight. The Fair wouldn't close for another two-and-a-half weeks. Tomorrow was a new day, a day of rest, fun, and fireworks, if all went as planned.

CHAPTER 18

As Matthew had promised, he knocked on Cedena's door at four the next afternoon. He wasn't crazy about the idea of camel races, donkey races, or horse races, but if they would make Cedena happy, he was willing to go along.

Cedena promptly opened the door. The circles Matthew had seen under her eyes last night had vanished, and he sensed renewed energy in her quick smile. "Are you ready for some camel races?"

"I am. And you?"

"Can't wait!"

Cedena stepped into the hall. A hint of white lilac came with her. Matthew's gaze swept over her, from her fawn-colored, upswept hair to her honey-brown eyes to her tawny-brown cape. "If I may say so, that cape looks particularly fine on you."

"Thank you. And your chestnut sack coat looks particularly fine on you. It appears we are ready to be tourists at the Fair today, rather than business people attending to a display."

He gave a nod and followed her down the stairs. The hack he'd hired earlier in the day waited for them at the curb. He opened the carriage door, gave her a hand up, and settled beside her on the single seat. Her nearness was almost enough to distract him from the next step in his plan. He needed to explain it before they went any farther.

"After we pass through the gate, we must go first to your uncle's display. There's something I must check on."

"I thought we were heading straight to the Midway Plaisance. It's our day off, eh?" She nudged him with her elbow.

"We'll be there in time for the races. Trust me."

She cast him a look full of suspicion.

He needed to change the subject, and fast. "Did I ever tell you about the first time I met your Uncle James?"

"You were five and he saved you from being hit by a train."

"And the first time he paid me to work for him?"

"You were thirteen and helped him out in the warehouse. And you told me about Spaulding College and becoming his assistant, and about your mother and the home where you've lived since you were two."

"So I did. You'd better tell me about yourself, since you know everything about me."

"Not everything, but those things. As for me, you already know most of it. I was born and raised in Fayette. Father worked at the furnace until the Jackson Iron Company shut it down at the end of 1890. He bought a used fishing boat—a sloop, and some nets. Father and David supposedly drowned two years ago in a storm but then resurfaced at the Fair. . . ."

Soon, they transferred to the train, and fifteen minutes later, they entered the fairgrounds.

"I still don't understand why we have to go to Uncle James's display."

MOUNTAINS OF LOVE 105

Matthew offered tight smile. "Believe me when I say you'll be glad you did." He placed her hand on his arm. As they crossed from the terminal to the Manufactures Building, he recalled his first day with Cedena three months ago. She'd been so impetuous. Now that she'd seen just about everything there was to see at the Fair and had proven herself to be an exemplary coworker, she was much more pleasant to be around. So pleasant that he found himself thinking about her whenever they were apart.

There was one troubling thought, though. Orin Young had been corresponding with her. Every couple of weeks another letter from him would be waiting for Cedena at Mrs. O'Donnell's. It could only mean one thing. Orin was sweet on her. But did she feel the same for him?

As they approached the pharmaceutical display, Matthew spotted what he had come for. It was visible behind the counter. Cedena saw it, too.

"Aunt Nancy, why are you sitting in a rolling chair? Are you all right?"

Mrs. Paxton quickly got to her feet. "I'm fine. I've been enjoying this chair since your uncle rented it early this morning. Matthew paid for it and insisted that James get it so you won't have to walk to the camel race. You know how it is with the rolling chairs. If you don't claim one early in the day, you're out of luck."

Uncle James rolled it out from behind the counter. "Cedena, have a seat, won't you? And enjoy the races. You, too, Matthew. Oh, and here," he reached into his pocket, pulled out some coins, and pressed them into Matthew's hand, "place some bets for me. I don't care who you pick. Races are no fun without bets!"

Just what Matthew needed—the responsibility to pick winning contenders in the races. Once Cedena was seated, he began to wheel her out of the building. She glanced at him over the back of the wicker chair. "You were sweet to rent a chair, but you needn't have done it. You could have saved your money. Maybe placed a bet on the races."

He shook his head. "I don't gamble. I wish your uncle hadn't asked me to bet for him."

"I don't normally gamble, either, but today is different. Did I ever tell you they used to race sulkies at Fayette and there was a whole lot of betting going on? I was just a kid, but I remember it well. It was so exciting!"

"Were you a gambler back then?"

"No, no. Mother was dead set against it. But I'll tell you a secret. Father used to place bets and she never knew it."

"I think I'm beginning to see where your interest in such things got a start." Conversation rolled along as smoothly as the chair Matthew was pushing, and soon they were at the racetrack at the west end of the Midway.

CHAPTER 19

"See those men?" Cedena pointed to a group of gentlemen a few yards away at the racetrack. "Go to them and put my quarter on Al Shroud." Cedena pressed the coin into Matthew's hand.

"Are you sure?" Lines grooved Matthew's forehead. "They don't look like gamblers to me."

"They are definitely making bets." Cedena pinned her gaze on Matthew. "Now go before it's too late. The camels are starting to line up."

Cedena watched Matthew approach the group somewhat hesitantly, but he was given ready reception, as she had been sure he would be. Then he returned.

Cedena grinned up at Matthew. "See! I told you they'd take your money."

Matthew shook his head. "Not *my* money, but yours and your uncle's. I think the both of you are throwing it away."

"Al Shroud means a camel that loves to escape and can't be caught. That camel has got to win!"

A few minutes later, when Al Shroud finished last, Cedena laughed. "I guess there's not much to a name, where camels are concerned. Maybe I'll do better on the donkey race. Put this quarter on Atum." She nudged Matthew toward the gamblers.

As Atum rounded the last curve in third place, Cedena urged him on. "You can do it, Atum! Hold on!"

He slipped into fourth just prior to the finish and Matthew offered a crooked smile. "Guess this isn't your day."

"It's not over. The Arabians are next." Cedena pulled out another coin. "Here's my last bet. Put this quarter on Ziyadah. It means superb in speed. Third time lucky, eh? That's what I always say."

"The other gamblers are starting to like me." Matthew walked away with much more confidence in his stride than she'd seen the last two times. He soon returned and was standing behind her chair when the race started. Ziyadah took the first turn at the head of the pack and then opened up the lead.

Matthew and Cedena's voices joined others in urging the horse on.

"Go, Ziyadah! Go!"

The horse's lead narrowed to two lengths at the second turn and then to one length at the third turn. Coming down the straightaway, Alfayiz ran almost even. Then Ziyadah pulled ahead by a nose and crossed the finish line.

Cedena looked back over her shoulder at Matthew. Wearing a grin as wide as the Midway Plaisance, he headed for the gamblers. He returned a few minutes later with a silver dollar. "This is your lucky day. You actually made money, and so did your uncle!" He placed the coin in her outstretched palm.

"Thank you, Matthew." Cedena gazed up at him. "For someone who wasn't particularly interested in attending the races today, you look as though you enjoyed yourself, at least during the last race."

He offered a wry smile. "Let's go find a café. We've got just enough time for supper before the grand illumination starts." He rolled her along on the Midway.

"Where are you taking me?"

"You pick the place."

"The Chinese café. We haven't been there since my first day at the Fair. Remember?"

"How could I forget?" Matthew turned into the Chinese Village.

Cedena placed an order for shark's fin, rice, fresh tomatoes, and ice cream for dessert. Matthew ordered corned beef, sliced tomatoes, and an éclair.

"That's the exact same thing you ordered last time." Cedena handed her menu to the waiter. "Don't you ever wonder what some of these exotic Chinese foods taste like?"

Matthew shook his head. "About now, I'm wondering what a Kansas City steak tastes like. It's been a long time since I've had one."

"You'll be back home soon . . . ." A lump formed in Cedena's throat, cutting off her words. Matthew had a home to return to. She envied him. There was no point returning to Fayette now that Mother had rejected her. Aunt Nancy was right. The best option was to go to Kansas City. But the ache in her heart brought tears to her eyes. She lowered her gaze and pulled out her handkerchief.

"Cedena, what's wrong?" Matthew spoke with a tenderness she'd never heard from him before.

She swallowed past the lump in her throat and forced herself to offer a smile. "I just had a really sharp attack of that biblical sin, covetousness. I'm jealous of you because you have a home waiting for you in Kansas City where you are wanted. I won't be returning to Fayette. My letter to Mother was 'Refused.' It looks like I'll be moving into Uncle James and Aunt Nancy's Kansas City home when the Fair closes." She still held hope that Father and David would take her in, but it was only a hope.

"I . . . I don't know what to say. I'm so sorry that your Mother is still angry with you, but you'll love your aunt and uncle's place. It's quite impressive. And I can tell that they love you very much."

Cedena drew a deep breath and let it out slowly. Her only hope for maintaining ties with her immediate family rested on Father and David. She didn't want to lose them again, regardless of Aunt Nancy's reminder that they had abandoned her. It was really Mother whom they had abandoned, wasn't it?

Matthew grew pensive. "You look like you have a lot on your mind right now, but please remember that God knows how you feel and he works all things for good."

Matthew was right. God knows. Maybe she needed to trust him more, even though He had seemed completely absent when she and Mother had been experiencing really hard times.

The waiter returned with their food and Cedena pushed heartache aside as she cut into the shark's fin and took a bite.

"What does it taste like?" Matthew cut into his corned beef.

Cedena tried to figure out what to compare the crunchy-chewy fin to. "It doesn't have much flavor, but the texture is interesting. Take a bite." She cut another piece and offered it to him on her fork.

Matthew shook his head. "I'll stick with good old American corned beef."

"Not much of a risk-taker, are you?" Cedena tucked the piece into her mouth.

He shook his head and chewed his corned beef.

~*~*~

Matthew rolled Cedena into the Grand Court in time to see the electric fountain display and illumination at seven. She'd seen it before, but she could never grow tired of the bright colors reflecting off streams of water darting up into the sky, or the marvelous lights shining on the white buildings. She wanted to memorize the display, for surely she would never see anything like it again once the Fair closed at the end of the month.

When the show ended, Matthew and Cedena returned the chair to the rolling chair kiosk and headed inside the Manufactures Building. Uncle James loaned them two canvas stools and they found the perfect spot on the beach to sit and enjoy the fireworks.

As Cedena watched the bursts of color unfold over the lake, she recalled the glorious display on the Fourth of July and how Alice and Orin Young had watched it with her and Matthew. Orin Young had been full of mischief, a risk taker, terribly good looking, and fun to be around. Against the wishes of Matthew and Alice, he had insisted on visiting the Joint Territorial Building of New Mexico, Arizona, and Oklahoma. In so doing, he had stirred in Cedena a real interest in the West.

After Orin had returned to Wisconsin, he had written several letters to her and implied some sort of future together. He could make her heart sing, but he was definitely not the sort of fellow she would want to cling to for the rest of her life. She never answered any of his letters. No point in encouraging him. But why hadn't she asked him to stop writing to her?

Matthew, on the other hand, was nearly Orin's opposite. Reliable. Responsible. Focused on business. Serious to a fault. Nice looking but not exactly handsome. Unlike the heavenly bursts of gold, red, blue, and green showing off over the lake tonight, Matthew didn't set off fireworks. Once the Fair was over, she might never see him again, unless she moved to Kansas City, but she was thankful for his friendship during these past three months.

But what would her life consist of after the Fair? Would she be caring for Father and David or moving in with Aunt Nancy and Uncle James?

CHAPTER 20

Late the following day, Cedena waited in the usual spot outside the Fisheries Building for Father and David. In their conversations over the past three months, they had often re-called the good times of their lives back in the Upper Peninsula. But whenever Cedena had asked about their plans following the Fair, their replies had been vague. Now, she needed answers. As Father and David approached, she offered them a bright smile. Each of them greeted her with a kiss on her cheek.

"How was your day, daughter?" Father started the conversation with his customary question.

"Busy, as usual. And how was your shift last night?" Her gaze slid from Father to David, who appeared more tired than usual.

"It was a late one." David ran his hand through the waves of his coffee-brown hair. "One of the tanks sprang a leak. We got off two hours late."

"I'm sorry to hear that." Cedena would have hugged him, but he had grown much more remote than he had been two years ago. Before his disappearance, they would finish each other's sentences, and each intuitively knew what the other was thinking. Now, she had to pry for information, which he parceled out as if it were gold.

Cedena fingered the envelope in her pocket and then slid it out. "I wrote to Mother a while ago to ask if I could come home after the Fair closes. Here's my answer." She held up her returned letter with the word "Refused" scrawled across Mother's name and address.

Father took the envelope from Cedena and studied it. He offered a deep sigh as his amber eyes narrowed. "Sorry to say this is just like Isabella. If she doesn't get her way, she gets back at you." He returned the missive to Cedena.

David pulled Cedena into a side hug. "I'm so sorry. But maybe it's for the best. Aunt Nancy and Uncle James have taken good care of you here at the Fair. I'm sure they'll do the same after it closes."

"That's what I wanted to talk to you about. I could live with you and Father and take care of your apartment for you— cooking, cleaning, laundry. And I could get a job part time to help with expenses, too."

David released Cedena, his gaze swinging to Father.

"That wouldn't work, Cedena." Father's words were firm.

"Why not? We're family! You and David are all I have left now that Mother has shut me out! *Please* don't turn your backs on me! I might never see you again after the Fair!" Moisture welled in her eyes.

"Go to Kansas City with James and Nancy. That's the best place for you." Father took a step back. "We have to get to work now."

David stepped off and then looked back over his shoulder. "See you again soon, Cedena."

As the distance increased between them, Cedena's heart broke all over again.

~*~*~

A few days later, another of the frequent letters from Alice Young arrived for Cedena. In this letter, she spoke of autumn in Wisconsin and the customary activities—husking bees, pressing apple cider, fish boils—and, as usual, she mentioned Matthew:

> Please remember me to Matthew. Orin and I had such fun with you and Matthew at the White City.
> Please keep in touch.
> Your friend,
> Alice

Cedena sat down to the writing desk and penned a reply, making sure to inform Alice of Aunt Nancy's address in Kansas City so her next missive wouldn't end up in the dead letter office.

~*~*~

On the last day of the Fair, Cedena waited impatiently for Father and David at their usual meeting place outside the Fisheries Building. As the minutes ticked closer to the start of their shift, her hopes sank. Surely they were expected to work tonight. There would be much to do to take down the aquariums and ship the fish to new homes. Why hadn't they shown up?

At last, she saw them hurrying toward her. A moment later, Father gave her a quick hug. "Sorry we're late. We've only got a minute. You take care of yourself in Kansas City, you hear?"

David pulled a scrap of paper from his pocket and shoved it into her hand. "Here's our address. Write real soon. Father says we'll be moving on before long."

Cedena pulled a folded note from her own pocket. "This is Uncle James and Aunt Nancy's address in Kansas City. I expect to hear from you. Understand?"

David nodded and shoved the paper into his pocket.

Father kissed her cheek. "Goodbye, Cedena. I'll sure miss you." He started toward the Fisheries Building. David followed, looking back to wave goodbye.

Cedena watched them go until tears blurred her vision. When would she see them again, and where? Why did life have to include such painful partings?

She headed back to the Manufactures Building. Uncle James, Aunt Nancy, and Matthew could use her help packing up the Paxton Pharmaceutical display.

CHAPTER 21

November 2, 1893

After an overnight train ride, Cedena was thankful to get off the California Express and plant her feet on the Union Depot platform in Kansas City. Even at half-past eight in the morning, people were everywhere. She was used to it at the Fair and in Chicago, but could she grow accustomed to big city life long-term?

Uncle James arranged for their baggage to be delivered to the house and went to find Lewis, the Paxton's chauffeur, who had been notified by wire when to pick them up. Soon, a beautiful red landau drove up and they headed home. A few minutes later, Lewis pulled in front of a modest two-story home and Matthew got out. Ten minutes after that, Lewis turned onto a wide boulevard of large homes.

The carriage came to a stop in front of a brick mansion. The sight of it took Cedena's breath away. It rose four stories in an ornate design that included more chimneys and dormers than she could count. A porch wrapped around the two visible sides, and the front lawn was spacious enough to accommodate Fayette's entire business district. How on earth had she ended up here? This was more unbelievable than the best fair-ytale.

Lewis opened the carriage door and Uncle James stepped out, set his valise aside, and then assisted Aunt Nancy. She poked her head back inside the open door. "Cedena, it's time to get out."

"I'm sorry. I'm still trying to take this all in."

Uncle James chuckled. "You'll do much better at that if you get out." He assisted her to the sidewalk and she followed him and Aunt Nancy to the huge, mahogany double-front doors. They had beveled and leaded glass windows in the de-sign of angels.

The doors opened and a woman in a black dress and white apron received them with a wide smile.

"Welcome home, Mr. and Mrs. Paxton!"

"Good morning, Mrs. Meyer!" Uncle James greeted her heartily. "Won't you meet our niece, Cedena Rossier? Cedena, this is Mrs. Meyer, our head housekeeper."

The woman's plump hand wrapped gently around Cede-na's. "I do hope you'll enjoy your stay here, Miss Rossier."

"I'm sure I will." Cedena barely got out the words, so speechless was she at the size and beauty of Uncle James and Aunt Nancy's home. In the front hallway, the cherry wainscot-ing was nicely paneled and cherry door frames were attractively fluted. Walnut molding outlined the decorative plaster ceiling. Hanging down from the center medallion was a brass chandelier with milk glass globes alternating with tulip shades.

Aunt Nancy turned to Cedena. "Do you like your new home?"

"Who wouldn't? But why didn't you tell me?"

"Tell you what?"

Cedena swept her hand wide. "About this mansion you live in. I had no idea your home was so huge."

Uncle James wrapped his arm about Cedena's waist. "Best not to boast, that's what I always say." He released her and adjusted his tie. "Now, won't you ladies excuse me? Lewis is waiting to take me to the office. Do you two need transportation today?"

Aunt Nancy nodded. "Please tell Lewis to be out front at eleven. I'm taking Cedena downtown. We have some shopping to do."

"I'll tell him, and I'll see you both tonight. Dinner at seven?"

"Yes, James. Don't be late. You know how it upsets Florence." To Cedena, she said, "Florence is our cook."

Uncle James headed out the door.

A girl in a maid's uniform who appeared to be in her late teens entered the front hall.

Aunt Nancy introduced her. "Cedena, this is Vivian. Vivian, my niece, Cedena Rossier." Aunt Nancy focused on Cedena. "Vivian is our upstairs maid. If you need anything, let her know. What do you say we go upstairs and unpack our valises? Vivian will help you put things away, and when our trunks arrive later today, she'll help you with that, also."

When they reached the second floor, Aunt Nancy paused outside the first door and turned to Vivian. "When you've finished settling Cedena in, would you please bring a tray of tea and scones to my suite? Cedena and I have to discuss our list for today's shopping trip."

"Yes, ma'am."

As Cedena followed Vivian down the hall and into her bedroom, she wondered whether she was dreaming. A wide bed with a spread of pale pink silk stood in the large room's center. Tall mahogany bedposts were carved in a reed design and topped with a curved leaf finial. Across the top stretched a pink silk canopy. It was trimmed with delicate lace a foot long that hung down on all four sides. Across from the bed was a bay window with a window seat. Its magenta velvet upholstery topped by several plump pillows offered a comfortable retreat and lookout. In the air hung the subtle scent of rose potpourri.

Vivian pulled a luggage rack from a huge closet, set it at the foot of the bed, and began unpacking Cedena's valise. Delicate unmentionables went into the carved mahogany dresser. A small bag of dirty laundry was set by the door.

When Vivian carried toiletries into the adjoining bathroom, Cedena followed her. What she saw took her breath away. A huge claw-foot tub stood against the outside wall. It was fitted out with a shower head. A curtain rod ran all the way around. Along the side wall was a marble countertop and a sink with silver fixtures. The floor and walls were tiled in pink marble. Decorative molding edged the ceiling, and in the very center was a painting of rose blossoms.

Vivian pulled clean towels from a cabinet above the commode and set them on the edge of the tub. "When you're ready for a bath, there are some wonderful bath crystals on the counter from your uncle's pharmaceutical company. Which is your favorite? I myself prefer the lilac-scented ones." She went to the counter and pulled one of the jars forward.

"To be perfectly honest, Vivian, I have only tried the rose-scented crystals. I think I'll give the lilac ones a try tonight."

With a curt nod, Vivian headed for the door. "I'll be going downstairs now to fix up the tray of tea and scones for you and Mrs. Paxton. I'll be back in about ten minutes. Oh, and before I forget, a letter came for you in care of your uncle. I put it inside the slant top desk over there." She pointed to the corner of the room. "Now, I'm on my way. I'll see you in Mrs. Paxton's suite soon?"

"Yes. I'll be there in ten minutes. Thank you for your help, Vivian."

CHAPTER 22

Cedena headed for the slant top desk and took out the letter. The handwriting and return address attributed the message to Alice Young. A gold-finish letter opener lay in a pigeonhole inside the desk. Cedena quickly slit the letter open.

A brief note to Cedena had been folded around a small sealed envelope bearing Matthew's name. Cedena read quickly.

> All is well here. I've had a cold, but I'm over it now. I must ask a huge favor. Would you please make sure the enclosed envelope gets to Matthew? I know it is forward of me to write directly to him, but I can withstand the criticism for doing so. It would mean so much to me if you would see that he gets it. Thank you a thousand times!
>
> Your loyal friend,
> Alice

Cedena slipped the note for Matthew into her pocket. She'd give it to Aunt Nancy this morning, and by tomorrow morning, it would be sitting on Matthew's desk. Uncle James would see to it, especially if Aunt Nancy made certain it wound up in Uncle James's work valise.

Cedena wandered to the window, sat down on the thickly padded seat, plumped cushions behind her, and leaned back. As she gazed out across the broad front lawn to the boulevard and watched a fancy carriage hauled by a stunning white horse roll past, she couldn't help wondering, *What have I gotten myself into?* This world was so far removed, so far beyond anything she had ever seen or imagined. How could she make herself useful here, when paid help attended to all the necessary chores? What would she do to earn her keep? At the Fair, it was simple. She worked, earned money, and paid for her room, board, and incidentals. Now what?

She heard her aunt and Vivian's voices in the hall. It was time for tea and scones, time to sort things out. Cedena headed down the hall and paused at the door to her aunt's suite. The sitting room combined the best of masculinity and femininity. Dark-brown leather covered a bulky chair and footstool, while shades of peach and apricot satin decorated two small balloon back chairs pulled up to a mahogany table where the silver tea tray rested.

Aunt Nancy beckoned to Cedena. "Come in. The tea is ready."

As Cedena joined her aunt, she pulled the note from her pocket. "This came from Alice. She wants me to make sure Matthew gets it. Would you ask Uncle James to take it to the office tomorrow?"

Aunt Nancy took it from her and placed it on her desk. "That Alice is getting a bit forward, I'd say. But more power to her. Perhaps a push from her is just what Matthew needs. I'll put the note in James's valise tonight. Now come and sit."

When the tea and scones had been served and Vivian had taken her leave, Aunt Nancy took a sip of her tea and then set the cup down. Her gaze on Cedena was direct. "Do you like your room?"

Cedena nodded.

"Good. Let's talk about what you need and make a list. You will need a nice gown for the formal occasions that constantly come up—dinner parties and balls. I'd like to take you to Thayer's Mercantile. We'll look at dress patterns and pick out some yard goods. And then, after lunch, we'll visit Alma—Mrs. Waren, Matthew's mother—who's been my seamstress almost as long as I've been living in Kansas City. She'll take your measurements and do the sewing."

Cedena nodded again as she munched on a scone. She had heard mention of Mrs. Waren over the years, just as she'd heard of Matthew before ever meeting him. But purchasing yard goods and hiring a seamstress for a formal gown sounded quite costly. How many weeks, months, years would she need to work, and at what, to pay for it?

Cedena set her scone aside. "Aunt Nancy, I don't want to be a burden here to you and Uncle James. I'd like to earn my keep, pay my own way as I did in Chicago. To do that, I'll need your help finding appropriate employment. I'm not sure I'll need a formal gown."

Aunt Nancy's sharp gaze pinned her for a moment. Then she set her cup and scone aside, got up from her chair, and paced to the window. In silence, she gazed out on the same boulevard Cedena had watched from her own room. A minute later, Aunt Nancy returned to her chair, her smile contrite.

"Cedena, I must apologize. I am so very pleased to have you here in Kansas City that I have barged ahead making plans for your needs without thinking to find out first what you prefer. The last thing I want to do is become as domineering as your mother was. Please, will you forgive me?"

Cedena reached for Aunt Nancy's hand and gave a gentle squeeze. "You're forgiven."

Aunt Nancy drew a deep breath. "Let me ask you a question. If you could go anywhere, do anything right now, and money was no object, what would be the desire of your heart?"

Cedena grinned. "I don't have to think long about that. I have a one-word answer: Travel. I want to see the Western states and territories. I saw lots of interesting displays in the Joint Territorial Building. The best one was Tiffany turquoise jewelry from stones mined in Los Cerrillos, New Mexico. It made me want to see the West for myself. But I don't know how I'll ever find the money for such a trip."

"Then we need to come to a compromise. If your Uncle James and I take you on a trip west, one that you plan out, would you be willing to accept that trip as our gift to you before you settle into 'appropriate employment,' as you put it?"

"You and Uncle James would do that? Take me out west?"

"Yes."

"But you haven't asked Uncle James yet, have you?"

"No, but there is nothing he would withhold from you if it were in his power to provide it. He loves you that much. So I think maybe a better idea for today would be to shop for fabric for a traveling suit and put Mrs. Waren to work on it right away. Is that suggestion to your liking?"

"Yes, yes, *yes!*" Cedena jumped up to give her aunt a hug, nearly upsetting the tea tray in her excitement.

Aunt Nancy hugged her tight and then released her. "Now listen to my plan. We must be careful to do this right. When we take the fabric for your suit to Mrs. Waren, we must not mention anything about traveling west. It would be very bad for us if Mrs. Waren mentioned it to Matthew and Matthew brought it up to James before we even had a chance to discuss it with him ourselves. We will probably be able to do that to-night unless James goes back to the office after dinner. Before we go to Mrs. Waren, we must see the ticket agent and get the train schedules for the lines going west. Then we can decide where we want to lay over for sightseeing on our way to California. What do you think?"

"I'm so excited I can hardly wait for Uncle James to come home tonight!"

A knock sounded on the door. Aunt Nancy opened it to find Vivian with a note in her hand.

"From Florence."

Aunt Nancy read it quickly. "She needs guidance on meal planning. Tell her Cedena and I will be taking lunch down-town, and dinner should be served at seven, prime rib with James's favorite vegetables and pumpkin pie with whipped cream for dessert."

With a nod, Vivian was gone.

Aunt Nancy grinned at Cedena. "Prime rib and pumpkin pie ought to put him in good humor. A prayer or two wouldn't hurt, either. Now go and get ready for our trip downtown."

CHAPTER 23

That evening, with some help from Aunt Nancy, Cedena managed to dress properly for dinner at seven. On their trip downtown, in addition to fabric for a custom-tailored traveling suit by Mrs. Waren, they had found a very attractive ready-made dress more appropriate for the dinner hour than the light-colored shirtwaists and dark skirts that had been Cedena's daily wear at the Fair.

Cedena turned this way and that, admiring the azure-blue, cotton bodice that had ruffles running in a V from her shoulders to just below her bosom, and white lace forming a standup collar circling her neck. The azure full skirt had several rows of ruffles running all the way around, and she turned this way and that, listening to the fabric's rustling, which sounded so rich to her ears. At the stroke of seven, she headed downstairs.

Uncle James was waiting for her at the bottom and offered his arm. "Let's go in to dinner, shall we?" Aunt Nancy, dressed in a burgundy wool gown with leg-o'-mutton sleeves, joined him on his other arm and they followed the hall to the dining room where a uniformed waiter stood by the sideboard.

An appetizer of shrimp cocktail was immediately served, followed by the main course exactly as Aunt Nancy had requested. Cedena couldn't remember the last time she'd eaten prime rib. It melted in her mouth almost as quickly as the silky smooth mashed potatoes. The only part of the meal that seemed off was Uncle James's mood. He was exceptionally quiet, and he looked strained. Cedena prayed that whatever was bothering him would pass, or be resolved soon. Although the pumpkin pie brought a modest smile, he seemed to shove it down quickly. Then he excused himself to go to his study.

When he was out of earshot, Aunt Nancy set her fork down with a clank. "Diddle-de-dum. It looks like this might not be a good night to talk about travel. Just to be sure, I'll go and visit his study in a little while. Meantime, let's go to the library. We might find some information about the West."

Cedena followed Aunt Nancy down the hall to the library. Her aunt stepped across the threshold and immediately turned about and pointed across the hall to a closed door. "That's the study. Your uncle must be doing something important. The door is usually open." She began browsing the shelves on the right wall. "Take a look down there." She indicated the back wall. "See if anything interests you."

Cedena found a bound copy of *Harper's Weekly* from 1890. She sat on a burgundy chair, or rather was embraced by the soft seat, back, and arms, and the leather aroma that surrounded her. Thumbing through the volume, a page of illustrations caught her eye. The caption read, "Las Vegas Hot Springs, New Mexico, drawn by Charles Graham—[See Page 499.]" She studied the depictions. One was of a castle-like structure labeled the Montezuma. Another showed hot springs, another was of a mud bath, and others were of a mountain view, a canyon view, and bath houses. She turned the page to the article and began to read.

"Find something interesting?" Aunt Nancy sat in a chair an arm's length away.

Cedena passed the volume to her aunt. "I most definitely want to visit this place, the Montezuma. Where's that train schedule we got today?"

"In the top left drawer of my dresser. Why don't you run upstairs and get it?"

Cedena returned a couple of minutes later with the train schedule and sat down to find the New Mexico stops on the route. "It takes about a day and a half to get to Las Vegas, and then we take a branch line up to Montezuma. What do you think?"

"May I see the schedule?" Aunt Nancy studied the route. "Yes, I think Montezuma is a wonderful destination. But we surely don't want to pass up the opportunity to see some of the other interesting stops along the way such as Denver, Colorado. And then, beyond the Montezuma, there are many more opportunities for sightseeing in New Mexico, Arizona, and California." She rose with the railroad schedule still in hand. "I think it's time I check in on your uncle."

Aunt Nancy knocked softly on the door across the hall and entered. The smell of cherry pipe tobacco drifted across the hall and into the library. Even though Aunt Nancy had left the study door open, her conversation with Uncle James was too hushed too hear. Cedena took quiet steps toward the study, catching her uncle's words.

"The recession that started earlier this year is affecting my business. In Chicago, all seemed well as long as the Fair was in operation. But railroad bankruptcies earlier this year along with bank panics and failures are putting a damper on druggists and pharmacists across the nation. I need to find new business to replace the accounts that failed, but how? No one has any money, it seems, and if this keeps up, I won't, either."

Cedena approached Uncle James, who was sitting behind a highly polished mahogany desk covered with papers and a ledger. He had removed his jacket and tie and unbuttoned his collar.

"I overheard what you just said, Uncle James. I have an idea for new business."

"What is that?" Uncle James came around to sit on the front edge of his desk.

"You need new accounts, so why not go out and find them on a cross-country trip? Many leads were gathered at the Fair, but few of them were from the West. Take a train trip out there. The train stops in all sorts of places. Many of them will have a druggist, pharmacist, or at the very least, a general store that needs the products Paxton Pharmaceuticals distributes."

Aunt Nancy handed Uncle James the railroad schedule. "I picked this up today after Cedena had said she'd like to travel west. Maybe you should take us out there and combine business with pleasure. If you don't find new accounts, at least you'll have taken a well-deserved vacation after months and months of long days at the Fair."

Uncle James began to look over the train schedule. "Some of these towns will be nothing more than a ten-minute stop, don't you know?"

"That's just enough time to leave off a brochure and business card at a mercantile or druggist." Cedena smiled.

Uncle James focused on her. "You really think you have this figured out, don't you?"

Cedena shrugged. "You'll have to be the judge of that. I'm just a country girl from the Upper Peninsula. I'm not trained for business, except what I learned at the Fair."

Uncle James returned to his desk chair and smoothed the train schedule open atop the ledger. "I'm going to take a good look at this, study the opportunities. Maybe I'll ask the company accountant to do an analysis." He looked up, his focus taking in both Cedena and Aunt Nancy. "It won't be easy finding new accounts in this economic climate. Making money is probably out of the question. Staying even or not losing so much that I go out of business is more realistic. I'll think about a trip west. Now let me get back to work." He dismissed them with a wave of his hand.

Cedena followed Aunt Nancy out of the study and into the library. Her aunt turned to her and shrugged. "At least he didn't say no. We'd better say our prayers, keep our finger crossed, and continue making plans as if our trip west were a sure thing."

CHAPTER 24

Nine days later

Cedena sat on a blue-velvet, balloon back chair in the parlor waiting for Matthew Waren to call on her. How had she gotten into this predicament? She had no romantic interest in him, and she hadn't been given an opportunity to decline his visit. He had *told* Uncle James that he was coming. She couldn't refuse to see him. Uncle James hadn't made a decision about going west yet, and she didn't want to jeopardize a possible "yes" to the trip with a firm "no" to seeing Matthew.

The parlor door opened and Matthew strode in. "Cedena, good to see you again. I've missed our time together since the Fair closed." He approached her, bringing a considerable waft of scented hair oil with him.

Cedena pressed her handkerchief to her nose, trying to block the fruity, flowery scent, but she couldn't avoid sneezing.

"Great Scott! I hope you aren't coming down with the nasty grippe that's been making the rounds." Matthew took a step back. "Your uncle has some trustworthy elixirs that will lessen the symptoms and shorten the duration." He sat on the sofa's edge, a considerable distance from her.

Cedena shook her head. "No illness, just allergies. It's your hair tonic."

Matthew ran his hand over his slicked-back hair. "My hair tonic? I've never heard of anyone being allergic to Thompson's Hair Oil. I bought it new from your uncle just yesterday. It's the best on the market. You can't get any better."

"Even so, it makes me . . . ." Cedena caught a second sneeze in her handkerchief.

"Bless you. My, my. I'm so sorry you aren't feeling well. I won't stay. I only wanted to come here tonight and make a proposal." He got down on one knee, keeping a distance of at least ten feet from her.

Cedena's heart raced. Surely he didn't intend to propose marriage. There hadn't been a romantic moment shared, not in the slightest, in the entire three months she'd known him.

He reached inside his coat pocket, pulled out a tiny black velvet box, and popped it open to reveal a stunning diamond solitaire of at least two carats. "I propose, my dearest Cedena, that we become husband and wife. I know you have deep and abiding feelings for me and I have met no other who could be a better match. You understand my work, you are kind, caring, and truly beautiful both inside and out. What do you say?" He extended the ring toward her; with it came another whiff of his hair tonic.

For the third time, Cedena sneezed.

Matthew chuckled. "That isn't exactly the answer I had hoped for." He stood up, set the ring on the table beside her, and backed away to sit again on the sofa.

Cedena blew her nose, cast a glance at the ring, and then focused on Matthew. "This is so unexpected."

He shrugged. "It shouldn't have been unexpected, Cedena. We're not getting any younger."

"But—"

"Marry me, Cedena. I will be good to you and a loving father to our children. God has brought us together. Let him bless us as husband and wife. I give you my word, I will never cause you one moment of regret."

Cedena's chest tightened. Her stomach knotted. Her nose ran. She dabbed it with her wet handkerchief and drew a shallow breath. "I need time before I answer."

Matthew's brows narrowed and then relaxed as the corners of his mouth tipped upward. "Of course you need time. Once the announcement is made and our wedding date set, your life will be a whirlwind of preparation. I'll call on you again in a week's time. Until then, take care of yourself and try not to sneeze." He stood and stepped toward the door.

Cedena tried to get to her feet, but her knees had turned to jelly.

Matthew put up his hand. "You stay put. I can find my way out."

She gave a nod and leaned back in her chair. How on earth had she ended up in such a predicament? She closed her eyes, drew a deep breath, and let it out slowly. In no way had she given Matthew any encouragement—not a hint of anything more between them than the need to tend to Uncle James's exhibit at the Fair. Matthew's ideas of a future together were entirely of his own making. And they were wrong. He was a fine man with excellent qualities, if a tad—or a ton—

presumptive. For *someone*, he would be a fine husband. Just not for *this* someone.

Footsteps entered the room. Cedena opened her eyes to find Aunt Nancy staring down at her.

"Are you all right, Cedena? You look whiter than an angel's wing." Aunt Nancy sat on the matching balloon back chair beside her.

Cedena picked up the open ring box. "Look at what Matthew left behind."

Aunt Nancy's eyes widened. "He wants to marry you?"

Cedena nodded and set the box aside. "He has swept me off my feet, but not in the way he intended. He's coming back in a week for my answer. I can't bear to hurt him, but neither could I bear to wed someone I'm not in love with. What am I going to do?"

Aunt Nancy drew a slow, thoughtful breath. "Your Uncle James will know what to do. And my goodness, if he knew Matthew was coming here to propose and didn't tell you, I'll give him a royal tongue-lashing." She called out in a voice loud enough to reach the study at the back of the house, "James, please come to the parlor! I must speak with you."

Uncle James entered the room whistling "Daisy Bell," caught the disapproving look on Aunt Nancy's face, and ended the tune mid-note. "Matthew is gone already?" His focus swung to Cedena. "Did you two have a tiff?"

Cedena shook her head. "No, Uncle James. Did you know about this?" Again, she held up the ring.

He let out an admiring whistle and shook his head. "Why isn't it on your finger? Doesn't it fit?"

Cedena snapped the box shut and set it firmly aside. "I don't know and I don't care. I'm not ready for marriage. I've seen the Fair, and it has only made me eager to see more of the world that has been beyond my reach until this summer. Matthew is such a nice, decent fellow that I hate to have to tell him his desire to marry me is an impossible dream. Yet that is exactly what I must do one week from today when he comes here for my answer."

Uncle James loosened his tie and slowly paced across the floor. When he reached the other side, he swung around and slowly made his way to the sofa. Sitting on the edge, he focused intently on Cedena. "I think we'd better start packing for that trip west we talked about a week ago. What if we leave next Friday? Then you won't have to see Matthew on Saturday. I'll return that ring before we leave town."

Cedena's heart raced. "Do you really mean it? Leave next Friday for the west?"

Uncle James nodded and turned to Aunt Nancy. "You can be ready, can't you, dear?"

"Absolutely! Diddle-de-dum! We're going west, and are we ever going to have fun!"

Uncle James howled. "That is just about the worst rhyme you've come up with in all the years I've known you . . . but it won't stop me from taking you along. Don't you think it's time to start planning and packing?"

CHAPTER 25

Matthew arrived at his office early Monday morning, but not earlier than Mr. Paxton. He had evidently come in extra early and left a note on Matthew's desk.

> Please see me first thing.
> Urgent business.—J.P.

What urgent business could have come up this early on a Monday morning? Or had something arisen since noon Saturday when he had ended his work for the week? The economy was shaky and growing less favorable each day. Matthew prayed Mr. Paxton's news was not of more closed accounts.

Matthew drew a deep breath and let it out slowly as he slicked back his hair, releasing his hair tonic's scent. Too bad Cedena had found it so irritating. He'd have to find an alternative before calling on her again this coming Saturday. His heart tripped over a few beats. Each thought of her increased his yearning to claim her as his betrothed. But he must be patient until Saturday. Right now, he needed to push thoughts of her as far from his mind as possible and concentrate on the business at hand, whatever that might be.

Standing tall, shoulders back, he strode confidently down the hall to Mr. Paxton's office. His boss sat behind his desk, studying a document. Matthew cleared his throat and raised the corners of his mouth.

"Good morning, Mr. Paxton. You wanted to see me?"

Mr. Paxton looked up with a half-smile. "Come in, Matthew. Close the door. Have a seat."

Matthew did as told. His boss set aside the papers he'd been reading, adjusted his tie, and leaned forward.

"Matthew, you have been my assistant for . . . what has it been . . . five years now?"

"Yes, sir. Five years."

"And in that time, you've proven yourself a very capable businessman with a dependable work ethic, good judgment, and above-average intelligence. As such, it is time for you to take on more responsibility here at Paxton Pharmaceuticals. Starting today, I want you to work alongside me to acquaint yourself more fully with our remaining accounts. You'll also spend time with Mr. Steiner to understand the company's financial condition and the challenges we face now that the country has sunk into a depression. On Thursday, we'll schedule time with Mr. Hammond in the warehouse where you will gain a greater understanding of our current inventory's status, his management, and our shipping and receiving procedures, which have improved greatly over the years since you were a boy and helped out there.

"Then, starting next week, your ownership in the company will increase to twenty-five percent and your salary will increase commensurate with added responsibilities. We will discuss all this in detail later this week. What do you say? Are you ready to get started?"

Matthew's pulse raced. He could hardly believe his good fortune. And so divinely timed, coinciding with his desire to take on more responsibility in his private life—that of a wife. He could hardly wait to celebrate the good news with Cedena. Surely with such promising prospects for his career, she would answer his marriage proposal in the affirmative.

He offered his boss a measured smile and a definitive nod. "Yes, sir. I'm ready. Eager, even."

"Good! I'll get in touch with the company lawyer and have papers drawn up."

~*~*~

By Friday afternoon, Matthew's head was spinning. The hours and days at work had flown by. He'd made notes. He'd spent a day each with Mr. Steiner and Mr. Hammond. With every moment of every day, his gratefulness to God and Mr. Paxton increased, knowing how much better he would be able to provide for Cedena, once they were wed.

Matthew pulled out his timepiece. In one minute, he was expected in Mr. Paxton's office for another conference. Matthew smoothed back his hair. The lemon scent of his new hair tonic drifted in the air. He hoped Cedena would find it more agreeable tomorrow night when he called on her for her answer to his marriage proposal.

Pushing that thought from his mind, Matthew rose and made the trip down the hall to Mr. Paxton's office where he paused at the open door.

Mr. Paxton gazed up and offered a smile. "Come in and close the door, if you would."

Matthew quietly latched the door and took the seat opposite his boss, who placed a document in front of him.

"Here is a contract for your new position and greater ownership in the company starting Monday. Please read carefully the responsibilities you will take on and the salary you will be paid. If you agree to the terms, sign at the bottom on the line provided."

Matthew studied the terms for Vice President of Paxton Pharmaceuticals. More responsibility, yes, but the salary Mr. Paxton proposed would more than compensate for the added work. Matthew pulled a pen from his pocket, rapidly scrawled his signature on the line, and slid the document across the blotter to his boss, hoping he wouldn't notice the slight trembling in his hand.

Mr. Paxton signed the contract also, set it aside, and handed Matthew a second document. "Here is your copy of what you have just signed. I'm very pleased to know I have someone here who is just about as knowledgeable as I am to keep Paxton Pharmaceuticals running smoothly whenever I am away. Speaking of which . . . I have news to share. I shall soon be taking an extended trip out west in search of new accounts. You will be in charge until my return. I am completely confident that you will do a splendid job of overseeing this operation in my absence."

Matthew's heart skipped a beat. "Thank you, sir. I'll do my very best not to let you down."

"I know that, Matthew. And I know that what I have to say next is not nearly as pleasant as what we have just discussed." He opened his drawer, pulled out a black velvet box, and placed it directly in front of Matthew—the very same box he had given to Cedena last Saturday night. "I'm sorry to be the bearer of bad tidings, son, but Cedena has declined your proposal of marriage."

Matthew's gut clenched as if a champion Irish boxer had landed a punch to his solar plexus. "But . . . how can that be? Cedena sent me a note several days ago. I found it on my desk one morning and assumed you had put it there. She told me how much she cared for me. She made it extremely clear that she wished for us to be together; how did she put it? 'Always until eternity.' If that isn't a declaration of love, what is? I think she must have been a trifle embarrassed to own up to her feelings, though. She signed it 'your secret admirer.' But I knew it was from her."

"Matthew—"

A new thought flashed into Matthew's mind. "It's my hair tonic. It made her sneeze. But I've changed to a different one. I need to see her—"

Mr. Paxton put his hand up, palm out. "It's not your hair tonic, son. In fact, her reason for turning you down has nothing to do with *you*. She's not ready for marriage, don't you know?"

"Not ready? She's twenty-three years old!"

His boss's thin smile was nearly obscured by his bushy silver mustache. "Let me explain. That note you received from a secret admirer was not from Cedena at all. It was from Alice Young."

Matthew's mind froze. "The note from my secret admirer was from Alice Young?" Hard as he tried, his heart kept rejecting the fact that the wonderful confession of love had come from a girl ten years his junior who lived two states away. His stomach soured. He felt no emotional attachment whatsoever to Alice Young. In fact, it had been quite the opposite at the Fair. He had tolerated her company for the sake of being with Cedena and keeping his eye on Orin.

Mr. Paxton continued. "Evidently, your secret admirer was quite successful in remaining undetected. But now that you know Alice has strong feelings for you, what could it hurt to write to her?"

Matthew shook his head. "Please let me call on Cedena. Let her tell me herself what her feelings are. It seems a bit cowardly of her to let you turn me down when she could have done that tomorrow evening."

Mr. Paxton sighed. "That's just it. By this evening, Cedena will be long gone. In fact, she and my wife are packing this very minute for a nine-thirty departure tonight on the California Express. The three of us are traveling west together. And I need you here to manage Paxton Pharmaceuticals until I return." He adjusted his tie and stood. "I must head home now and pack my own bags. I'll wire you when we make our first overnight stop. The itinerary is somewhat informal, completely at the whim of my wife and Cedena, so I can't tell you where we will be. But you'll hear from me, I promise."

Matthew stood, tucked the velvet box into his jacket pocket, and extended his hand to his boss. "Have a safe trip, and don't you worry about Paxton Pharmaceuticals."

Mr. Paxton grasped Matthew's hand for a firm shake. "I have full confidence in you, Matthew." With a pat on the back, he ushered Matthew out of his office, closed and locked the door, handed Matthew the key, and strode quickly down the hall and out of the building.

Matthew returned to his own office and slumped onto his chair, head down. His mind might be devoted to Paxton Pharmaceuticals' operation, but his heart would be leaving on the train with Cedena.

CHAPTER 26

Cedena checked the silver tray on the front hall table for a letter from Father and David. As usual, it was empty. She'd been hoping to hear from them before going west. As she climbed the stairs to her room, she pushed disappointment aside in favor of anticipation for the wonderful trip she was about to embark on.

Back in her room, Cedena relaxed on the velvet-cushioned window seat while Vivian carefully folded shirtwaists and placed them in her trunk. Cedena would miss the girl. She was always cheerful, a hard worker, and completely trustworthy. Too bad she wasn't coming on the trip. But Aunt Nancy had a practical side and had decided against taking any staff along. She hadn't forgotten her early days in Kansas City when Uncle James was building his business, putting most of his earnings back into Paxton Pharmaceuticals, and they were living frugally. She knew how to get along without, and besides that, she wanted the trip to be a special time together for just family.

"Do you wish to take this along, Miss Rossier?" Vivian held up the black cotton skirt that Cedena had worn many times at the Fair.

Cedena shook her head. "You may leave that in the closet. The hem is nearly worn through."

"I'll be glad to refurbish it for you while you're gone, if you wish."

"You would do that for me?"

"Certainly. I don't think there will be much for me to do here while you and Mrs. Paxton are away. I'd be glad for the work. Besides, I've done many a new hem for the worn ones on Mrs. Paxton's skirts. She's more practical than she appears."

"Then by all means go ahead and redo the hem."

Vivian hung the skirt back in the closet and paused to gaze at the new tweed traveling suit Mrs. Waren had finished a few days ago. "This new suit will look wonderful on you. It's just the thing for your trip." She moved to the dresser and pulled out unmentionables to add to the trunk. "Someday I want to travel west, but I don't believe I will ever be able to afford it. I spend almost all of my earnings on groceries for Mother and my younger brother and sister. Mother has had a rough time of it since Father died last year." She drew a sharp breath and looked up at Cedena. "Forgive me. I shouldn't be spillin' my troubles. Please don't tell your aunt."

Cedena dismissed Vivian's concern with a wave of her hand. "My lips are sealed."

Vivian closed and latched the trunk. "I believe everything you need is packed. I'd better go and check with your aunt one last time and then I'm off. You have a wonderful trip. Godspeed." She slipped out the door.

~*~*~

Cedena had been on the California Express overnight, and now she was hungry for breakfast. The conductor had come through with menus, taken orders, and wired them ahead to the restaurant. The thought of it made Cedena's stomach growl. When the train came to a stop at the Hutchinson, Kansas station, Aunt Nancy and Uncle James led the way to the trackside dining room.

Inside, the aroma of coffee filled the air. The tables were covered with white linen and set with sparkling silverware. Waitresses in black dresses, white aprons, and black shoes and stockings stood at attention until guests were seated in their section, and then they seemed to fly into action.

"You'll like this place," Uncle James told Cedena as the hostess led them to a table beside a window.

A waitress approached, her gaze centered on Aunt Nancy. "What may I get for you, ma'am?"

"I'm having coffee, eggs over hard, ham, toast, and orange juice."

Without writing anything down, the waitress looked at Cedena. "And you miss?"

"The same, except I'd like tea instead of coffee."

"Black or orange pekoe?"

"Orange pekoe, please."

The waitress turned Cedena's cup upside down and pointed the handle to nine o'clock.

Uncle James placed his order the same as Aunt Nancy's and the waitress took off. Instantly, another waitress showed up to pour drinks. It seemed strange that she didn't have to ask who wanted what, as in other restaurants. Cedena inquired about this and Aunt Nancy explained.

"A cup right side up means coffee, a cup upside down in the saucer means tea, and the direction of the handle tells the waitress which kind. If the customer wants iced tea or milk, the cup is positioned differently."

"How ingenious. But I'm worried. Will we be able to get back on the train in time? We only have thirty minutes."

Aunt Nancy dismissed Cedena's concern with a wave of her hand. "This is a Harvey House. Service is fast because the food is being prepared while we are still rolling down the track, and it is of exceptional quality."

"Those girls you see working here are called Harvey Girls," said Uncle James. "They are much better trained than ordinary waitresses. The standard is very high to become one of Fred Harvey's girls. I understand he advertises in Eastern newspapers for new hires as well as across the Midwest, and he's adding staff right now for new locations opening up in New Mexico. With all this expansion, he moved his office from Leavenworth to Union Station, Kansas City."

Aunt Nancy nodded. "Fred Harvey takes good care of his girls, too. The waitresses stay in dorms run by a house mother and there are strict curfews. All of their meals are provided, of course, as part of their contract. I understand the tips can be quite lucrative. Some of these girls, besides supporting themselves, send money home to their families."

Cedena was impressed, not only with the description of the waitresses, but also with the efficiency of the dining room and the taste of the food. Her eggs and ham were cooked to perfection, the orange juice was fresh squeezed, and the tea was as good as what she'd had at the Chinese café.

But the restrictions on the girls sounded burdensome. Living in a dormitory with a curfew would be oppressive. Cedena

had to respect the Harvey Girls' energy, though. They could
move fast. She was still thinking about that when she got back
on the train and started rolling west again.

~*~*~

"Next station Denver!" the conductor called out early the
next morning as the train rolled north.

Cedena caught her first glimpse of the Rocky Mountains in
the grayness of dawn. What did these magnificent peaks look
like in full daylight? She could hardly wait to see. Now that
she had reached the land of the Rockies, she really was in the
West, a place she had only dreamed of months ago. The
thought put a smile on her face.

Aunt Nancy took the vacant seat beside Cedena. "You'll
like the hotel we're going to, the Brown Palace. It's the tallest
building in the city and has a triangular shape. Mr. Brown
stipulated that the construction should be of sandstone, red
granite, and steel so it would be fireproof. Inside is an atrium
that I understand is especially gorgeous."

Uncle James stood and began collecting their bags. "Time
to go, ladies. I'll arrange for transfer to the hotel. And I'd better wire Matthew and let him know where he can reach us for
the next three days."

A while later, a carriage delivered Cedena, Uncle James,
and Aunt Nancy to the hotel's front door. Inside, it was as
Aunt Nancy had said—too beautiful for words. The nine
floors rose up in row after row of balconies that circled an
atrium. At the very top, a glass ceiling admitted the first light
of the new day. The intricately carved staircase was so beautiful Cedena might have climbed all the way to the top just to

admire it. But once Uncle James had finished registering, the bellhop grabbed their bags and led them to the elevator.

They got off at the top floor and entered a richly decorated suite with leather chairs, a velvet sofa, a fireplace, brocade draperies, and two bedrooms exquisitely furnished with poster beds. The brocade bedspreads, hunter green in Aunt Nancy and Uncle James's room and gold in Cedena's, complemented the draperies hanging at the windows. The bellhop delivered Uncle James and Aunt Nancy's bags first, and then carried Cedena's bag to her room, set it on a luggage rack at the foot of her single bed, and exited.

Cedena wandered to the window. From this height, the mountains were visible, but only because, as Aunt Nancy had said, the hotel was much taller than all the other buildings in the city. The tall summits looked so permanent, unchangeable, and stable.

Aunt Nancy wandered in. "How do you like your room?"

Cedena turned to face her aunt. "It's beautiful. Of course, it's not as nice as my bedroom back in Kansas City. Then again, we can't see mountains from your place on the boulevard." She strolled over to her bed and ran her hand over the rich brocade spread. "I wonder if our rooms at the Montezuma will be this nice."

Aunt Nancy drew a quick breath and then shook her head. "There's something I need to tell you. I didn't want to say this before we left home. I was afraid to disappoint you. When your uncle bought our train tickets for this trip, he was talking with the agent about the places we planned to visit. It seems the recession has hit the railroad pretty hard and they closed the Montezuma Hotel on the first of September. I'm sorry."

Closed. Cedena tried to take it in. The beautiful castle in the mountains of New Mexico, the one place she wanted to see more than any other, was not serving guests. No mineral baths. No trail rides on a donkey. She forced a smile. "I'm sure we'll find other interesting places to visit."

"Of course we will. There's Santa Fe, Albuquerque, and plenty of interesting stops in Arizona and California." Aunt Nancy closed the distance between them and gave Cedena a hug. "I'm sorry. I was looking forward to visiting the Montezuma, too."

Uncle James appeared in the doorway. "Would either of you like to go downstairs with me to find some reading material?"

Cedena shook her head. "I'm going to unpack my bag and continue reading the magazines I brought along."

"You go ahead, James. Since this is Sunday morning; you might inquire about church services nearby. I saw a tall church spire about a block down the street from here. We could easily walk that far. And why don't we hire a driver to take us around the neighborhood this afternoon? I understand there are some impressive homes not far from here."

"I'll look into it."

CHAPTER 27

Following church service and lunch in the hotel dining room, Cedena accompanied Aunt Nancy and Uncle James on a carriage ride. The driver, who claimed to be quite familiar with the neighborhood and the residences of the city's wealthiest citizens, drove about a block and pulled to a stop in front of a Queen Anne home with an impressive onion dome tower.

"This is the residence of Mr. George Schleier, a real estate developer. His house was designed by the famous architect E. F. Edbrooke."

"The one who designed the Brown Palace Hotel?" Aunt Nancy asked.

"The very same."

Uncle James studied the architecture. "Evidently Mr. Edbrooke and Mr. Schleier favor sandstone because they've used quite a lot of it on the exterior of this place, and if I'm not mistaken, there is some sandstone on the Brown Palace Hotel."

"Yes, sir, native Colorado sandstone, to be exact. Many of Denver's finest homes have some sandstone in them."

"What does this house look like inside?" Aunt Nancy asked. "Have you seen it?"

The driver shook his head. "I've never been inside, but I hear it's quite something. The stairway has carvings of gargoyles and swans. They're good luck symbols in Bavaria, where Mr. Schleier is from. And there's a huge stained glass window in the dining room, so I'm told." He slapped the reins and pulled away. "I'll take you to the Capitol Hill neighborhood. There are plenty of impressive homes there."

A few minutes later, the driver pulled down Pennsylvania Avenue and made a stop in front of another large stone house on a street lined with similar homes. "The owners of this place are looking to sell, I understand—victims of the decline in the price of silver—and they're not the only ones. I hear tell that Henry C. Brown is in serious financial trouble with his Brown Palace Hotel."

A shiver slid down Cedena's back. Things were far worse than she had imagined. Here in Denver, the wealthy were selling mansions and struggling to keep the city's finest hotel afloat. In New Mexico, the Montezuma had closed. In Kansas, Uncle James's pharmaceutical business was dropping off. How bad would the situation get before it turned around? All she could do was pray that these hard times would soon end.

The next morning, Uncle James headed out to make calls on pharmacies. He returned early in the afternoon glum-faced. As he shucked off his coat and tossed it into the chair nearest the door, he said, "Business conditions are so bad in Denver that druggists are not placing any new orders for merchandise. Out-of-work miners have set up a tent city near the river and are pan-handling on the street. There's no business to be had here, pharmaceutical or otherwise."

Cedena's stomach turned. Her idea to find new business in the West was a colossal failure. She rose from the winged back chair in the farthest corner of the sitting room, crossed to her uncle, and gazed straight into his troubled blue eyes.

"I'm so sorry. I had no idea things were so bad. You've come all this way because of me, and for what?" Heat flushing through her, she slammed her fist onto the top of the chair. "We should have stayed home. I should have faced Matthew myself and told him there would be no engagement. Instead, here we are, hundreds of miles from Kansas City, spending loads of money on this trip that you'll never earn back." Her throat closed off as moisture welled in her eyes and began to trickle down her cheeks.

Uncle James reached out, pulled her close, and handed her his handkerchief. "Stop blaming yourself. You couldn't have known conditions here."

Aunt Nancy joined them. "Your Uncle James is right. Diddle-de-dum. We need to forget business for a while and just have some fun!"

Uncle James groaned. "I thought you'd laid that miserable rhyme to rest. However, what you say is true. I'm going to relax with some good reading." Uncle James sank into the sofa, plumped pillows behind him, stretched out his legs on the hassock, and opened his book. Aunt Nancy joined him.

Cedena returned to the winged back chair, her mind in a whirl. Uncle James was going to a lot of trouble and expense because of her. And what about those poor miners? How would they make it with winter coming on? Then there were the businesses forced to close up shop. Could it get any worse than this? Her spiraling thoughts were interrupted by a knock on the suite door.

Uncle James sighed as he extracted himself from his comfortable spot to open the door. A bellhop stood on the other side with an envelope in hand.

"Mr. Paxton, a cable has just arrived for you."

Uncle James thanked him, gave him a tip, and closed the door. A moment later, seated again on the sofa beside Aunt Nancy, he tore open the missive. "It's from Matthew." As he silently read the news, his mouth dropped open and his face grew ashen.

Aunt Nancy, who had leaned closer to see the cable, began to read out loud.

"'Seventy percent of orders cancelled. Bank failed. Return immediately.' What does this mean, James? Are we ruined?"

Uncle James got up and paced to the window. Silently, he stood there looking out as he rubbed the back of his neck. Cedena glanced at Aunt Nancy. Her lips were pinched together, her color gone.

Cedena took shallow breaths. As her mind raced through possibilities, her feet sped to Uncle James. "Will you lose the business? Will you lose the house? How can I help? What can I do?"

After what seemed like minutes, but was probably only a handful of seconds, Uncle James glanced at her from the corner of his eye and pointed. "That mountain out there looms large and casts a long shadow. Most folks wouldn't dream of climbing to the top, but I've already scaled that peak. I stood in that shadow and clawed my way to the top of my business. Now, a great big rock slide is trying to take me down to the bottom, but I won't go, not without a lot of scrambling." He turned toward her, his gaze shifting to Aunt Nancy. "You ladies start packing. I'm going downstairs to find out when the next train leaves for Kansas City."

~*~*~

On the long, somber, joyless train ride to Kansas City, Cedena mulled over her future. She must not remain dependent on Aunt Nancy and Uncle James. They had troubles enough. But what type of employment would a woman find in Kansas City when even men were out of work? Maybe she could find a job caring for children. She'd done it in Fayette. Or perhaps nursing was a possibility, but she had no training and would be unpaid while she trained in a hospital.

Maybe she could find work as a domestic, but even the wealthy were cutting back on staff. She'd heard Aunt Nancy discussing it with Uncle James. Some in the Paxton household were going to be dismissed soon. Poor Vivian. Such a sweet girl, and so in need of the money she was earning.

When the train stopped for dinner at the Hutchinson, Kansas Harvey House, the Harvey Girls again performed their duties efficiently and flawlessly. The baked ham with raisin sauce, sweet potatoes, and stewed tomatoes were delicious and filling. As Cedena boarded the train, she only wished there were time for a short walk before being confined to her seat for the next several hours.

As the train rolled along, the rhythmic click-clack made Cedena drowsy. Just as she was about to doze off, it suddenly hit her. There was a very good solution to her employment problem, one that might also help Vivian once she had been let go. They could become Harvey Girls. It was perfect. Room, board, and a decent income all came with the job. Cedena's heart pitter-pattered. It was the perfect way to gain independence, go west, and relieve a burden from Aunt Nancy and Uncle James. The strict rules might be irksome, but Cedena could get used to them. She could hardly wait to get home and start looking into it.

~*~*~

The day after Cedena returned to Kansas City, she was at her desk writing a letter to Alice when a knock sounded on her open door. She looked up to find Vivian.

"Please come in."

As Vivian entered, she dabbed moisture from her cheeks. "I've come to say goodbye. I . . . I'm going miss this place. Mrs. Paxton was always . . . so kind."

Cedena went to Vivian, hugged her briefly, and then stepped back, her gaze fixed solidly on the red-nosed girl. "What will you do now?"

Vivian shrugged. "It will be hard to find a position with everyone cuttin' back."

"I have an idea for a job, one that will give you your dream of traveling west. Have you heard of the Fred Harvey eating houses along the Santa Fe line?"

Vivian shook her head.

"They are expanding and need girls—Harvey Girls—to wait on train passengers during meal stops. Harvey Girls are no ordinary waitresses." Cedena described the excellent training, the room, board, and uniforms that came with a job that provided a good paycheck and the potential for tips. "There's one thing more I must tell you." She crossed the room to close her bedroom door and then returned to face Vivian. "I haven't said anything to Aunt Nancy or Uncle James yet, but I myself plan to apply to be a Harvey Girl. When I heard of Uncle

James's business trouble, I made up my mind not to remain a burden to him and Aunt Nancy. Of all the jobs I could think of, being a Harvey Girl seems the most promising for getting hired and for financial independence. You and I could apply together at the Fred Harvey office down at the Union Depot. Aunt Nancy gave you a reference, didn't she?"

Vivian nodded and pulled an envelope from her apron pocket.

"Good. Tomorrow, we could go straight to the Union Depot and see if we can get ourselves hired. What do you think?"

"I . . . I don't know what to say."

"Think it over. If you want to go together tomorrow to apply, meet me out front of the Union Depot at two o'clock. It would be so much better for the two of us to go together." Cedena walked Vivian to the door. "See you tomorrow, if you're willing."

Vivian dipped her head and then slipped quietly down the hall toward the back stairs. Cedena silently prayed that Vivian would join her in her Western adventure, but before two o'clock tomorrow, she had other challenges to conquer.

CHAPTER 28

Very early the following morning, Cedena rode with Uncle James as he drove his smallest buggy to his office and warehouse. It seemed strange that he was handling the reins, but the chauffeur had been let go the previous afternoon. As they covered the two miles to Paxton Pharmaceuticals, Cedena thought back to her conversation with Aunt Nancy and Uncle James last night. They fully supported her desire to apply for a position as a Harvey Girl, agreeing that it was probably for the best in this time of economic depression. And they admitted that avoiding bankruptcy would be tricky, but they had a plan.

At home, Aunt Nancy, the groundskeeper, and the head housekeeper were hard at work closing off all but the first floor of the house to save on heating costs through the winter. When that was done, the head housekeeper and groundskeeper would be let go. At Paxton Pharmaceuticals, only Matthew remained on staff with a drastic cut in pay, all others having been discharged yesterday.

Cedena's offer to work unpaid alongside Uncle James and Matthew until she could obtain a paid position elsewhere, and her request for a job reference written by Matthew had been met with approval. Now, she must face the suitor she had re-buffed.

Cedena's heart beat erratically as Uncle James parked the buggy and led her through Paxton Pharmaceuticals' front door. He paused outside Matthew's locked office door.

"He'll be here any minute. Come with me to the ware-house, won't you? I could use your help."

Cedena followed Uncle James across an alley and into a large building behind the offices. The temperature was barely any warmer than outdoors, in the low- to mid-fifties at best, and dust almost started her on a sneezing binge. She prayed she wouldn't soil her dark skirt and cape before her afternoon interview.

Standing just inside the door, Cedena rubbed her arms to keep warm as Uncle James went around the room lighting the gas ceiling fixtures. Their anemic beams seemed insufficient to clearly read labels on low crates and shelves, let alone bot-tles of elixir. He had just finished when Matthew came through the door, almost bumping into her. Even in the dim light, Cedena caught the look of surprise on his face.

"Cedena, I wasn't expecting to see you here."

Uncle James approached them. "Cedena has volunteered to help us temporarily. But before the two of you get started to-day, she has a request to make."

Cedena attempted to smile but caught a whiff of Matthew's hair tonic and sneezed.

"Bless you." Matthew took a step back. "Sorry. Had I known you were going to be here, I'd have chosen a different hair tonic this morning."

She waved his concern aside, blew into her hanky, and stuffed it into her pocket. "No need to apologize. I have a favor to ask. I'd like a reference from you for employment purposes. I'm going to apply for a job as a Harvey Girl."

Matthew's gaze instantly swung to Uncle James, who answered his unasked question.

"You heard right, Matthew. Cedena is going to apply to become a waitress for Fred Harvey. Her chances will be much better if she has a glowing report in hand from her work at the Fair. You are the only one who can supply that, since a reference from a relative is not worth the paper it's written on. So if you would be so kind as to go to your office right now and take care of that, Cedena will assist me here."

"Yes, sir. I'll be back shortly."

Uncle James showed Cedena how to pack the wooden crates used for shipment to keep products from breaking. Excelsior, cloth bags, paperboard, and newsprint each had a purpose. And although many orders had been canceled, several waited to be filled. Uncle James pulled the first order and set several brown bottles on the shipping table for Cedena to pack. As he turned away, Cedena caught him by the hand.

"Uncle James, I want to thank you for all you've done for me."

His gaze met hers, a question in his blue eyes.

"You showed me the Fair. You gave me a chance to prove that I could do more with my life than just while away the years in Fayette. For that, I am exceedingly grateful."

Uncle James drew her near. "I offered you an opportunity and you succeeded beautifully. But you paid a high price, as does anyone related to your mother." A muscle jumped in his cheek and his gaze hardened.

"What is it, Uncle James? What are you thinking?"

He gave a narrow shake of his head and released her. "Just remembering what Isabella did to your Aunt Nancy and me a long time ago." His jaw clenched. "Because of her spiteful ways, our marriage was delayed by five years." He kicked the leg of the shipping table, rattling the bottles waiting to be packed.

A chunk of ice landed in Cedena's stomach. "Mother delayed your marriage? But how?"

Uncle James drew a deep breath and released it slowly. "I won't go into it now. I shouldn't have brought it up. I just pray that someday your mother will welcome you back with open arms." He headed off to pull another order.

Fifteen minutes later, Uncle James paused beside Cedena. "I think you'd better go and see what's keeping Matthew. He should be done by now, don't you think?"

With a nod, Cedena headed back to the office building. She paused outside Matthew's open door. His office furnishings reflected the practical, tidy man she had come to know. A plain pendulum clock hung on the wall to the right. Beneath it stood a straight back chair. An illustration of a mortar and pestle in a simple pine frame hung on the left wall. In the corner, a small table on wheels held some sort of machine. Matthew sat at a small oak desk with pen in hand, bent over a sheet of stationery, evidently unaware of her presence. Uncharacteristically, the top of his desk was a mess. Wads of paper littered his blotter.

Cedena stepped through the door. "Matthew, how are you coming with my reference?"

Matthew motioned for her to enter, his gaze steady on her. "Truth be told, I'm having a devil of a time. I just can't seem to find the right words."

Cedena took a seat on the straight back chair, pulled out her handkerchief, and suppressed a sneeze. "Just describe my work habits when we were at the Fair. Did I arrive on time? Did I follow instructions? Did I work hard? Was I reliable? Did I work well with people? Did I have a good command of proper English? Was I honest?"

He poised his pen over the paper, but before making a single stroke, he capped his pen, dropped it on the desk, and sighed. "Yes, yes, yes. Yes to all of that." He lifted his gaze until it rested gently on Cedena. His tone softened. "I just keep thinking that if I tell the truth about how good a worker you are, you'll be gone from Kansas City. At least while you're here, there's a chance that someday . . . maybe not this year or next year, but in the future . . . perhaps you'll feel differently about me. Please stay."

Cedena closed her fist around her hanky. "Yours is an impossible dream, Matthew. I'm not going to stay, nor am I ever going to want to have anything more than a simple friendship and good working relationship with you. I hope that will make it easier for you to write a reference, because I really need it."

"It's Orin, isn't it?" Matthew's gaze bored into her. "He's been writing to you. You have feelings for him, don't you?"

Cedena rose. "Orin has nothing to do with the way I feel about you. Now I beg you, write an honest description of my work at the Fair. It's the last thing I'll ever ask of you. Please." She hurried out the door and back to the warehouse.

CHAPTER 29

Shortly after Cedena had left Matthew's office, he brought his letter of recommendation to her in the warehouse. She read through it and then gazed up at him.

"Thank you, Matthew. I couldn't have done better if I'd written it myself."

He gave a slight nod.

Uncle James approached them. "Matthew, why don't you take Cedena to your office and show her how to write up billings."

"Yes, sir." Back in his office, he set a stack of blank invoice forms and a stack of orders on his desk, pulled out the desk chair, and gestured for Cedena to sit. As he leaned over her to explain her job, she tried not to sneeze.

Matthew pointed to one column at a time as he explained the form. "List each item number here, the description here, the quantity here, the unit price here, and the total for the item here. Don't bother to calculate the grand total. I'll do that later on the Registering Accountant when I check all your numbers." He indicated the equipment on the table in the corner. "Any questions?"

Cedena shook her head and Matthew left. At midday, Uncle James treated her and Matthew to a light lunch at a nearby restaurant; then she resumed her work until a quarter to two.

Beneath a partly cloudy sky, Cedena walked the short distance to Union Station. There was no sign of Vivian. After thirty minutes of pacing, Cedena decided to go to the Fred Harvey office alone. Her pulse quickened as she entered the depot's annex. Eventually, she found the door marked Fred Harvey Company and knocked. A businessman in his thirties with light hair, blue eyes, and a longish nose opened the door.

"Yes?"

Cedena swallowed hard and offered a smile. "Good afternoon, sir. I'm Miss Cedena Rossier, and I would like to apply for a position as a Harvey Girl. I've brought a letter of reference from my former employer." She pulled out the recommendation Matthew had sealed in an envelope and prayed his words would please the Harvey Company.

The man smiled and opened the door wide, revealing a cramped office. "Come right in. Have a seat." He pointed to a leather chair laden with papers. It faced a desk strewn with books and documents. He quickly scooped the papers off the chair and Cedena sat, taking in the essence of aged leather.

"I'm Mr. Benjamin, and that fellow," he indicated a man sitting at a desk facing the back wall, "is also Mr. Benjamin. He's my younger brother." The older Mr. Benjamin deposited the documents on a corner of his messy desk, sat down, and swiveled to face his brother. "Henry, a Miss Cedena Rossier is here to apply for a job. Why don't you take a break from correspondence and interview her. We had two training positions come open this morning in New Mexico. Maybe we will be able to fill at least one of them today."

The younger Mr. Benjamin set his pen in a holder and swiveled toward Cedena and his brother. His friendly smile and gentle blue eyes put Cedena at ease. He swapped places with his older brother, who grabbed documents from his desk to work on.

Cedena offered the younger Mr. Benjamin her letter of recommendation. "This is a referral from my former employer."

"Thank you. I'll take a look." Mr. Benjamin slit the envelope, opened the letter, and began to read, pausing to glance up at her from time to time and smile. When he finished, he folded the letter and tucked it back inside the envelope. "Miss Rossier, I don't think any applicant has come to us with a higher recommendation. You are off to a good start. Now I must ask you a few questions that we ask of every potential Harvey Girl." He took out a form, placed it on the blotter, and picked up his pen. "What is your age?"

"Twenty-three."

Mr. Benjamin marked it down. "Did you finish high school?"

"Yes, sir."

"Do you attend church?"

"Yes."

Mr. Benjamin checked off her answers on his form and returned his focus to Cedena. "If hired, will you agree to follow all instructions given you, go to whatever location the company assigns you, and stay unmarried until your contract expires? You may choose either six or twelve months for the duration of your contract."

"I can agree to all that."

"Good." He flashed a smile and quickly looked all business. "You must satisfactorily complete thirty days of training, unpaid, before you will be assigned a location. You will live in a dormitory above or next to the restaurant and work twelve hours per day with one day off per week. Your uniform will be provided. If you are assigned a location after your training period, you will qualify for a month's vacation after six months of service, at which time you will be given a rail pass to any stop on the Santa Fe, either home or a vacation destination. Do you have any questions?"

"When do I start, and where will I be assigned for training?"

Mr. Benjamin pulled open a desk drawer, slammed it shut, pulled open another desk drawer, slammed it shut, and then turned to his brother. "Dave, where are the contracts and the rail passes?"

"Bottom left drawer. I'll get them." He swung around and pulled out the needed items.

The younger Mr. Benjamin placed the contract in front of Cedena. "Sign on the appropriate line." He pointed to the choice between six months and a year and handed her a pen.

Cedena considered her options. Though she had no plans to marry within a year, she wanted the possibility of doing something different after six months if the job wasn't to her liking. She placed her signature on the six-month line.

Mr. Benjamin slipped a rail pass into an envelope printed with the Fred Harvey Company name and address in the upper left corner and offered it to Cedena. "Here's your rail pass to Raton, New Mexico. Be on the train that departs tomorrow evening. Upon completion of your training at Raton, it will be determined which of our locations needs you."

"Thank you, sir!" Cedena's heart leaped for joy. As she rose from her chair, a knock sounded on the door.

The younger Mr. Benjamin instantly rounded the desk and swung the door open.

Cedena drew a quick breath. "Vivian, you came! Guess what! I'm going to New Mexico for training as a Harvey Girl! I leave tomorrow night!"

Mr. Benjamin's focus alternated between Vivian and Cedena. "Obviously, you two ladies are acquainted."

"We know each other well." Cedena's gaze pinned Mr. Benjamin. "Sir, I am going to say something right here and now that I hope you will consider carefully. Vivian is a hard worker, and she has a recommendation from her former employer. You said you have another opening. You would do well to hire her and send us out together on that train tomorrow night."

Mr. Benjamin smiled. "I'll take your suggestion very seriously." To Vivian, he said, "Come in, young lady, and have a seat." His gaze shifted to Cedena. "Thank you for coming today, Miss Rossier. Goodbye, and good luck."

Cedena closed the door behind her and headed out of the annex. Tomorrow, she was heading west. Her knees grew weak. It was one thing to talk about it and another to actually do it. She found a bench in front of the annex where she could wait and watch for Vivian. And pray.

Cedena had been waiting for about twenty minutes when Vivian came out of the annex door. Her gaze seemed riveted to the walkway, so Cedena feared the worst as she approached her former maid.

"Vivian, how did your interview go?"

The girl made no reply, nor did she look up. Her face remained partially obscured by the brim of her felt hat, but her lips were visible and they were trembling as she gave a shrug and dabbed at her cheeks with her handkerchief.

"I'm sorry. I was so hoping we would be going to New Mexico together to start training." Cedena put her arm around Vivian's shoulders. "Chin up, my friend. Something will come along."

Vivian reached into her pocket and pulled out an envelope identical to the one Cedena had received from Mr. Benjamin. She lifted a mischievous gaze to Cedena and giggled. "Just teasin' you, Miss Rossier. We *are* going to New Mexico together!" She opened the envelope and waved her rail pass back and forth.

Cedena's heart danced. "You naughty girl! You scared me almost to death thinking I would have to go alone!"

"Looks like we'll both be on the nine-thirty train tomorrow night, headin' for Raton."

"Meet me by the clock inside the depot at nine so we can board and sit together, all right? And don't you dare call me 'Miss Rossier' again. You are no longer my aunt's employee. You are my friend and fellow Harvey Girl."

"Yes, Miss . . . I mean Cedena. Now, I must go and tell Mother the good news. See you tomorrow night!" She headed south at a brisk pace.

Cedena stepped off in the opposite direction toward Paxton Pharmaceuticals. There was still time this afternoon to be of help to Uncle James and Matthew before they closed up for the day. But tomorrow would be devoted to packing for her new adventure.

CHAPTER 30

Thirty hours after Cedena and Vivian had boarded the Santa Fe train at Kansas City, they arrived at Raton. At three-twenty in the morning, wan lights at trackside barely lit the platform in front of the depot. Cedena and Vivian picked up their handbags and carried them off the train. Cool mountain air tinged by smoke from the train's stack greeted them on the platform as a short, plump woman approached.

"Miss Rossier? Miss Duncan?"

"I'm Miss Rossier, and this is Miss Duncan."

The woman offered a welcoming smile that belied the severe look of her slicked back silver hair.

"I'm Mrs. Edwards. Follow me and I'll get you settled into the dormitory." She led them to a door at the back of a two-story plain wooden structure just beyond the depot.

Once inside, Mrs. Edwards spoke quietly. "Miss Rossier, you will be in Room One with Bertha Norris. She's been working here for almost a year. Miss Duncan, you will reside in Room Ten with Grace Trumble. Grace has been here about eight months. They are both lovely young ladies. I'm sure they will be very helpful in getting you adjusted. Please be very quiet as they are both required to get up at five o'clock. Your trunks will be brought up to your rooms later this morning. Come and see me for uniforms and further instructions at ten. My office is right there." She pointed to a door left of the entrance. "You'll begin training during lunch hour. Now please follow me upstairs."

Steps creaked as Mrs. Edward's ample weight landed on them. Upstairs, the weak light in the hallway allowed just enough visibility for Cedena to find her bed in the first room to the right. She said goodnight to Vivian and Mrs. Edwards who headed down the hall.

Cedena quietly set her small bag at the foot of her iron bed, hoping not to disturb her roommate, but the girl rolled over and mumbled a greeting.

"Welcome. We'll talk more tomorrow." Bertha pulled her blanket almost all the way over the top of her head.

The bedroom was quite cool. Aside from two beds, the compact space included two wardrobes and two chests of drawers. Cedena took off her traveling suit and hung it in the wardrobe on her side of the room. Within a couple of minutes, she had removed her corset cover, corset, chemise, petticoat, high top shoes, garters, and lisle stockings, and put on her nightgown. As she slipped between the cool muslin sheets, she silently prayed for a few hours of refreshing sleep.

Cedena wasn't sure what time the dormitory began to hum with activity, but all she wanted was more peace and quiet before her ten o'clock meeting with Mrs. Edwards. The frenzy grew until six o'clock with talk echoing in the wooden hallways of soiled cuffs and wrinkled collars. Then the mass exodus occurred with the girls descending the creaky stairs.

Suddenly, the dormitory was quiet as a ghost. Cedena's next awareness was of someone jiggling her.

"Wake up! It's a quarter to ten!"

Cedena pushed off the covers and bolted upright. Vivian stared down at her. "Quarter to ten? Uh, oh!" Her feet hit the cold floor. She reached for her stockings and pulled them on.

Vivian handed Cedena her corset and began tightening the laces as she had done in Kansas City.

"You shouldn't be doing this, Vivian. You're not a maid anymore."

"Can't help it. We don't want to be late for our meetin'. Besides, I have a feeling that once a maid, always a maid. It's the way of the world according to my mum. Being a Harvey Girl will mean a different set of rules and routines, but we'll still be waitin' on others the whole day through."

The truth of Vivian's words stung. Cedena reached for her hairbrush and pulled her hair up atop her head while Vivian made her bed. Then they headed downstairs for their meeting with Mrs. Edwards.

The woman came from behind her desk as they entered her office. "Good morning, ladies! I have lots to cover, so let's get started by finding you some uniforms." She took them to a closet that held plain black dresses in various sizes. When two each had been issued, Mrs. Edwards got out the regulation white bib aprons. In addition, she issued stiff white collars and cuffs. As they returned to the office, two fellows, each carrying a trunk, came through the front door.

"Where to with these, Mrs. Edwards?"

"Rossier's goes in Room One. Duncan's in Room Ten."

Up the stairs they trudged.

Mrs. Edwards gestured toward two chairs in front of her desk. "Have a seat, ladies. Let's go over what is expected of you for the next month." She sat down and leaned forward, her hands clasped atop her desk. Her gaze swiveled between Cedena and Vivian as she spoke.

"You are to live in harmony with your roommates and hall mates. Your uniforms will be laundered for you. Wear black stockings and plain black shoes that will be comfortable when you stand on your feet all day. Your hair will be worn pulled back from your face into a simple bun at the nape of your neck. No Gibson Girl styles like yours, Miss Rossier." She paused as if to emphasize the point and then continued.

"Makeup is not allowed. If I suspect you are wearing any, I will wipe your face with a damp cloth. Be helpful to one another at all times both at work and in the dormitory. No fraternizing with customers or with the male employees of the Harvey staff. Your meals will be provided. Have either of you eaten breakfast yet?"

"No, ma'am," Cedena and Vivian replied in unison.

"Go upstairs, put on your uniforms, and then go to the dining room and eat. As soon as you are finished, report to Miss Keller, the head waitress. She's in charge of training. In the hours between lunch and dinner, unpack your trunks and drag them into the hallway. They will be taken to the attic for storage. Good luck, girls!"

Upstairs, Cedena quickly rid herself of her traveling suit and pulled on the plain black dress. As she stood in front of the mirror, fastening her collar and cuffs and tying on the apron, she began to look and feel like someone else. Even though she would have preferred to keep her upswept hairstyle, she removed the pins, shook out her hair, and then twisted it into a knot at neck level as required. No longer was she the girl from the Upper Peninsula who had never been more than fifty miles from home until last summer. She was a Harvey Girl in the West.

Cedena went to find Vivian and they headed to the dining room. A tall, slim woman immediately introduced herself and guided them to the table closest to the kitchen. Her narrow face cracked a momentary smile, softening the severe look that seemed to come naturally.

"Enjoy your breakfast, girls, and see me as soon as you finish."

The efficiency of the service during this off-peak hour was so swift that it seemed like in no time Cedena and Vivian had finished their bowls of oatmeal and were reporting to Miss Keller for duty.

CHAPTER 31

One month later

As the last dinner customer hustled out the door, Cedena breathed a sigh of relief. Her training period was officially over, but had she passed the test? Would she be approved to go out to one of the Harvey Houses as a full-fledged, paid Harvey Girl? And what about Vivian? They both had encountered their problems during training. Cedena had struggled to remember orders. Vivian had fought to control her temper when difficult customers had complained for no good reason. Both of them had been called aside and corrected by Miss Keller a few times, especially during that first week when everything seemed so strange. But Miss Keller had used the utmost tact, never belittling or berating either of them. In fact, Miss Keller always offered positive encouragement, saying she was certain they would catch on and become efficient over time. But had they done well enough?

Two girls had been dismissed in the last two weeks for failing to uphold the Harvey House standard—one for squeezing orange juice before the orders were placed, and the other for repeatedly failing to dump the coffee urn after two hours.

Those were two avoidable mistakes, but the girls were young, probably younger than the minimum age of eighteen. They had likely lied about their ages. Either their judgment was lacking, or they were testing the system to see how much they could get away with.

"Cedena?"

She turned to face Miss Keller. Vivian was with her.

"I have good news for the two of you. A telegram arrived from Kansas City with approval for both of you to go to your first assignment. Are you ready to fulfill the remaining months of your six-month contract?"

Vivian bounced up and down, her face engulfed in a smile. Cedena simply nodded, praying they'd be sent to the same location.

Miss Keller pulled the telegram from her pocket and studied the message. "You'll both be leaving tomorrow for Las Vegas, New Mexico. Come with me and I'll issue your rail passes."

Cedena couldn't believe it. She and Vivian would be going to the same place. Surely God was smiling down on them.

Back in Cedena's room, her roommate, Bertha, a spinster in her late twenties, looked up from the sweater she was knitting. "Where are you off to, Cedena?"

"Not far. I'll still be in New Mexico Territory; Las Vegas to be exact."

Bertha, resumed her knitting, the needles clacking. "I hear Las Vegas is a good location to gain some experience. It's a lot safer there now than it was twelve years ago. Back in that day, it was definitely a wild place."

Cedena sat on her bed, her enthusiasm suddenly waning. "What do you mean?"

"For a while after the railroad reached the town, some of the most famous—or infamous—names of the West congregated there. Doc Holliday, Jesse James, Billy the Kid, Wyatt Earp, and a group of so-called peace officers called the Dodge City Gang all wound up in Las Vegas, New Mexico Territory at one time or another." Bertha paused to look up from her knitting. "Cedena, are you all right? You're white as a sheet."

"I . . . uh . . . ."

"You're not worried about Las Vegas, are you? It's not a bad town anymore. The townsfolk got tired of lawlessness and ran the bad men out. It's quite safe today, so I hear, though personally, I've never ventured there myself. I'm sure you'll be fine."

As Bertha's needles resumed their clacking, Cedena tried to push thoughts of danger from her mind. No point worrying when there was so much to look forward to, and the Harvey Company wouldn't send girls into danger, would it?

As Cedena packed her trunk for her early morning departure, she tossed in the letters Aunt Nancy had written, one each week. As soon as Cedena got settled in Las Vegas, she'd send her new address. But why hadn't Father or David written? Were they still in Chicago?

CHAPTER 32

Las Vegas, New Mexico Territory
December 27

Cedena and Vivian stepped off the train at half-past seven in the morning, tired but hopeful. In less than a minute, a smiling, short, and slightly plump woman approached them. Her black dress and pulled-back sandy hair marked her as a Harvey employee.

"You are my new Harvey Girls from Raton, I presume. I'm Miss Upton, head waitress and matron. Which of you is Cedena and which is Vivian?"

The girls introduced themselves.

"Come with me, girls. I'll show you to your room, and then I must get back to the dining room. Come down at a quarter past eight for breakfast and then I'll introduce you to the manager, Mr. Vetsch, and get you started on your assignments here." She turned and headed for the dormitory door at a pace just shy of a run.

Inside, Miss Upton pointed out her small office to the left of the stairs. "Come to me at any time with your concerns. My door is always open." She hurried up the stairs, beating out a quick tempo on treads that sounded remarkably free of creaks.

Midway down the hall, Miss Upton gestured to a room on the right. "This is your home, girls. Your trunks will be brought up by this afternoon. See you in the dining room in a bit."

The room was exactly as Cedena had expected, except a tad larger than the one in Raton. Its furnishings were nearly identical. Two single iron beds, two wardrobes, two small chests of drawers. The best part was that Vivian would be her roommate.

~*~*~

When Cedena and Vivian returned to their room after lunch, their trunks were waiting to be unpacked. Girls they had not met in the course of their work in the dining room stopped by to welcome them. Sally Pederson, a petite blonde, and Rachel Owen, a tall brunette, introduced themselves as roommates next door on one side. Franny and Georgina Turner, redheaded sisters, lived on the other side. They soon left to let Cedena and Vivian unpack—all but Sally. She lingered as Cedena unbuckled the straps of her trunk and turned the key in the lock.

When Cedena stepped away to deposit the key in her top dresser drawer, Sally lifted the trunk's lid. "Oh! Look at this! Such a lovely shade of blue!" She held up the azure ruffled dress Aunt Nancy had bought for Cedena in Kansas City.

Cedena took the dress from Sally. "I prefer to do my own unpacking, if you don't mind."

Sally moved away to pause beside Vivian, who had opened the lid on her trunk.

Vivian instantly slammed the lid down and riveted her gaze on Sally. "I, too, prefer to do my own unpacking." Vivian offered an obviously forced smile.

Sally backed toward the door, her hands palms out. "Just trying to be helpful, ladies; just trying to be helpful."

Vivian shut the door behind Sally and approached Cedena, keeping her voice to a whisper. "Sally is not helpful. I've got a feeling about her. I don't trust her. Maybe you'd better find a different place for your trunk key."

Cedena's brows knit. "Do you really think she'd steal something?"

Vivian shrugged and continued in a whisper. "Better be safe than sorry. And watch what you say aloud. The walls are paper thin, and I'm sure Sally will be listenin'."

Cedena wasn't convinced that Sally was as bad as Vivian suspected, but just in case, she moved her trunk key to the toe of her right winter boot.

~*~*~

The next day when Cedena and Vivian arrived back in their room following the lunch shift, Sally appeared in their doorway. She was holding her hands behind her back as she smiled brightly. "May I come in? I brought you each something." She stepped past the threshold, dramatically whipped out a peppermint stick in each hand, and offered one to Cedena and the other Vivian. "I apologize for being so nosey yesterday. I pray you'll forgive me. I hope we can be friends."

Cedena exchanged glances with Vivian, who still appeared suspicious. Despite Cedena's own apprehension, she reached for the peppermint stick. "Thank you, Sally. Of course I forgive you." She sent an encouraging smile Vivian's way.

Vivian hesitantly accepted the candy. "No need for a gift, but thank you."

Sally pulled a third candy stick from her pocket, sucked on it for a moment, and then sat down on Cedena's bed. "Say, where are you two from, anyway?"

"We're from Kansas City. And you?" Cedena bit off a piece of the stick and rolled it around on her tongue.

"Ellington, Kansas, once the wickedest cowtown in the West. My pappy was a cowboy. He drove longhorns up from Texas to Ellington twenty years ago. One time he met Buffalo Bill Cody and Wild Bill Hickok at Joe Brennan's Saloon, even bested them in a poker game!"

"You lie." Rachel Owen, Sally's roommate, stood in the doorway, a huge grin on her face. "You're from Emporia, same as me, and your father was never a cowboy. He's always been a farmer, just like mine."

"Oh, hush. You've spoiled my fun." Sally yawned and then headed for the door. "Come on, Rachel; let's take a nap."

Cedena closed the door behind them and turned to Vivian, keeping her voice low. "I don't know what to make of Sally."

Vivian responded in an equally quiet tone. "I do—liar." She pulled back the covers on her bed and began unbuttoning her uniform.

CHAPTER 33

January 7, 1894

Ten days after Cedena had started work at her new assignment, she pulled out a sheet of paper and picked up her pen. It was time to let Aunt Nancy and Uncle James, Father and David, and Alice Young know where she could be reached for the next five months. Father, David, and Alice didn't yet know she had left Kansas City to become a waitress. Cedena began with the letter to Aunt Nancy and Uncle James.

Dear Aunt Nancy and Uncle James,

Thank you so very much for your Christmas greetings last month. Sorry to be so long in making a reply. The holidays were quite a challenge for us Harvey Girls. First, there was Christmas at Raton where we served three seatings of a full house for dinner. I've never been so exhausted in my life as when we finished that day.

Then Vivian and I packed up and moved to our first assignment in Las Vegas, New Mexico, only a hop, skip, and jump from the Hot Springs. Too bad about the Montezuma.

Even though it's closed, perhaps I'll take the branch line up there and look around.

Two good things about our assignment in Las Vegas: We are roommates now, and we will get paid for our hard work since our training period is over. Vivian is eager to send earnings home to help out her mother. The girl is such a dear. I am so glad the two of us came on this adventure together. It has eased the transition for both of us.

That's about all the news for now. I wish you happiness and good health this coming year, and I hope business will pick up for Paxton Pharmaceuticals.

Write to me soon and tell me your news.

Your loving niece,

Cedena

Cedena set the letter aside and penned two more notes before the evening meal. Tomorrow, she would find out where the post office was located. Perhaps she could walk there between the lunch and dinner shifts, buy postage, and send the letters.

~*~*~

The following day after lunch, Cedena inquired of Miss Upton how to find the post office. Cedena tucked the handwritten map into her pocket and hurried up to her room to fetch the letters needing postage stamps. Vivian was already there, relaxing on her bed and reading a dime novel.

Cedena pulled her coat from the wardrobe, slipped the letters into her pocket, and pulled out the map. "I'm going to the post office. Want to come?"

Vivian replied without looking up. "No, thanks."

"Anything I can get for you?"

Vivian shook her head.

"See you later." As Cedena closed the bedroom door behind her, Sally Pederson popped her head out of the room next door.

"Where you off to, Cedena?"

"The post office. Want to come?"

Sally's blue eyes sparkled. "Sure! I'll get my coat."

As the two women stepped outdoors in front of the dormitory, the bright sun warmed the cool winter air. Cedena paused to consult her map.

Sally snatched it from Cedena's hands. "Who drew this?"

"Miss Upton. She says we go across the street and make a left."

Sally wadded the map and tossed it on the ground. "I know a shortcut. Come on."

Cedena scooped up the wadded paper, shoved it into her pocket, and caught up with Sally's brisk pace through an alley. "Sally, are you sure this is the way?"

"I've been this way a dozen times. I know where I'm going."

As they approached the back door of a barn, Sally caught Cedena by the elbow and pointed. "Go right on down there and wait at the corner. I'll catch up with you in a couple of minutes. I've got to see someone."

"Are you sure? Maybe I should wait right here for you."

"No. Now go." She gave Cedena a nudge.

Reluctantly, Cedena continued on her way, pulling out the map and smoothing away the wrinkles. As she studied Miss Upton's drawing, her foot suddenly gave way. Her heart caught in her throat as she plummeted to the bottom of a deep pit.

Cedena groaned. Every breath sent shooting pain through her chest. Blood trickled down her cheek.

Slowly, Cedena pushed up to a sitting position. She pulled out her handkerchief, pressed it to her face, and prayed the blood hadn't stained her coat. With her free hand, she pressed against the cold, hard dirt in an effort to stand. After a considerable struggle, she managed to get to her feet. The edge of the pit came to eye level. It had to be five feet deep. There was no way she could pull herself out. She tried to raise her arm to wave her hand in the air, but only got it halfway up before severe pain set in. When she attempted to shout, it was as if a knife went straight through her ribs. Her voice rose barely above a whisper.

"Help! Someone, please!"

A couple of minutes later, Sally appeared.

"Cedena, what are you doing down there?"

Tears trickled down Cedena's cheeks. She dabbed them with her bloody hanky. "Get help. Please!"

"I'll be back in two shakes of a lamb's tail!" Sally disappeared.

Breathing hurt so much that Cedena took only shallow breaths. At least the bleeding had stopped. She tucked her messy handkerchief into her pocket and hugged her ribs. It seemed like an eternity before Sally returned with a rather handsome, sturdy fellow dressed in a blue denim jacket.

"Cedena, this is Will Adams. Will, meet my unlucky friend, Cedena. Can you pull her out?"

"No problem at all!" Will squatted down, hooked his arms beneath Cedena's, and began hauling her up as his barnyard odor wafted around her.

Cedena bit her tongue to keep from crying out. When her feet reached street level, she silently thanked God that the pain subsided. She gazed up at Will. Though he'd been helpful and friendly, there was a hard look about him. "Thank you, Mr. Adams."

He gave a slight nod and turned to Sally, grasped her by the elbow, and fixed his dark eyes on her in a glare that could have chilled a polar bear. "You owe me, girl. You know what I mean." He released her as if he were tossing off a dirty rag and then hurried away at a near trot.

Sally watched him go, her previously cheerful countenance falling into a frown.

Cedena fished for the coins meant for postage. Thankfully, they were still in her pocket along with the letters. She held out the money. "For Mr. Adams."

Sally pushed her hand away. "He doesn't want your money. Come on. Let's get you back to your room and then I'll fetch the doctor. He'll know what to do for you." She hooked her arm with Cedena's.

Every step sent jarring pain to Cedena's ribs. After a few minutes of silence, Sally cast a sideway glance at Cedena. "That pit wasn't exactly small. I'm just curious. How was it that you missed seeing it?"

Cedena gritted her teeth as much because of her stupidity as because of the pain. When she was able to loosen her jaw, she spoke rapidly. "I was looking at Miss Upton's map. Next thing I knew, I was face down in dirt."

A few minutes later, they entered the door to the dormitory. Miss Upton looked up as they passed her office door.

"Cedena, what happened to your cheek?" In an instant, Miss Upton joined Cedena and Sally in the hallway.

"Cedena took a little tumble into a pit. She was studying your map so carefully that she didn't notice the ground was about to disappear right beneath her feet. She's pretty banged up."

"I'm so sorry." Miss Upton flanked Cedena on the other side and the two women helped her slowly climb the stairs.

When they entered Cedena's room, Vivian looked up from the pages of her novel and gasped. "Cedena, what happened? You look awful!"

"She fell." Miss Upton pointed to Cedena's bed. "Would you please pull back her covers?"

Vivian scrambled off her bed, pulled back the covers, helped Cedena off with her coat, and hung it in the wardrobe.

Sally headed for the door. "I'll fetch the doctor."

Miss Upton nodded. "Thank you, Sally."

Vivian and Miss Upton helped Cedena to undress and put on her nightgown. Then they eased her into bed, fluffed the pillow, and pulled up the covers.

Vivian headed for the wash basin. "I'd better clean up your cheek before the doctor gets here."

"I'll fetch some Witch Hazel." Miss Upton left the room.

Vivian gently dabbed Cedena's cheek with the cold, wet washcloth. It stung and Cedena couldn't help wincing.

Miss Upton returned to apply Witch Hazel. Cedena tried not to react, but a muffled "ow" escaped her lips.

Miss Upton capped the bottle and headed for the door. "I'll be back when the doctor gets here."

When she had gone, Vivian stared down at Cedena. "So sorry you got hurt. Is there anything else I can do for you?"

Cedena nodded. "Tomorrow." Every breath hurt. She minimized her words. "Letters. Money. Coat pocket. Can you mail . . . ." Cedena grit her teeth.

"I'll mail them for you tomorrow afternoon."

"Don't let Sally . . ."

" . . . lead me into a pit? I won't." Vivian sat on the edge of her own bed. "I'm a little confused. How was it that *you* ended up falling into a pit and Sally *didn't*?"

In as few words as possible, Cedena described how she and Sally had separated for a few minutes, the fall, and the rescue. Because it hurt so much to talk, she didn't say how Will Adams had treated Sally or what he'd said, but it weighed on Cedena's mind. Will Adams didn't seem like the sort of fellow any respectable girl should befriend.

Vivian went back to reading her novel, and within a few minutes, Miss Upton and Sheriff Watts entered the room.

"The doctor is out of town delivering a baby," Miss Upton explained. "Sheriff Watts has some doctoring experience and a key to the doctor's medicine cabinet. He'll look you over."

The sheriff, armed with two six-shooters at his waist, approached Cedena's bed. A modest smile appeared beneath his brown mustache. "So sorry to hear about your accident. Aside from that nasty abrasion on your face, where do you hurt?"

Cedena ran her hand across her chest.

Sheriff Watts' huge hands gently pressed against Cedena's ribs, eliciting a string of "ows." Then he checked her arms and legs. "I'd say you have some ribs that are badly bruised. You need rest for the next couple of weeks. Keep that abrasion on your face clean so it won't get infected." He turned to Miss

Upton. "You'd better call in a replacement. Don't let this young lady work in the dining room for the next two weeks. After that, she can return to her duties. In about three weeks, she should be completely free of pain. I'll send over some medicine that will help her sleep."

Miss Upton took a step toward the door. "Come to my office, Sheriff, and we'll settle up."

"I'll take a free dinner as full payment if it's all right with you."

Miss Upton smiled. "I'll be more than happy to issue you a voucher."

Several minutes later, Miss Upton returned with a small brown bottle of liquid. "This is to control the pain so you can sleep at night. Use only a drop or two in a glass of water. Understand?" She set the bottle on the small stand between the two beds.

Cedena nodded. "Thank you, Miss Upton."

When the head waitress had left, Sally appeared in the doorway. "Cedena, I'm so sorry about all of this. I had no idea that pit was there. Sounds like you're going to be okay in a couple of weeks, and at least you didn't have to pay for the doctoring or the medicine." Sally's gaze shifted to the small brown bottle on the bedside table.

With considerable pain, Cedena drew a breath to reply. "I'll be okay."

Vivian got off her bed and headed to the door. "We're going to take a nap now, Sally. See you at the dinner shift."

Sally backed into the hallway. "Sweet dreams."

Vivian closed the door and returned to her bed. Her words barely broke a whisper. "That girl is pure trouble."

Cedena nodded, then closed her eyes and tried to pretend that every breath didn't hurt.

CHAPTER 34

Several weeks later, end of February

At the end of the lunch shift, Cedena stepped outside for a breath of fresh air. The day was cool and crisp, but the sun was shining and the sky was bluer than the most beautiful turquoise imaginable. One thing she had learned during her two weeks of bed rest was to take time to appreciate the beauty and relative warmth of a New Mexico winter. Compared with all the years she'd suffered harsh storms in the Upper Peninsula of Michigan, this was glorious.

Another thing she'd learned was that some mysteries seemed impossible to solve. She had only taken one dose of the pain medicine Miss Upton had provided when the little brown bottle had disappeared from her bedside stand. Vivian had urged Cedena to ask for a replacement, but she had refused, not wanting to cause any further expense. Eventually, the pain had subsided enough for Cedena to sleep well and heal.

A second puzzling aspect of Cedena's recovery was that during that two-week time of healing, Sally Pederson never stepped foot in her room. Why was the girl who had been so nosey and then helpful and apologetic suddenly so absent? Was it guilt over Cedena's fall that had kept Sally away?

No matter. Life had returned to normal now that Cedena had been back to work for a while. She had collected pay for the days she'd worked in January, and lately was making some very good tips. Every day, she thanked God for these blessings.

The cold air was starting to make Cedena shiver. When she went back to the dormitory, she found four letters waiting for her. The first was from Uncle James, the second from Aunt Nancy, the third from Orin Young, and the fourth was her letter to Father and David that had been returned. Stamped across their Chicago address were the words, "No forwarding address on file." Where had they gone?

Cedena's brows pinched together as she set the returned letter aside and stared down at the envelope with Orin's return address. He must have learned of her whereabouts from Alice, but why hadn't *she* written? Cedena sat down on her bed, put all but the letter from Uncle James aside, and was about to open it when Vivian came through the door. Her gaze immediately fell on Cedena's letters.

"You got mail!" Vivian came closer. "Four letters? In one day? Nobody gets four letters on the same day. Who are they from?"

Cedena grinned up at Vivian, who was already staring at the envelopes, trying to read the return addresses. "Only three letters. They're from Uncle James, Aunt Nancy, and Alice Young's brother, Orin. The fourth is a return of my letter to Father, who has evidently moved from Chicago."

"Sorry to hear that his letter came back. Maybe he'll write soon with his new address. Now tell me about Alice's brother!" Vivian's eyes twinkled.

"Don't get any ideas. There's nothing between us. That's all I'm going to say about it."

Vivian made an exaggerated frown and flopped onto her bed.

Cedena opened the letter from Uncle James, and began to read silently.

February 12, 1894

Dearest Cedena,

I hope all is well with you in New Mexico. Your Aunt Nancy is writing to you also, but I wanted you to receive a letter just from me as well. You are a very special niece and I am so proud of you!

Your aunt was down with the grippe for a time. She is back to good health now.

She wrote to your mother about your job with the Harvey Company. Your mother blames your Aunt Nancy for allowing you to take a waitressing job. Nancy assured her there is no shame in you working for Fred Harvey, but you know how stubborn and opinionated your mother is.

Nancy and I miss you terribly. I believe your mother misses you, too, but she hasn't admitted it yet.

Love, Uncle James

P.S. Due to the recession, I am no longer able to send money to your mother. Maybe you could send a few dollars to her now and then to help her make ends meet.

Cedena folded the letter and set it aside. No surprise Mother disapproved of Cedena's job. It was troubling, though, that Uncle James was not sending money.

Cedena picked up the letter from Aunt Nancy, carefully broke the seal, and unfolded it. Out fell an envelope from Father and David that had been sent to her in Kansas City with no return address, only "C. Rossier" in the upper left corner. The postmark read "Cripple Creek, Colorado." She ripped open the letter and began to read.

Dearest Cedena,

David and I have moved to Cripple Creek, Colorado. We are gold miners now, working for a small mining company and earning $3 per day. The only thing good about it is the pay. The work is dangerous. We never see the light of day. I'd work for a third that amount if I could find a job outdoors in the sunshine.

There is much suffering because of the recession. We had to do some pretty fast talking to get jobs. Gold mines are overrun with men from silver mines that closed down. Are you and the Paxtons all right?

Write to us soon at General Delivery, Cripple Creek, Colorado.

Love, Father and David

So Father and David were miners. Cripple Creek wasn't too far from New Mexico, if she remembered her geography correctly. She set aside the letter and opened the one from Aunt Nancy.

February 20, 1894

Dearest Cedena,

Enclosed is a letter from your father.

I do hope you and Vivian are both well and prospering in your new assignment in Las Vegas. I must bring you up to date on some interesting developments.

At Christmastime, Matthew surprised us all by asking for two weeks off so he could take a trip to Kenosha to call on Alice Young. About a month after his return, Alice traveled here with her mother to visit Matthew and his mother. When Alice went home, she was wearing a diamond ring on her left fourth finger, the very same ring you had refused.

Soon after the Youngs returned to Wisconsin, a wedding date was set and on February 14th, Matthew and Alice were joined in holy matrimony in Kenosha. From there, the newlyweds boarded the train for Kansas City. They now reside with Matthew's mother. After such a whirlwind romance, you would think they would have planned a honeymoon, but no. Matthew evidently felt so guilty about all the time off he had been given that he decided to get right back to work. He probably needed the money, too, with a wife to provide for on a salary that has been cut in half due to the depression.

Speaking of the depression, James and Matthew have just barely managed to keep Paxton Pharmaceuticals running. Times are still very challenging. Certainly, the company would have gone under by now if not for Matthew's loyalty, long hours, and good business sense. For that, we are grateful.

Our household, down to the main floor with the study, library, and dining room closed off, is running about as lean as can be. Mrs. Meyer comes in once a week to assist with tidying up, but that is the extent of paid staff. James is taking care of the grounds now, but with everything dormant, there is little needing attention except for the occasional snowfall. I do not know what will happen come spring if we cannot afford a gardener. Hopefully, things will improve or James and I will be up to our elbows in yard work.

Enough about us. Do write and keep us up to date on your own doings. I pray you are making friends and enjoying your work.

All our love,

Uncle James and Aunt Nancy

Cedena folded the letter and slipped it back inside the envelope. It was a lot to think about. Matthew and Alice married, and so quickly. Was that Matthew's reaction to Cedena's refusal, or did he discover that he really cared for the girl who had pursued him with such vigor?

Vivian, who was sitting on her bed reading a dime novel, looked up. "How is your Aunt Nancy?"

Cedena handed her the letter. "She has some interesting news." While Vivian read Aunt Nancy's letter, Cedena picked up the envelope from Orin and stared at it. Memories flooded her mind—trying to get into the Life-Saving Station to see the fireworks; getting cheated by the farmer with the wagon; watching the spectacular show from the roof of the Music Hall. She opened the envelope and unfolded the letter.

February 18, 1894

Dear Cedena,

Maybe you know by now Alice and Matthew have tied the knot. I didn't think I'd miss her half as much as I do since she left for Kansas City.

I don't know why you don't write to me. We had a fine time together at the Fair. I think about you every day.

I am not too surprised you went west. My younger brother Paul and I have been hankering to go out there. We are saving our pennies for train fare and to get a ranch, but money is scarce. My wages at the mercantile have been cut. Business is way off and no hope of it picking up soon. There is no reason for Paul and me to stay here. Prospects are better out west for young men.

I have to ask a favor. Take a look around Las Vegas and see what we might do when we get there. Read the paper and tell me what the Help Wanted ads say. We'll have to work or go gold mining to get enough $$ to buy land and cattle and all. We'll work at just about anything and we both have plenty of experience in Father's mercantile. We're coming by the middle of April. So don't be surprised if we show up there at the Harvey House one day.

Write to me now. I'm counting on your help. Don't let me down. You were good about writing to Alice. Now write to <u>me</u>.

Your friend,

Orin

Cedena stared at the letter. Orin and his brother Paul were coming to Las Vegas?

Vivian folded Aunt Nancy's letter and returned it to Cedena. "That's quite some news about Matthew. And givin' his fiancée the ring he bought for you? I hope Alice never finds out or she might give him the boot!" Vivian shifted her focus to the letter from Orin, still in Cedena's hands. "What does Alice's brother have to say?"

Cedena passed the page to her. "You might as well read it for yourself."

While Vivian read, Cedena took off her uniform. She could use a nap, but with the news from so many letters swirling in her head, would she be able to get any sleep? She was pulling back the covers when Vivian finished reading.

"From the sounds of it, Orin is quite interested in you. You're going to write to him, aren't you? Send him the information he asked for?"

"I don't know." Cedena lay down and pulled up the covers.

"You should write to him. He says you had a good time at the Fair. Didn't you enjoy his company?"

"I did, but I don't want to encourage him. For a fellow in his late twenties, he's not particularly responsible or even mature. And trouble? He can find it faster than a fly can find a cow patty!"

Vivian laughed. "Maybe he's changed." She set the letter on the nightstand between their beds and picked up her dime novel again. "What's Orin's brother Paul like? Did you meet him at the Fair?"

"No, he didn't go to the Fair. The only thing I know about Paul is that he gave up his opportunity to go to the Fair with Orin so that their younger sister, Alice, could go instead."

"Sounds like a very thoughtful brother. You should write to Orin. Help him and Paul out by sending some ads from the paper."

"Like I said, I don't want to encourage Orin. Now let me get some sleep." Cedena pulled the covers over her head.

"Sweet dreams—of Orin." Vivian giggled.

The sound was so infectious that Cedena began to laugh, but the news from each of the letters vexed her. Mother still disapproved. Matthew had wed seemingly in haste. The depression had put Aunt Nancy and Uncle James, and, therefore, Mother, in a difficult position. Father and David had gone into the dangerous job of mining. And Orin wanted her help. She would send a few dollars to Uncle James and ask him to send it on to Mother and let her think it came from him. Otherwise, Mother would refuse it. Cedena would answer Aunt Nancy and Father, but there was no good reason to write to Orin. She asked God to guide each of the circumstances that had been brought to her attention and then she drifted off to sleep.

CHAPTER 35

April 23, 1894

Orin Young tried to find a comfortable position on the hard wooden board and scratchy straw pillow in the emigrant car on the California Express. Riding overnight without the benefit of costly Pullman accommodations was exhausting, and this was his third night on the train since leaving Chicago. As on the previous two nights, he and Paul had converted two benches for sleeping by reversing the back of one to make them face each other. Then they had bought a board and straw-stuffed cushions from a railroad servant who appeared nightly to hawk his wares. The cushions and the unwashed passengers made the place smell like a barn.

Only one thought eased Orin's discomfort—make that two thoughts. First, he and Paul each had several gold pieces that Mother had sewn into their undershirts. The small stash of cash should be more than enough to tide them over until they landed jobs and earned wages. Second, they were only nine hours away from Las Vegas. Nine more hours of foul body odors, crying babes, foreign tongues, and a board for a bed. He looked forward to exchanging all these for fresh air and a glimpse of Cedena Rossier.

As Paul slept beside him, Orin tried to do the same. On the back of his eyelids, Cedena's face appeared. As soon as he reached Las Vegas, they'd pick up where they'd left off at the Fair. Life would alternate between the sweat of hard work and the sweetness of Cedena's company. Nine more hours.

The train slowed down as if to stop, but why? The next station was a half-hour away. As the train came to a standstill, Orin looked around. In the extremely dim light of the one overhead lamp that remained lit at night, passengers exchanged puzzled looks.

The car's rear door opened. The conductor, carrying a lantern, made his way forward. Somehow, he managed not to trip over satchels, carpet bags, and a small chest that cluttered the floor.

As the conductor approached, Orin spoke up. "Sir, why are we stopped?"

Paul blinked awake. "What's wrong?"

Questions from other passengers followed in quick succession.

"Where are we?"

"Weren't we supposed to go through to Timpas?"

The conductor paused briefly at the front of the car. "Water stop. Take your ease. We'll be underway again shortly." He quickly disappeared out the front exit.

Water stop? It made no sense. They were only a few miles out from La Junta. Surely they could make it through to Timpas without taking on more water. Or had the well run dry at the last station?

Orin swung his feet to the floor. "Paul, stay here. I'm going to find out what's going on."

Paul started to get up.

Orin pushed Paul back down. "Do as I say. I'll be right back."

Paul grumbled and stayed put.

As Orin started toward the front of the car, loud voices could be heard outside.

Shots rang out.

Orin's pulse raced. Just as he was about to open the front door, an armed man masked by a black bandana burst into the car, pushing him back. The armed man fired a bullet into the ceiling with a loud bang.

A woman shrieked.

A second masked villain entered holding a bag in one hand, a pistol in the other.

The armed man yelled in a low gravelly voice, "Quiet! Do as we say, and you won't get hurt!"

Muffled sobs came from the women and children.

The robber continued. "Everybody get out your valuables—cash, jewelry, watches—and toss them into my partner's bag. Don't make no quick moves or you'll be the final restin' place of one of my bullets. You!" He indicated Orin. "Empty those pockets!"

A shiver crawled up Orin's spine as he reached into both front pants pockets. He pulled out a few small coins from his right pocket and a badly soiled handkerchief from the left.

"Into the bag with the coins!" The robber's steely gray eyes pinned Orin.

Orin tossed in the coins and the robber moved on.

In the first seat, a baby began to cry. His mother tried to comfort him, but she was crying, too. Her husband slipped his arm about her.

"Make that brat shut up 'fore I shut him up!" The crook brandished his pistol. As he did, Orin caught sight of a scar running across the back of the robber's gun-bearing right hand.

The woman tried to stifle her babe's crying. Her husband spoke quietly in a foreign tongue.

"Hand over your money, Dutch!" the robber demanded.

The man shook his head rapidly and put both hands in the air. "Ich habe kein Geld!"

The robber pistol-whipped him across the face. His wife screamed. His baby wailed. Blood trickled down the foreigner's cheek.

"Don't argue. Gimme your money!"

The man turned his pockets inside out. They were empty of all but a handkerchief, which he pressed against his wound.

The crook kicked at the bag beside the man. "Open it!"

The emigrant unlatched the bag and spread its jaws. The second bandit dumped its contents on the floor. Finding nothing of value, the robbers grumbled and moved on.

The routine was repeated with the next passenger and bag. Orin glanced past the robbers to Paul. Even from a distance and in the dim light, Paul's darting eyes and tight shoulders told Orin his brother was as scared as he was. If only there was a way to stop the pair of villains. But it would be foolhardy. They were both armed and ready to shoot. Orin prayed Paul would follow his lead and turn over his small change without hesitation.

A few minutes later, Paul did just that and the robbers finally confronted the last man at the rear of the car, an ornery cuss
who had griped and complained ever since he had gotten on at
Topeka.

"Hand over your cash, fella."

The man reached into his pocket, coming up with a Derringer. Before he could even get off a shot, a bullet landed in his
chest. He slid off his bench to the floor.

Women screamed.

The robbers opened the rear door and then the armed bandit
turned to the passengers. "Everybody stay put. If you step outside this car, you're dead!"

The two exited quickly and slammed the door behind them.

Orin made his way to the back. Paul and several other men
gathered around the fellow on the floor. A man with a grizzled
beard, a miner, probably, placed his fingers against the vic-
tim's neck and then shook his head.

"Dead as a doornail, the fool."

"I'll go find the conductor." Orin headed toward the front
of the car wondering how many cars he would have to go
through to find him. Before he reached the front exit, the train
had started to move and the conductor came into the emigrant
car.

Orin pointed toward the rear. "Man shot dead by the train
robbers."

The conductor headed straight to the corpse, Orin at his
heels. Blood had formed a large stain on the man's shirt.

The conductor turned to those gathered around. "Leave him
be. When we get to Timpas, someone at the station will take
him out." The conductor exited at the rear without a single
word of sympathy.

A woman who had been sitting in front of the dead man offered a blanket. "Least we can do is cover 'im."

Paul took the blanket from the woman, unfolded it, and laid it atop the man. Then he and Orin returned to their board bed and straw pillows. When Orin closed his eyes, the image of blood soaking through the man's shirt burned into his mind. There was no escaping it. And there was no escaping the fact that he and Paul had chosen to move to a very dangerous part of the country. In an instant, a life could be snuffed out.

Orin had never seen a man die before. He never wanted to repeat the experience. A lead weight settled in the pit of his stomach.

Dangerous or not, Orin wasn't about to turn tail and run home. He'd make good in the Southwest, and he wasn't going to die young doing it. He was going to work hard, earn his way into ranching, make a success of himself, and prove all the naysayers back in Wisconsin wrong. A whole passel of Kenosha friends and family thought he was nothing but a slacker, a jokester, always out for a good time, but he'd make a success of himself if it was the last thing he did. Most importantly, he'd prove to himself that he could take life seriously and succeed on his own terms. But first, he needed to find Cedena and a paying job. That's what he'd do starting the minute this train pulled into the Las Vegas Depot.

CHAPTER 36

The next morning as Cedena and the other Harvey Girls prepared the beverage bar and dining room for breakfast, their head waitress, Miss Upton, called them together.

"We've had word that the seven-thirty train will be about half an hour late. It was robbed last night after it left La Junta. A passenger was shot and killed and removed from the train at Timpas. Your customers will understandably be somewhat disturbed by the experience as they come to breakfast. Please remain pleasant, and as usual, do not engage in conversation beyond that necessary to take their orders. That is all."

Vivian came alongside Cedena and whispered, "Can you imagine? A passenger shot dead? Thank the Lord nothing like that happened when we were on the train."

Cedena caught sight of Miss Upton watching them. "We'd better get back to work or risk a scolding." Cedena returned to folding a stack of napkins that had come back from the laundry and Vivian made haste to the beverage bar, but Cedena's mind was on the train robbery. What an absolute nightmare. If she had been on that train, she would never want to go anywhere by rail again. She prayed for the poor passengers who would soon arrive, and the unfortunate fellow who had already seen his last meal.

At eight o'clock, the train rolled in and customers quickly filled the tables. Cedena could hardly believe her eyes when she saw the first person to be seated in her section: Orin. And the fellow with him had to be his brother Paul. Cedena's heart raced. Her cheeks burned. Never would she have believed he'd show up here, especially since she had made no reply to any of his letters. But here he was. Smiling. Gesturing for her to come to his table. If ever there was a possibility of getting into trouble for having a conversation with a customer, this was it.

Cedena approached the Young brothers' table, catching a whiff of lemon grass. She gazed into Orin's wide-set blue eyes. They were rimmed with circles of fatigue. She'd never seen him looking so tired, and his perpetual smile so unconvincing. Had the robbery taken a toll? She didn't want to know, didn't want to be his waitress, but she must do her job as she had been trained to do.

"Good day, gentlemen. What may I get for you?"

Orin's brow rose. "Cedena, is that the best you can do for your old friend, Orin?"

Cedena kept her smile stiffly in place. "Welcome to Las Vegas, Orin. As I said, what may I get for you?"

Orin nodded toward his brother. "Meet my brother, Paul. Paul, Miss Cedena Rossier."

Paul's smile was just as charming as Orin's, but everything else about him was different. Paul was taller, slimmer, and had dark curly hair instead of waves of taffy.

"Pleased to make your acquaintance, Miss Rossier. I'm having two eggs over easy, ham, fried potatoes, corn muffins, and coffee."

Cedena had been so busy noting the brothers' differences that she almost forgot the order. Her gaze returned to Orin.

"My order is the same. What time do you get off work? I'd like to talk with you."

Paul's grin widened. "And I'd like to talk with that girl pouring coffee at the next table." He nodded toward Vivian.

Cedena glanced furtively across the room. Miss Upton was watching. "We're off at two. You'll have to clear a meeting with Miss Upton. She's right over there. I'll be back shortly with your orders." As Cedena stepped away, Orin's voice trailed her.

"Send Miss Upton over on your way to the kitchen."

Cedena ignored his request and headed straight to the kitchen. She didn't really want to meet with Orin, but she didn't want to be rude.

As Cedena took orders from her next table, she saw Orin and Paul try to engage Vivian in conversation. As she made her way back to the beverage bar, she took a detour past Cedena, pausing to whisper in her ear.

"Orin is quite keen on you, I can tell. I could be keen on his younger brother, Paul."

Just what Cedena needed—a roommate who was interested in Orin's brother.

Cedena placed more orders and then went to Miss Upton. "The two brothers over there wish to see Vivian and me after work." She indicated Orin and Paul's table. "I met the older one last summer at the Fair in Chicago. I told them they'd have to clear it with you. Vivian has already said she's keen on the younger one."

Miss Upton's gaze held Cedena's. "Are they just passing through, or staying awhile?"

"I didn't ask." No point in going into the content of Orin's letter from two months ago. Besides, maybe the Youngs had changed their plans.

"I'll ask them to come see me after they've eaten. Now you had better get back to work." Miss Upton set a rapid pace toward the Youngs' table.

~*~*~

Evidently, the Young brothers had turned on the charm and convinced Miss Upton of their honorable intentions, for she not only granted them permission to visit with Cedena and Vivian, but she suggested the privacy of her own small office for the two o'clock meeting, which was to last no more than half an hour. When Cedena and Vivian walked through the door, Miss Upton's desk had already been pushed back against the wall and two additional chairs had been brought in, making a tight arrangement of four chairs facing each other in pairs.

Orin had been talking, but he stopped mid-sentence and rose to his feet, along with Paul. Both of them were without jackets now. Their shirts bore the wrinkles of having been slept in.

Miss Upton stood and gestured for Cedena and Vivian to take the seats facing the brothers.

"Enjoy your chat. I'll be down the hall putting away uniforms. Keep the door open at all times. I'll be back in thirty minutes." She pushed the doorstop against the door to hold it as wide open as possible before she exited.

Orin and Paul sat again. Orin's smile seemed to hide his fatigue. "Cedena, you're looking well. Work here must agree with you." He started to rest his leg on his knee, but the chairs were so close, his boot heel brushed Cedena's apron, leaving a dark smudge, so he quickly planted it back on the floor. "I'm so sorry. I didn't mean to muss your apron." He started to brush off the dirt.

"No need to do that. You'll only make things worse." Cedena tried to push his hand away, but he caught her hand in his and held it firmly, sending a surge of warmth through her. "I've missed you, Cedena, missed the good times we had at the Fair. I must say, after receiving your letter, I'm a bit baffled by your cool behavior toward me now that I'm here. Have I done something wrong?"

Cedena yanked her hand from Orin's. "My letter? I didn't—"

Vivian cut in. "Surely you remember the letter you sent to Orin after he wrote to you about coming here this month." She smiled sweetly. "You bought a newspaper and asked me to cut out advertisements from Rosenthal's Mercantile, the livery, and the mill so you could send them on." Her cheeks began to color.

Cedena's pulse sprinted. Obviously, Vivian had written a letter and signed Cedena's name. She was about to clear up the confusion when Orin spoke again.

"The advertisements were extremely helpful. Paul and I will go right down the street after we leave here to see if we can get positions at one of those places."

"Perhaps you'll each have positions by the end of the day." Cedena folded her hands in her lap, wishing the lingering warmth of Orin's touch hadn't sent a heat wave right to her heart, and that Vivian hadn't been so deceitful.

Paul's gaze had remained almost exclusively on Vivian, but now he shifted it to Cedena. "I'm so glad you spoke of Vivian in your letter. It gave me something to look forward to on the long train ride. Now that I've met her, she is everything you described and more." His focus returned to Vivian. "I hope the four of us will be able to deepen our friendship over time. I'm especially looking forward to this Saturday night and the dance being held in the restaurant. Miss Upton heartily encouraged Orin and me to attend. She said all of you girls would be there."

Cedena grinned. "We'll be there, and so will a few dozen local gents. Here in the West, men outnumber women by about four or five to one. It's the bane of Mr. Harvey's existence, constantly losing his girls to marriage." Why had she mentioned marriage? It made her sound desperate.

The conversation turned to reminiscences about the Fair and talk of family. Cedena explained about her reunion with her father and brother, both presumed dead until she discovered them alive at the Fair, and that Father and David now were miners in Cripple Creek. Vivian spoke of her mother, brothers, and sisters back in Kansas City. The half-hour passed so quickly that when Miss Upton came to the door, Cedena consulted the wall clock to see if she were cutting off the conversation earlier than promised. Such was not the case.

Miss Upton aimed her smile at Cedena and Vivian. "I hope you ladies have enjoyed your chat with your Wisconsin friends." She turned to the fellows. "Sorry to bring this to an end, but these ladies need rest before the dinner shift. Didn't you say you had job applications to tend to?"

Orin was the first to rise. "Yes, ma'am, we do. Thank you for allowing us the use of your office."

Paul stood. "We'll see you all again on Saturday night. Good afternoon, ladies." With a modest bow, he headed out the door, followed closely by Orin.

In no mood for questions from Miss Upton, Cedena quickly exited the room. Vivian caught up with her on the stairs.

"I hope you're not angry with me. Please say you're not!"

Cedena paused and looked straight into Vivian's mischievous green eyes. "Promise me you'll never do anything like that again, writing a letter in my name. I had no idea you harbored such a deceitful streak."

"But wasn't it good that I did? Orin and Paul seem like such nice fellows, and quite handsome, too."

Cedena laughed. "That doesn't sound like a promise not to do something similar again." She slipped her arm about Vivian's waist. "Come on; let's get some rest."

CHAPTER 37

Saturday night

When the last dinner customers exited the dining room, Cedena and Vivian pitched in along with all the other girls and the fellows from the kitchen to convert the dining room into a dance floor. Tables and chairs were lined up against the walls. Refreshments were brought out and attractively displayed on the tables—cookies, small cakes, a punch bowl and cups. Dried red and green peppers had been scattered on the table as decorations. They looked out of place to a Michigander who would have expected dried flowers or evergreens tied with fancy bows. But as Cedena was learning, the small peppers were a regional specialty and perpetually present in main dishes and sauces. Why not as part of the décor?

At eight o'clock, all the girls were sent upstairs to change out of their uniforms and into their street clothes. Saturday night dances were the only time Harvey Girls were allowed to wear street clothes in the restaurant, and the variety of costumes were amazing and quite indicative of each girl's taste and status before she had signed a contract with Fred Harvey.

Cedena put on the azure-blue cotton dress Aunt Nancy had bought for her at Thayer's Mercantile, and the little white lace collar that added such femininity to the high neckline.

Vivian exchanged her black dress and white apron for what looked almost like another uniform—a black skirt and white shirtwaist. She stood in front of the long mirror on the wardrobe door and frowned. "I look better in my Harvey Girl dress than I do in these old things. But what can I do? It's all I've got besides another shirtwaist that looks almost identical to this one."

Cedena rummaged in her trunk and pulled out the pink silk ribbon she had worn on her first day at the Fair. "Tie this on. It will add some color."

Vivian worked the long, narrow silk scarf into several soft loops that brought out the natural blush of her cheeks.

Cedena stood behind Vivian as they both studied her reflection in the mirror. "Paul is going to like the way you look."

"Honest?"

Cedena smiled and squeezed Vivian's shoulders. "Honest."

"And Orin won't be able to take his eyes off you in those blue ruffles."

Cedena shrugged. She was not about to admit that she hoped Vivian was right.

Giggles and chatter in the hallway, followed by footsteps clacking down the stairs, indicated that the other girls were on their way to the dining room.

Cedena headed for the door. "We'd better go down. You wouldn't want Paul to be snatched up by someone else for the first dance, would you?"

Vivian lifted her skirt and practically flew out the door, making Cedena laugh out loud.

At the bottom of the stairs, Miss Upton, who had shed her Harvey uniform for a navy blue dress adorned only by a tiny ruffle around the high collar, held an impromptu meeting. She took a close look at each girl to assess necklines, hem lengths, and whether anyone was wearing makeup. With a white wash-cloth in hand, she wiped Amy Cotter's face, only to discover that her blush had resulted from pinching her cheeks, not rouge.

"You all look very nice, and I wish each of you an enjoya-ble evening. Remember to be extra courteous to the Santa Fe employees. Never forget that our jobs depend on the railroad. Above all, keep circulating so that every gent has a partner as often as possible, even the gun rackers."

"Gun rackers?" someone asked.

"That's the masculine version of a wallflower. Sometimes it's up to us ladies to invite the shy ones onto the dance floor. Now go, have a good time, and remember that a Harvey Girl is a lady at all times."

The girls hurried across the street. In the west end of the dining room, a violinist, guitar player, and cornetist were tun-ing up their instruments. Mr. Vetsch, the restaurant manager, stood at the door, collecting a quarter from each guest and making sure no firearms were brought inside except by Sheriff Watts, and no troublemakers were allowed to enter. Orin and Paul were among the first guests admitted. They hung their hats on pegs just inside the door and set a straight path to Cedena and Vivian, walking past a bevy of Harvey Girls whose expressions ranged from curiosity to bewilderment to disappointment.

"Good evening, ladies." Paul aimed his smile at Vivian.

Orin focused on Cedena. His gaze swept over her from head to toe and then held hers, his blue eyes and smile radiating appreciation, not the mischievousness she'd so often seen at the Fair. "You look lovely tonight. I must say that in my humble opinion, blue is definitely more beautiful when worn by you."

Warmth flooded Cedena's cheeks. Last summer, she would have dismissed the compliment as one tossed off his overly glib tongue. But tonight, his words and his gaze held unmistakable sincerity. He seemed to be much improved from the Orin she remembered. Was this new version here to stay? She prayed it was so. He'd been a fine-looking fellow when they'd met six months ago. Now, with nobleness radiating from the inside out, he was becoming irresistible.

"And you, sir, are looking mighty fine in your red-checked shirt, neckerchief, blue jeans, and—are those new leather boots?"

He grinned. "As my boss at the mercantile said, 'A man ain't taken seriously in New Mexico 'less he's got a pistol, a good pair of boots, and a wide-brimmed felt hat.' Then he offered me a discount and is allowing me to pay for everything over time." He pointed to the pegs by the door. "My hat is over there. Oh, and there was one thing more he said. I need to cultivate a taste for red or green chile."

"So which is your favorite? Red or green?"

Orin grinned. "Haven't been here long enough to give a fair assessment. What about you? Red or green?"

Cedena moved closer and spoke quietly. "Neither. Don't you dare tell a single soul or I might get kicked clear out of the territory."

Orin's grin widened and his eyes twinkled. "My lips are sealed."

The musicians began to play "The Blue Danube" waltz. Orin offered his hand, inviting her to dance, and Cedena quickly accepted, catching the scent of lemon grass. She marveled at how perfectly they fit together with his right hand at her back and his left hand cradling hers. They matched each other's steps as they whirled around the floor.

Vivian and Paul were among the other couples dancing. They were looking into each other's eyes as if no one else existed. But too soon, Joe, the telegrapher for the Santa Fe, cut in on Paul. Poor Vivian. Joe had two left feet, it seemed, and Vivian looked miserable. Then Sheriff Watts cut in on Orin, and Cedena found herself in the arms of a partner whose dancing skill was no better than the horse he rode.

The waltz finally came to an end. Sheriff Watts led Cedena off the floor as Joe did Vivian. The "Washington Post March," a two-step, started to play, and Sheriff Watts quickly partnered with Vivian.

Joe offered Cedena his arm. She glanced across the room. Orin was partnering with Miss Upton. Mr. Vetsch had his eye on Joe and Cedena. She had no choice but to accept Joe's invitation. Onto the dance floor they went. In no time, they had collided with Sally and her partner Ted from the ticket office. With apologies exchanged, Joe was about to lead Cedena off in a different direction when Mr. Vetsch cut in.

"Why don't you take some refreshments, Joe?" Mr. Vetsch said. "The polka is up next, and we both know you're an ace at that." Joe lumbered off to the refreshment table as Mr. Vetsch led Cedena in the two-step with the skill of a professional dance instructor.

When the two-step came to an end, Mr. Vetsch walked Cedena to the edge of the dance floor and made a slight bow. "Thank you for the dance, Miss Rossier. Enjoy the rest of the evening." He turned to go.

"Thank *you*, Mr. Vetsch!"

He gave barely a backward glance and nod as he moved quickly across the floor to Miss Upton.

Cedena tried to find Orin in the crowd, but before she could locate him, the polka started and Joe was at her elbow.

"May I have this dance? It's the 'El Dorado Polka.' I promise not to step on your feet or run into anyone. Mr. Vetsch was right truthful when he said I'm an ace at the polka."

Cedena smiled. "Then let's dance!"

Joe placed his hands on her waist and she rested her hands on his shoulders. With a heel, toe, heel, toe, they were off, gliding three long steps between the short ones. The lightning tempo made her feel as if she were dancing on air. When it was all over, she wasn't sure but what Joe must have lifted her off the floor a few times. She tried to catch her breath as he led her toward the punch bowl.

Cedena filled a cup for Joe and one for herself of the fruity tea punch. Before she had finished her drink, the band struck up a waltz. Not far away, Vivian and Orin began circling the room. Paul beat a path to Cedena, edging out Sheriff Watts as they crossed from the other side of the dining room. Before Cedena and Paul could enter the flow of dancers circling the floor, a shot rang out from the street and someone shouted.

"Come out here, Sheriff. Stop hidin' behind them s-s-skirts, or I'll come get ya!" The sound of shattering glass followed the slow, sloppy words that could only be those of a drunk, but whom?

CHAPTER 38

Another shot rang out.

Girls screamed. Cedena's heart pounded.

"Girls, go to the back! Now!" Sheriff Watts shouted.

Paul nudged Cedena toward the kitchen. As he did, she turned to the girls closest to her. "Sally, Rachel, Georgina, Franny, hurry!" She pressed them firmly toward the swinging door. Vivian and Miss Upton made haste from the other side of the room. As Cedena followed her boss through the door, another shot rang out.

Cedena's right foot flew out from under her. She plummeted to the floor. Pain seared up her right leg. "I've been shot!"

Orin picked her up and carried her into the kitchen. The door swung closed.

Sally brought a stool and Orin carefully lowered her onto it.

"Where'd you get hit?" His gaze bored into Cedena.

"Right foot."

He lifted her skirt to ankle height, unbuttoned and removed her shoe, and began inspecting her stockinged foot. "Where does it hurt?"

"It doesn't. My foot is numb. I can't even feel your touch."

Sally held up Cedena's shoe. "Look at this! The heel's blown clean off!"

"Let me see that." Orin took the shoe from Sally and studied it, then focused again on Cedena. "That explains it. The force of impact numbed your foot."

Miss Upton inched closer. "Cedena, you are the luckiest lady here tonight!"

Cedena didn't feel lucky, but she nodded as she massaged her foot.

Mr. Vetsch pressed through the swinging doors. "Everybody all right back here?"

Half-a-dozen voices told what had happened, and Orin held up the damaged shoe.

Mr. Vetsch rested his hand lightly on Cedena's shoulder. "Glad to hear it was only a shoe. A replacement will be provided." His gaze shifted to the others. "It's perfectly safe to come back to the dining room. Sheriff Watts has taken Mr. Zimmerman to jail, and we're about to resume the dance. Ladies, I'm counting on you to go out there and show our guests a good time!"

The others filed out, all but Vivian and Orin.

Vivian eyed the damaged shoe. "I'll go and get your work shoes."

"But—" The last thing Cedena wanted to do was return to the dining room where bullets had flown.

Orin shook his head. "No buts. You heard Mr. Vetsch. Besides, you can't let fear win the night."

Cedena wanted to argue but held her tongue. At least feeling was returning to her foot.

In the dining room, a waltz began to play. One part of Cedena wished she were in Orin's arms dancing, the other part wanted to run as far from Las Vegas as she could go.

Orin found another stool and sat beside Cedena. "Don't let what happened tonight rule your mind."

Cedena glanced sideways, unwilling to listen as she continued kneading her foot.

"I know what it's like to see danger," Orin said. "A man died before my very eyes on the train. I'll never forget it, but I won't let it ruin my life."

Orin was right. Cedena couldn't let a pistol-happy drunk make her afraid from now on.

Vivian returned with Cedena's work shoes; Cedena tied them on and let Orin escort her to the dining room. When the waltz came to an end, Mr. Vetsch made an announcement.

"Musicians, strike up a square dance! Folks, make up your sets! Barney, you do the calling, please!"

Cedena and Orin, Vivian and Paul, Sally and Joe, and Mr. Vetsch and Miss Upton made up their set. The peppy music was enough to lift anyone's spirits, with the calls coming in rapid succession, but the gunshots remained on Cedena's mind as the instructions were called out.

"Circle left, right grand, dosey doe, promenade, allemande left, forward and back, swing . . . ."

Cedena pushed fear back and focused on the dance moves. They took her back to Fayette where she had last attended a square dance. It must have been three years ago when Father was still alive. He had partnered with her when Mother had grown tired and taken a seat along the wall. Would Cedena live long enough to see Mother again?

Three more square dances followed, and then Mr. Vetsch called for a Virginia reel to be the last dance. Miss Upton and Mr. Vetsch started as the head couple. The band struck up "Old Zip Coon" and the routine began. Forward and bow, swing right elbows, swing left elbows, two hands and circle clockwise, and on it went exactly as Cedena remembered it. The memory tugged at her heart. But those days were gone. She was a Western woman now. What would the Fayette folks think of her being shot at?

When the reel ended, Cedena walked Orin to the door. He took both her hands in his and gazed straight into her eyes. "I'll see you real soon. Everything will be all right, I promise. Good night." He squeezed her hands and disappeared out the door with Paul.

Cedena had only time to exchange glances with Vivian, who had a dreamy look on her face, before the rush began to reposition tables and chairs and set up the dining room for breakfast. By half-past midnight, all was in order. Cedena, Vivian, and the other girls headed to the dormitory and up the stairs.

Vivian yawned. "I'm ready to drop into bed."

Cedena tried to suppress a yawn of her own. "I couldn't agree more." She swung open the door to their room. A cool breeze brushed passed her, but why? She hadn't left the window open. She stepped inside and lit the pendant lamp hanging in the center of the room. The answer to her question became clear. The window was shattered. Shards of glass littered the floor. Cedena stooped to pick up a white object the size of her fist.

Paper had been tied with string around a rock. Cedena slipped the string off and read the note out loud. "You owe me." She handed the note to Vivian. "Who could have written this? What does either of us owe anyone?"

Sally appeared in the open doorway, her gaze landing on the shattered glass. "What's going on?" She entered without invitation.

Vivian gave the note back to Cedena and brushed past Sally on her way to the door. "I'm going to fetch Miss Upton. She'll know how to take care of this mess."

Sally approached Cedena, stole a glance at the note, and disappeared without a word.

A few minutes later, Vivian returned with Miss Upton, Mr. Vetsch, and a fellow carrying a broom and a dustpan.

Mr. Vetsch beckoned to Cedena and Vivian. "Ladies, if you will wait in Miss Upton's office, we'll get the glass cleaned up and the window boarded over."

Cedena tucked the note into her pocket. As she followed Miss Upton and Vivian down the stairs, a question circled through her mind. Why would anyone break the window and send such a message?

Miss Upton took the seat behind her desk and gestured for Cedena and Vivian to fill the two chairs facing her. "Ladies, have either of you had a problem with our customers or anyone else in town since you arrived?"

Vivian shook her head vigorously.

"No problems." Cedena fingered the note in her pocket. "Who is that Zimmerman fellow who was shooting his gun off? Could he have thrown the rock at our window? I was sure I heard the sound of glass breaking after he called for Sheriff Watts to come out of the dance."

Miss Upton centered the blotter on her desk and folded her hands atop it. "He has a reputation for spending a good deal of his time in the saloon down the street. When he's not drinking and gambling, he takes odd jobs around town. Rumor has it he's accused Sheriff Watts of cheating him in a card game. Rock-throwing doesn't seem likely, although it isn't beyond the realm of possibility."

Cedena reached into her pocket and pulled out the note. "This was attached to the rock that broke our window."

Miss Upton studied the note and then lifted her gaze to take in both Cedena and Vivian. "Do either of you have a debt to someone in town?"

Cedena and Vivian shook their heads. Then a thought flashed into Cedena's mind.

"Remember the day I fell into the pit? Sally's friend, Will Adams, pulled me out. Afterward, he took Sally by the elbow none too gently and said, 'You owe me, girl.' Then he released her as if he were tossing off a stinking rag. After Will had gone, I tried to give Sally money to pay for Will's help, but she refused. She said Will didn't want my money. What do you make of that?"

"I'll speak with all the girls about this at breakfast. If no one offers information, I'll speak with Sally privately. If she can't shed light on the problem, at the very least I might be able to make discreet inquiries about Will Adams."

Mr. Vetsch appeared in the doorway. "The broken glass has been swept up and a board installed on the window. It's safe to go to your room now, Miss Rossier, Miss Duncan."

Cedena offered a tired smile. "Thank you, Mr. Vetsch."

Vivian followed Cedena out the door. "Quite a mystery, don't you say, Cedena?"

"It won't be solved tonight, not by me, anyway." Once upstairs, Cedena headed straight to her side of the room, took off her dress, and hung it in the wardrobe. Moments later, she had put away her undergarments, pulled on her nightgown, and climbed beneath the covers. Only with the help of God would she be able to push the troubles of this night aside and sleep.

~*~*~

The following morning, Cedena kept her eye on Sally as Miss Upton spoke with all of girls prior to breakfast. "Last night, a rock broke the window in Cedena and Vivian's room and attached to it was this note saying, 'You owe me.'" She held up the paper. "Does anyone know of a disgruntled individual who had reason to throw the rock and this message into an upstairs window?"

Sally covered her cheeks with her hands. Cedena would have bet an entire month's pay that beneath those hands was a ruby red blush, but neither Sally nor anyone else offered any information.

Miss Upton continued. "Except for Sally, you are all dismissed to go to breakfast. Sally, I'd like a word with you in my office."

Cedena would have loved to be a fly on the wall in Miss Upton's office, but it was her day off, so she wasn't going to waste time thinking about trouble she had not invited. She followed the others into the dining room and sat down to enjoy a bowl of oatmeal topped with maple syrup. She had eaten only a few spoonsful when Sally entered. Evidently, her conference with Miss Upton had been quite brief. Either Sally had unraveled the mystery in a hurry or denied any knowledge of the situation. If bets were taken, Cedena's money would be on a denial.

CHAPTER 39

One week later

Cedena sat on her bed, lowered the latest issue of the *Las Vegas Daily Optic*, and looked out the window at the crystal blue morning sky. It was Sunday, her day off, eight days since the night of the dance. She hadn't heard or seen anything of Orin all week. Was he working at the mercantile on Sundays, too? And who had tossed the rock through her window last Saturday night? So far, no light had been shed on the mystery and Sally had been keeping her distance. That friend of hers, Will, must have done it, mistakenly hitting the wrong window.

Pushing that thought away, Cedena focused again on the beautiful day. She needed to get outdoors and enjoy the fine desert air. She probably should walk to church, but she longed to see more than the same Las Vegas streets she'd been over dozens of times since moving from Raton.

The branch line train to Hot Springs six miles north began to roll out of the station. Perhaps next week, she would take that train. Vivian might even go with her. She glanced at her roommate. Vivian was sitting on her bed, absorbed in another of her dime novels.

"Vivian, I'm thinking of going up to Hot Springs next Sunday. I've always wanted to see the Montezuma, even if only from the outside, and I'd like to hire a donkey for a trail ride. Want to go with me? We could take the nine-thirty train in the morning and return in the afternoon or evening. The kitchen would pack us a box lunch if we asked."

Vivian kept on reading as if she hadn't heard a word Cedena had said. Cedena was getting used to being ignored. Ever since Vivian had fallen in love with dime novels during their time at Raton, she'd spent almost every free minute absorbed in their ridiculous stories. Cedena couldn't blame Vivian. Her life had never been easy, and if reading some love story by Bertha M. Clay gave her enjoyment, so be it. Cedena raised her newspaper and resumed reading about the possibility of a coal miners' strike and the effect it could have on the railroads.

Someone knocked on the door. Cedena set her newspaper aside and hurried to open it. Miss Upton stood there smiling.

"Cedena, Vivian, Orin and Paul Young have asked for permission to escort you to church. They're waiting out front. Should I tell them you'll be down?"

Vivian tossed her novel aside and hopped off her bed. "Be right there, Miss Upton. Cedena, you're coming, aren't you?"

Cedena's heart skipped a beat. Orin's offer was just what she needed to perk up her boring day off. "Yes, I'm coming. Miss Upton, please tell the Youngs we'll be there in a minute."

Cedena pulled her hair up in the Gibson Girl style that wasn't permitted when she was working, and then she put on her straw boater. She smoothed her black cotton skirt and tied a narrow black ribbon about the collar of her white shirtwaist.

Vivian, similarly attired except for the ribbon, threw open the wardrobe doors and searched through the contents with a sigh.

"What are you looking for, Vivian?"

"Do you have a ribbon I can borrow to perk up this plain white shirtwaist?"

"Do you want to borrow the pink one again? Or maybe you would rather wear a pin?" Cedena retrieved the key to her trunk from where she'd hidden it inside her right winter boot, unlocked the trunk, and reached deep into the bottom corner finding her silver pin. It was shaped like a maple leaf, a cheap piece with an elegant look that she'd bought for herself from the Montgomery Ward Company's catalog for twenty cents. She offered the pin to Vivian.

"How lovely! It's perfect!" She fastened it at the center front of her high collar.

"You may keep it, if you like, providing you give me borrowing privileges."

"Absolutely! Thank you!" Vivian put on her boater and gloves and assessed her image in the mirror.

"You look very nice. Now come along; we'd better not keep our callers waiting." Cedena grabbed a pair of lace gloves and led the way out the door and down the stairs.

Orin and Paul rose from the bench out front the moment Cedena and Vivian emerged from the dormitory door. Each wore a wide-brimmed felt hat, a brown sack coat, matching pants, boots, and most importantly, a big smile.

Paul's gaze settled on Vivian. Orin's captured Cedena as he spoke.

"Ladies, we would be honored to escort you to church this fine morning."

"We would be pleased to have your company," Vivian replied before Cedena could ask which church they had in mind.

Cedena quickly cleared up any confusion. "We've been attending the Methodist Episcopal Church since we moved to Las Vegas. It's on Blanchard Street a few blocks from here. Services start at eleven o'clock, if that meets your approval."

Paul nodded and offered his arm to Vivian. "We have plenty of time for a leisurely stroll, then."

On the walk home, Vivian and Paul paused to face Cedena and Orin. A sparkle lit Vivian's eyes as she focused on Cedena. "Paul says he and Orin would be glad to take us up to Hot Springs next Sunday."

Cedena was stunned. Her gaze slid to Vivian. The girl had been listening to her after all, and right now she was wearing an "I fooled you again, didn't I?" grin. Cedena couldn't help smiling.

Orin's expression swiftly turned bright. "Sounds like a very good time if you ladies are willing."

Paul focused on Orin. "Vivian says she and Cedena will get box lunches for all four of us. And we can rent some burros and spend the day on the trail." He turned to Cedena. "Is that all right with you?"

"It's more than all right with me, if Miss Upton approves."

When they reached the dormitory, permission was granted by Miss Upton for the plan and promises were made to meet at the depot at 9 a.m. the next Sunday.

CHAPTER 40

As the branch line chugged out of Las Vegas, Orin's hand rested on the pistol hanging from his hip. After the train robbery, he'd made a decision never to step onto a train unarmed, even though this run up to Hot Springs on a Sunday couldn't possibly be dangerous. There was no mail car, no express car, only passengers. It wouldn't be worth a robber's attention.

Orin pushed thoughts of danger aside to focus on the lovely woman sitting beside him. Her hair was drawn up atop her head like spun honey, and her lips were curved upward as she watched the scenery out the window. When she turned to him to speak, her brown eyes sparkled.

"Have you ever seen anything so quaint as those flat-roofed adobe huts and the tiny village they make up?" Her focus pivoted to the window again. "Look at that donkey pulling a cart, the old man walking beside it, and the tiny little dog chasing behind."

"I like his wide-brimmed straw hat. This is like stepping back to a time before farm equipment and steam engines were invented." Orin reached for Cedena's hand. Warmth spread through him.

"You're right, Orin. It *is* like a trip into the past. You've got to admit these folks are surrounded by great scenery, though, with the beautiful hills and mountains all around."

"Beauty certainly is abundant here." He squeezed her hand.

Her gaze flitted to him and back to the window. Had she caught the double meaning?

A while later, as the train neared the depot in Hot Springs, the castle-like Montezuma came into view.

Cedena drew a sharp breath. "Look at that, Orin! The Montezuma really *is* just like the picture I saw in an old *Harper's Weekly* magazine! There's a tower, and a veranda that goes on forever. I bet the view from the tower is spectacular. Too bad the place had to close. It's probably the most romantic location in all of New Mexico Territory."

"Maybe times will improve and it will reopen."

"I certainly hope so. It's a dream of mine to see it from the inside."

The train came to a halt at the depot, and within a few minutes, Orin and Paul began to haggle for burros owned by a short, dark-skinned fellow wearing a sombrero. At first, it seemed he was not going to allow the animals to go without him as their guide. His proficiency in English was lacking, or maybe he was just pretending not to understand when Orin explained that he was very competent with both burros and trail riding. Or did he sense that those claims were overstated? With an offer of more money than a day's rental was worth, the transaction came to a successful conclusion.

While Paul helped Vivian mount one of the donkeys, Orin led a donkey to Cedena. "I'll help you get on. I see you've wisely chosen to wear a split skirt."

"Franny and Georgina, the sisters who live next door, loaned their split skirts to Vivian and me. Franny said we'd be much more comfortable riding astride than side-saddle."

Orin knelt on one knee and pointed to the other. "Use this as a stepping stool to mount."

Cedena swung her right leg up over the donkey so enthusiastically she overshot and began slipping off the other side.

Orin sprang up and grabbed her left leg, helping her to center her weight atop the animal; then he mounted another of the donkeys.

Paul handed the lunch basket up to Orin, swung up onto the fourth donkey, and led the others. They passed a bath house, an old hotel made of stone, and the Montezuma, finally reaching the hill behind the castle. Orin rode at the rear, keeping an eye on the ladies and watching for anything that might pose danger. As the trail rose higher, Orin paid close attention to their whereabouts, memorizing landmarks along the way—a fallen pinyon, an old stump, a sandstone outcropping. Mostly, though, juniper dotted the hillsides.

The sun beat warmly upon Orin's shoulders. He wished he could strip off his shirt. Cedena and Vivian must be feeling hot, too, with their extra layers of undergarments beneath their shirtwaists, but they hadn't offered a single word of complaint. He was fairly certain, though, that he'd caught a glimpse of Cedena pulling out her handkerchief, and that she was mopping her brow beneath her straw boater.

At noon, Paul found a spot in the shade of a circle of pinyons for lunch. With the help of Mexican blankets off the burros' backs, they created a picnic area. Cedena and Vivian distributed the box lunches that included ham sandwiches, celery and carrot sticks, orange slices, sugar cookies, and lemonade still icy from the careful way it had been insulated with flour sack towels.

Conversation dwindled as each bit into a sandwich. From the "mmms" going around the circle and the speed at which the sandwiches disappeared, it seemed the others had worked up appetites as hearty as Orin's. He took out a carrot, and as he gnawed on it, his mind chewed over the present scene. He'd have to be blind not to see that Paul was completely smitten with Vivian and that she was equally taken with him.

Orin's gaze met Cedena's. She paused as she raised a celery stick to her lips, offering a modest smile before taking a bite. He swallowed and asked a question that had been on his mind for some time.

"How long do you ladies plan to work for Fred Harvey?"

Vivian's gaze swung from Paul to Orin. "Until a better offer comes along." Her focus returned to Paul and she followed up with a grin and a giggle.

Cedena focused on pulling strings off her celery stick. "Our contracts are up on the twenty-fourth of this month. We'll get a month off to visit family, and then we'll start another six-month contract on the twenty-fourth of June. Right, Vivian?"

"Right." Vivian seemed lost in the embrace of Paul's rapt attention.

"Do you fellows plan to continue at the mercantile?" Cedena crunched on her celery.

Orin nodded. "For a while. We're trying to help Mr. Rosenthal solve the mystery of disappearing merchandise— ammunition, cartridges, and the like. We think the thief is a fellow from the livery, Will Adams."

Cedena's eyebrows rose. "Will Adams?"

"Do you know him?" Paul's gaze pivoted to Cedena.

"I met him briefly last winter. He's a friend of our neighbor, Sally."

Orin swallowed the last of his carrot stick. "Is she a little mite of a thing with blonde hair and blue eyes?"

"That's her," Vivian answered before Cedena could reply. "She's nosey, too. I don't trust her. How do you know her?"

Paul spoke up. "She's been in the store the same time as Adams."

"She does dumb stuff." Orin's brow lifted. "Like knocking over the checkerboard Mr. Rosenthal keeps on a stand, and sending the pieces scattering."

"Or running into a stack of stove shovels that clatter to the floor," Paul added.

"While we're distracted with her mess, Adams disappears," Orin explained. "Later, we discover ammo or powder is gone, too."

"They're working together?" Cedena asked.

Orin shrugged. "Probably, but enough about that. So you ladies will be working at least until the end of the year for the Harvey Company, right?"

"That's our plan," Cedena replied.

Paul's gaze momentarily met Cedena's and then swung back to Vivian like a compass needle following a magnet. "Maybe by then we'll be able to buy some ranch land."

Orin picked up another carrot stick. "We'll have to start small—twenty acres or so at first and a few stock animals—and ranch part time until we can build up a herd."

Cedena reached for a cookie. "So you fellows will raise beef cattle?" Her gaze landed on Orin. "Don't you need to get some experience, learn the business by working on a ranch first? And what about water rights and grazing land? There are stories about fights over those things in the newspaper almost every week."

Orin offered Cedena a confident smile. "We're looking into all that. Mr. Rosenthal knows just about everybody and everything to do with ranching hereabouts. He'll advise us."

Paul swung his focus from Vivian to Cedena. "We'll find out about branding, how to pick the right stock animals, the right grazing land, and the like."

Cedena offered an encouraging smile. "Will you call it the Young Ranch?"

Paul's gaze sought Orin, who nodded and answered. "The Young Ranch sounds good. We'll have to check the registry of brands and see what we can come up with for a branding iron."

A wry smile curved Vivian's lips. "Meanwhile, Cedena and I will continue on with the Harvey way, running our feet off and making sure every customer is satisfied."

Cedena's gaze sought Vivian. "But we get paid well, something your mother appreciates in these hard times."

Vivian brightened. "You're right. I don't mean to complain. Enough about work. Let's get back on the trail. The view is too beautiful for words." She pointed to a high peak that stood alone in the distance with perpendicular sides and a flat top. "What did Miss Upton call that mountain?"

"Hermit Rock," Cedena answered.

"Hermit Rock, here we come!" Paul sprang to his feet and helped Vivian up.

Orin did the same for Cedena. Her hands clasped his and his pulse quickened. Too soon, she was on her feet, releasing her touch.

Everyone pitched in to clean up. Paul put the blankets on the donkeys' backs. Soon, everyone was aboard his or her animal and Paul led the way from the dry, dusty trail into a pine forest. Orin welcomed the change from the hot sun to the cool and fragrant woods.

A few minutes later, they emerged from the trees to follow a narrow ridge. A steep cliff rose fifteen feet or so on the right. A deep ravine marked the edge of the trail on the left. All was quiet save the chirps of sparrows and songs of warblers.

Suddenly, Paul's voice interrupted the peaceful concert. "Whoa! Easy, boy!"

Vivian screamed.

"It's a rattlesnake!" Cedena shouted.

Orin's heart raced. Ahead, Paul struggled to control his burro. The animal danced dangerously close to the edge, upsetting Vivian's donkey, which began backing toward Cedena. Orin fingered his pistol. On this narrow ledge, with three burros and three riders separating him from the snake, there was no way he could safely get off a shot, and Paul was too busy trying to stay on his donkey to make use of his own weapon.

Gunfire rang out from above.

Orin gazed up. A fellow stood with his gun aimed at the snake.

"You got him!" Paul shouted.

The shooter holstered his weapon and began his descent to the trail.

Orin dismounted. With his hand resting on his pistol, he made his way past the others to where the snake lay motionless.

The shooter approached, coming to a standstill on the opposite side of the dead rattler. "Guess he won't bother no one ever again." He kicked the snake off the ledge.

The man's gravelly voice sounded familiar. When he looked up, his steely gray eyes met Orin's. Tied about the fellow's neck was a black bandana. The man's shooting hand rested lightly on his pistol, a scarred hand. A chill ran down Orin's spine. This was the same man who had robbed the train near Timpas and killed a passenger. Orin's grip tightened on his weapon.

In a flash, the snake-killer drew his gun and aimed it at Orin. "Take your hand off that pistol, son."

Orin raised his hands.

The robber waved his pistol toward Hot Springs. "You and your friends turn around. Go back where ya came from. Ain't nothin' but trouble waitin' for ya farther up this trail. Now git!"

Orin's heart pounded. He backed away.

Vivian whimpered.

Cedena hushed her.

Orin made haste back to his donkey, mounted it, and started toward Hot Springs. When he had gone a few yards, he cast a backward glance. Paul and the women had turned their donkeys around without incident and were following close behind. The robber had climbed partway up the incline. His gun was still drawn and pointed at them as he watched them go.

A few minutes later, once they were off the ledge and out of sight of the gunman, Paul called out, "Orin, wait up!"

Orin pulled off the trail.

Paul told Cedena and Vivian to continue a few yards ahead and then stop and wait. He came to a halt beside Orin and spoke quietly. "Did you recognize that man? He's the one who robbed the train."

"I know. We've got to get back as soon as possible and tell Sheriff Watts where we saw him. Don't say anything to Cedena or Vivian. They've been frightened enough. Why don't you resume the lead now that the trail has widened, and I'll bring up the rear?"

Paul gave a nod and rode ahead.

Orin prayed they would all make it back to Hot Springs without further incident, and that he'd never see the killer again.

CHAPTER 41

Back in Las Vegas, Orin and Paul walked Cedena and Vivian to the dormitory and then made a beeline to the sheriff's office at the jailhouse. As they came through the door, Orin was surprised to see that one of the jail cells was occupied not by Zimmerman, the town drunk, but by Will Adams.

Sheriff Watts, who was sitting in a chair with his feet propped on his desk, turned his gaze from his prisoner to Orin and Paul. "What can I do for you fellows? The Young brothers, right? Orin and Paul, is it? You work for Rosenthal. Saw you at the dance a couple of weeks ago." He swung his feet off his desk and rose to his full six-foot height.

Orin gazed up, hating how short the sheriff made him feel. "Sheriff, do you remember the train that got robbed coming down from Colorado last month?"

"Sure do. What about it?" He sat on the edge of his desk.

Paul stepped beside Orin. "We know where one of the robbers is hiding out."

The sheriff's brow rose. "Is that right?"

"We saw him on a trail about three miles north of Hot Springs," Orin replied.

"What's he look like?" The question came from Will Adams.

The sheriff shot him a scorching gaze. "Who's askin' the questions here? Shut up, Adams. I'll handle this." He turned back to Orin. "What's he look like?"

"He's about your height. His eyes are like steel, gray and cold. There's a scar on the back of his shooting hand, and he was wearing a black bandana around his neck. When he was robbing the train, he used it to mask his face. But the thing I remember most is the sound of his voice."

Paul spoke up. "It's real deep and gravelly, one you'd never forget or mistake for someone else."

"I know that son-of-a-bull." Adams paused his pacing, grasped two of the bars of his cell, and pressed his face in between. "And I know how you can take him in without ever firing a shot."

Sheriff Watts glared at the prisoner. "Is that so?" Skepticism dripped off each deliberate word. "I'm waitin' to hear your plan."

"I'll give it to ya on one condition. Drop all charges against me and let me outta here. Ya got nothin' to lose. I already told you and Rosenthal where I stashed his goods. He oughta be by any minute to say he's recovered his losses, less he's a worse deceiver than me." Adams grinned.

Sheriff Watts stood and wandered toward Adams. "Why would you want to cooperate to bring in this train robber? How did you get mixed up with him? And what's his name?"

"How I got mixed up with him ain't none o' your business. I wanna bring him in 'cause he's a cold-blooded killer. Other gangs rob trains and no one gets hurt. Bloody Burt takes pure delight in murderin' folks that never done him no harm. He killed my best friend just 'cause he didn't like the way he looked at him one day. That's when I left his gang, came here to start over."

"You started over, all right, as a lone thief. Well, almost lone. Ya got some female distractin' the store clerk while ya make off with the goods."

"But I ain't hurt no one. Deputize me. I'll help ya capture that whole gang of four alive without a shot being fired. They're the ones on that wanted poster over there." Adams pointed to the wall beside the door.

Sheriff Watts wandered over to the poster that had four sketches of train robbers, stared at it, then turned to Orin and Paul. "Do either of you recognize any of these men?"

Orin and Paul joined Sheriff Watts in front of the poster. It said "Wanted Dead or Alive. $5,000 Reward." Orin pointed to two of the sketches. "These are the ones we saw during the train robbery."

"Those two came through the car we were on," Paul said. "The one on the left killed a passenger right before our eyes. He's the one we saw on the trail."

Adams spoke up. "Take him in. Put him on trial. I'll testify against him. And with the testimony of these two, he'll be hanged."

Orin's stomach turned. He didn't want to testify. He didn't want anyone hanged. But he didn't want Bloody Burt killing anyone else, either.

Mr. Rosenthal came through the door. "Well, well. It's the Young brothers. What are you doing here? I thought you were spending your day off at Hot Springs with your girls?"

Sheriff Watts grinned. "They did, and they came back with the location of one of the men in the gang on that poster." He pointed to the sketches. "Bloody Burt is up in the hills beyond the Montezuma."

Will Adams spoke up. "Rosenthal, did you get your goods?"

"I got 'em."

"Sheriff, let me out; put a badge on me, and we'll get Bloody Burt and his gang." Will rattled his cell door.

Mr. Rosenthal chuckled. "Don't you do it, Sheriff. He's got his eye on that reward money. It'll slip through his fingers quicker than water, and then he'll be back to his old pilfering ways."

"Not in this town, he won't." Sheriff Watts sauntered toward the cell. "Adams, I'll let you out and I'll deputize you 'cause I know you're a good shot. But there's one more thing. Once this gang is caught and the reward money split, you get out of San Miguel County and don't ever come back, or I'll bring you up on charges for stealing from Rosenthal. Understood?"

"Deal!" Will stuck his hand through the bars. The sheriff sealed the deal with a handshake and then unlocked the cell.

Rosenthal headed for the door. "I've got work to do, and so do you. Good luck bringing the bad boys in." He hurried out the door.

Sheriff Watts turned to Orin and Paul. "I'm deputizing both of you, too. We'll leave on the nine-thirty train tomorrow morning for Hot Springs. I'll order an extra boxcar for us and our horses, and a couple of days' worth of provisions. Make sure you pack plenty of ammo. Adams, get down to the livery and reserve the three best riding horses for you and the Youngs. And don't you breathe a word of our plan or you'll be right back in that jail cell. Understood?"

Orin put his hands up. "Whoa, there, Sheriff. I want no part of any posse."

The sheriff's gaze bored into him. "Did I hear you right? You don't want to be deputized?"

Orin nodded. "I don't want to get into a shootout tomorrow. I just want to go back to work for Mr. Rosenthal. He's counting on me and Paul to be there or we'll get fired."

Adams was halfway to the door when he reversed his direction. "Who says it will be a shootout? We'll get the jump on Bloody Burt easy if we know where he's at, but that'll take you showin' us. Without you, we're just wanderin' in the mountains. As for Rosenthal, the sheriff will make sure your jobs are safe."

Orin took a tight breath. "Why can't I just draw you a map?"

Sheriff Watts, hands on hips, approached Orin until his chest nearly pressed against Orin's chin. "See here, Mr. Young." The stink of chewing tobacco blew down on Orin's face. "You and your brother are going to show us exactly where you encountered this Bloody Burt scoundrel. If you don't, word will get out just how lily-livered you are. Folks will run you two out of town as the worst cowards Las Vegas has ever seen, and I won't lift a finger to stop 'em."

Paul spoke up. "We'll show you," he glanced at Orin, "won't we?"

Orin's head bobbed. He had no choice but to go along with the sheriff's plan.

The corner of the sheriff's mouth curled upward. "Good. Tomorrow morning, I'll pin badges on each of you. Go now and get a good night's sleep. We'll meet at the livery at half-past eight in the morning."

Orin and Paul followed Will out the door, and then Will turned to face them. "Are you fellows experienced riders? Can you handle hot-blooded stallions? Or should I reserve a couple of gentle mares?"

Orin would have been glad for a mare, but he didn't want to look weak. "Stallions are fine. We spent a lot of time around high-spirited horses back in Wisconsin." He exaggerated. He'd had one encounter with a hot-blooded stallion and had landed on his backside in the mud.

"Stallions, it is. See you two in the morning." Will headed for the livery.

CHAPTER 42

The next day following lunch, when Cedena and Vivian opened the door to their room, they discovered a letter had been slipped beneath their door. Vivian scooped it up, studied it, and passed it to Cedena.

"From your father, you lucky lass."

Cedena opened it and sat on her bed to read. It was brief. Both Father and David were well and were saving much of their pay for the day when they could quit mining and go into some other line of work. As Cedena shoved the missive back into its envelope, Sally appeared in the doorway.

"I've got something really important to tell you." Her blue eyes had lost their usual sparkle and her lips curved down-ward.

Vivian rolled her eyes.

Cedena stifled a yawn. "Could it wait until we take our naps? We're really tired."

Sally shrugged. "I suppose so, but if I were you two, I would want to know if my gentleman friend had been depu-tized by the sheriff and joined his posse to arrest Bloody Burt and his gang of train robbers." She whirled around to leave.

Vivian sprang to her feet, grabbed Sally by the elbow, and turned her about. "Are you saying Paul and Orin Young have gone to chase down a gang of train robbers?"

"That's *exactly* what I'm saying. Will Adams is with them, too. They left on the nine-thirty train this morning."

Cedena's heart raced. "I can't believe it! Why would Orin, Paul, and Will put themselves in such danger?"

"Money," Sally stated confidently. "There's a five thousand dollar reward for bringing in Bloody Burt and his three accomplices. Five thousand dollars split four ways is still a good sum of money. Will had another reason, too. It got him out of jail for stealing from the mercantile."

Vivian sat on the edge of her bed and crossed her arms. "Wait a minute. How do we know you're not just making all this up?"

Sally smiled. "Go ask Mr. Rosenthal. He was at the sheriff's office yesterday afternoon when Orin and Paul told the sheriff that Bloody Burt was hiding out up in those mountains beyond the Montezuma. And then this morning, the sheriff bought provisions from Rosenthal for the posse on the promise that he wouldn't fire the Youngs for taking time off to go after Bloody Burt. Mrs. Rosenthal spilled the whole story when she and her friends were in for lunch at my table. It's the buzz all over town, the sheriff and his three deputies loading their horses onto a special box car this morning headed for Hot Springs. I hope they all make it back alive." She headed out the door.

Cedena's mind whirled as she turned to Vivian. "I can't believe it. Orin and Paul helping to chase down a dangerous gang all for reward money?"

Vivian kicked off her shoes, swung her legs up on her bed, and turned to face Cedena. "I'm really scared for them. What if . . ." She pressed her lips together.

" . . . they come back dead?" Cedena finished Vivian's sentence.

"Or wounded."

Cedena clenched her fists. "If they make it back unharmed, I'm going to be really angry with Orin for taking such a chance. Just when I thought he'd started acting more responsibly, he goes and does something completely foolish."

Vivian drew a deep breath. "If they make it back safely, I'll be too happy to waste any time being angry."

Cedena considered Vivian's words. "I guess you're right. I thought I was too tired to do anything except take a nap, but now, the only thing I want to do is pray."

Vivian nodded, got up off her bed, and then knelt beside it, hands folded, head bowed.

Cedena did the same, begging God to keep Orin and Paul safe while fear iced her veins. Her narrow escape from a gunshot wound at the dance had given her new respect for the power of firearms. Bullets didn't respect justice, only the shooter's aim. She begged God to spare Orin and Paul any harm.

By the time supper was served, Cedena's stomach was in such a knot that she could eat only a few bites of the ham, sweet potato, and peas that filled her plate. She headed to her station at the beverage bar and wiped down the silver coffee urns, even though they were immaculate. Her hand shook as she poured coffee and tea for her customers. She spilled coffee on her apron and had to run back to her room to put on a fresh one. When she returned, it was obvious that Vivian had dropped a customer's order on the floor. It was being cleaned up by a busboy while she placed a new order from the kitchen.

Sally came to Cedena and whispered in her ear. "Joe was in." She referred to the telegrapher for the Santa Fe. "Sheriff Watts sent a wire. It said, 'Three captured. One dead. Returning at seven.'"

"One dead? But who?"

Sally shrugged and pointed to the clock on the wall. "We'll find out soon enough."

It was only half-past six. All Cedena wanted was to see the branch line from Hot Springs pull into the station at seven and to find out if Orin was alive. But she would have to serve customers until eight when the dining room closed, and then set up for breakfast. Perhaps she could beg a few minutes to go out to the platform before the eastbound California Express arrived at seven-fifteen and the dining room filled again with hungry passengers.

As Cedena stood at her post by the beverage station trying to keep an eye on which customers might need more coffee or tea, Mr. Vetsch approached her and pointed to one of the urns. "When was the last time that was dumped?"

Cedena's face grew hot. "Four o'clock, sir."

"And what time is it now?" Mr. Vetsch pointed to the clock above the door.

"Twenty-five minutes until seven, sir."

"I'm disappointed in you, Cedena. You know the coffee must be made fresh every two hours, and until now, you've been punctual about it. Don't let it happen again." He pivoted on his heel and strode off.

Cedena hastened to dump the urn, refill it with water, and measure out fresh grounds. In no time, the small hand on the clock had moved to seven and the unmistakable rumble of the branch line grew louder. Cedena's palms grew moist. From across the dining room, Vivian's gaze sought hers. She looked as if she were about to cry, which was exactly how Cedena felt.

Miss Upton approached Vivian, spoke into her ear, and then Vivian hurried outside. Next, Miss Upton made a beeline for Cedena.

"You may go out to see if your friends, the Young brothers, have returned. But you must be back here in five minutes. Now go!" She gave Cedena a nudge.

CHAPTER 43

A crowd had gathered trackside. Cedena searched for Vivian among the faces and hurried to her. Moments later, Sally joined them. Cedena wrapped one arm around Sally, to her left, and the other around Vivian, to her right, as they waited with moist eyes for the train to come to a halt. A few seconds later, the boxcar stopped directly in front of them. The door rolled back, a ramp was lowered, and Will Adams, with his left arm in a sling, led a horse down the ramp. Over the saddle was draped a man, face down and motionless as his black bandana fluttered in the breeze.

Sally pointed. "That's Bloody Burt on the horse. He's dead!" Sally ran up to Will.

Cedena exchanged worried looks with Vivian, who let out a quiet whimper. Then their focus returned to the boxcar ramp. Sheriff Watts walked off next. He led three prisoners, handcuffed and roped to one another, in the direction of the jailhouse. The crowd began to cheer. Behind the sheriff, Paul led two horses down the ramp. He appeared unscathed. Vivian ran to greet him.

Where was Orin? Cedena's heart raced. Then he started down the ramp with two more horses. She ran to him.

"Thank God you're all right!"

Orin dropped the reins, pulled Cedena into his arms, and squeezed the air right out of her lungs. "I didn't think I'd live long enough to see you again." His voice broke.

Cedena wrapped her arms about Orin's neck, kissed his cheek, and then released him.

Moisture clouded his eyes. He wiped it away with the cuff of his shirt and picked up the reins. "I've got to take these horses and three others to the livery. See you when you get off work tonight—nine o'clock in front of the restaurant."

"See you then!"

Cedena hurried back to the restaurant, Sally and Vivian catching up with her on the way.

"Looks like there'll be a four-way split of that reward!" Sally grinned.

Cedena turned to face Sally. "Is Will going to be all right?"

"Oh, goodness, yes. Nothing but a flesh wound. The doc will fix him up in no time. Then, soon as he gets his money, he'll be gone from Las Vegas, never to return, Sheriff's orders."

When they returned to the dining room, Mr. Vetsch called Sally aside. He didn't look pleased. Word spread that she hadn't been given permission to leave her duties to meet the train, and furthermore, she'd been told some time ago that she was to keep her distance from Will Adams. Her roommate, Rachel, even suggested to Cedena that Sally might be fired that very night.

~*~*~

It was already a few minutes past nine when Cedena and Vivian finished setting up the tables for breakfast and headed out the door of the restaurant. Orin and Paul were waiting on a bench and immediately sprang to their feet. Sally followed close behind Vivian and Cedena and kept walking straight across the tracks to the dormitory.

Paul took Vivian by the hand and led her toward the end of the boardwalk, leaving Cedena and Orin standing alone in front of the bench. The air had taken on a chill and Cedena shivered.

Orin gestured for her to sit down, and then he sat close beside her and wrapped his arm about her shoulders. His touch brought more than warmth. As she relaxed into his embrace, a sense of belonging washed over her.

Orin leaned his head against hers. "Wish I had a jacket to loan you."

"I don't." Cedena cast a sideways glance and grinned. "Your arm is jacket enough."

Orin gave her a squeeze and looked deep into her eyes, as if searching for something. "When we went up to Hot Springs this morning, I was worried this moment might never come, that I might never see you again."

"When I heard where you'd gone and why, I was terribly worried, too." A lump formed in Cedena's throat. She struggled to force her next words past it. "I prayed for you all afternoon. Why did you do it, Orin? Why did you put yourself in such danger?" Her eyes filled with tears.

Orin reached for her hand, cradling it gently in his as he raised it to his lips and pressed a kiss against it. Then a somber look settled over his features. "On the train coming down here from Colorado, I saw a cold-blooded killer murder a man. It changed me. It made me put aside foolish ways and try to make the most of my life. Then, on the trail with you and Vivian, that cold-blooded killer came out of nowhere and shot the rattlesnake. Paul and I recognized him from the train robbery and reported his whereabouts to Sheriff Watts. He roped us into going after him."

Cedena wiped a tear from her cheek. "That's the part I don't understand. Why you and Paul? Couldn't other men have gone?"

Orin drew a deep breath. "No. Paul and I knew where Bloody Burt was. Will Adams said we could get Bloody Burt without anyone firing a shot. Too bad Adams got hit, but his own quick draw took down Bloody Burt. It was Adams who shot first. Bloody Burt had already been hit when he shot back, which is probably why the shot wasn't fatal."

Cedena shook her head, trying to rid it of the violent story. "No more talk about gunshots. I need to get back to the dormitory before I'm late for curfew." She glanced down the platform to where Paul and Vivian were standing face to face at very close range, and then Cedena stood, pulling Orin to his feet. "Come help me get that besotted roommate of mine away from your equally besotted brother, or Vivian and I will both be in hot water."

CHAPTER 44

When Cedena and Vivian reached the second floor a couple of minutes before ten o'clock, Sally followed them into their room, her gaze on Cedena. "Mr. Vetsch fired me tonight. He said I left the restaurant without permission and had fraternized with an undesirable sort after being warned not to go near Will Adams."

Cedena looked Sally straight in the eye. "Is it true? Did you leave without permission? Had Mr. Vetsch told you not to go near Will Adams?"

Sally's gaze dropped momentarily and then bounced back to Cedena. "Mr. Vetsch has had it in for me almost from the start, scolding me for the tiniest little spot on my apron, or for being too friendly with the customers."

Vivian laughed mirthlessly. "Those are basic rules taught during training. Mr. Vetsch was right to hold you to the Harvey standard."

"Yes, but—"

Cedena had no more patience for excuses. "Sally, your disobedience has earned fair and just consequences. The best thing you can do right now is to start packing."

Sally turned and headed toward the door.

"Sally, wait up." Cedena approached her. "Regardless of what you've done, I wish you the best for your future. And there's one thing more, one thing I wish you'd tell me. The rock that broke our window a couple of weeks ago—did Will Adams throw it? And what did the note mean—'You owe me'?"

Sally offered a half-smile. "Will's aim with a rock isn't nearly as accurate as his aim with a pistol. As for the note, he misunderstood something I said to him. He thought he was due a favor woman to man. That's all I'm going to say about it." She quickly exited the room.

Vivian closed the door, approached Cedena, and spoke in a whisper. "I'm not sorry she's leaving." Vivian began unbuttoning her uniform.

Cedena could have echoed Vivian's statement. She had never really liked Sally, but she wanted to put that subject to rest. She sat down on her bed and began unlacing her shoes. "I'm thankful this day is over. It's been long and hard, and I'm looking forward to getting some sleep."

The following evening when the seven-fifteen train arrived, Cedena glanced out the restaurant window. Miss Upton was ushering Sally onto a passenger car. How sad.

With customers coming into the restaurant for dinner, Cedena pushed thoughts of Sally from her mind and focused on taking orders. The next two hours passed quickly, and then the staff set up for the following day. It seemed to Cedena that the atmosphere was more somber than usual. With a heavy heart and even heavier feet, she crossed the street to the dormitory and climbed the stairs to her room. Vivian and several others had arrived ahead of her and were gathered in the hall-way.

Vivian turned to Cedena. "Everybody seems to be missing something. That silver maple leaf pin you gave me is gone from my dresser drawer."

"I'm missing the silver hairbrush I always kept on my dresser," said Georgina.

"My mirror is gone," said Franny.

"The book I got from my grandmother for Christmas is gone, too," said Rachel.

Other girls were missing items also—a hair comb, a pearl necklace, a paperweight, and more. Every girl on the floor was missing something.

"I'm going down to see Miss Upton right now." Vivian turned toward the stairs. "Anyone coming with me?"

All agreed to go except Cedena.

Vivian took a couple of steps and cast a backward glance. "Cedena, you'd better check to see if anything of yours is missing. If so, come down and tell Miss Upton."

Cedena had started to go through her drawers when Rachel returned carrying a brown bottle. "Does this look familiar?" She handed it to Cedena.

Cedena read the label. "That's the bottle of medicine Miss Upton gave me after I fell in the pit. It went missing after the first day." She shook the bottle. "But it's empty."

Rachel grinned. "Now you know where the bottle went, and I know why I had such a hard time getting Sally to wake up in the morning that first week after your fall. She must have been taking nips off that bottle each night before she went to bed. I found it sitting on her dresser tonight after the dinner shift. She must have decided to clear up the mystery of your missing medicine as one of her final deeds before moving out."

Rachel left and Cedena continued going through all her drawers and the wardrobe. Nothing was missing. She dumped the key to her trunk from her right winter boot and picked it up off the floor. It seemed like a waste of time, but she'd check her trunk anyway. She inserted the key into her trunk lock. It turned too easily. The trunk was already unlocked. Cedena's pulse raced. She couldn't have left it unlocked. How did it get that way? Nobody but *nobody* knew the whereabouts of her key, not even Vivian. Cedena threw the lid open.

On top lay a handwritten note. Cedena snatched it up and looked at the signature. Sally Pederson. But how had she unlocked the trunk to put her note inside? The girl was full of surprises. Cedena sat on her bed and began to read the scrawl on the page.

Dear Cedena,

I am sory for the truble last Jan when you fell in the pit. I didn't no the pit was there. I never ment for you to get hurt.

I have always looked up to you. I wish I could be good like you. My mama sed I had the devil in me. She was rite. Good by. Good luck.

Your frend,
Sally

Cedena shook her head. Never would she have expected a note like that from Sally. She set the note on the dresser and then searched through her trunk, but nothing was missing or disturbed. Perhaps the note explained why nothing of Cedena's was missing. She put on her nightgown, washed her face, and climbed into bed.

Within minutes, the girls returned from downstairs. Vivian entered the room followed by Rachel. Cedena sat up.

"What did Miss Upton say?"

Vivian untied her apron. "Everybody thinks Sally stole from us while we were working the dinner shift, Miss Upton included."

Rachel drew closer. "Mr. Vetsch is sending a wire to Springer. The agent there is going to hold Sally and her belongings until they can make a thorough search for the missing items."

Vivian hung up her apron. "The train doesn't arrive in Springer until nine-fifty-two. It will be eleven o'clock or later before they know if Sally is our thief. Were you missing anything, Cedena?"

Cedena shook her head. "No, but I found an interesting note from Sally. It's on the dresser. I found it inside my trunk—which was locked until tonight. I don't understand how Sally got into it without the key."

"I do." Rachel smiled wryly. "Sally has a set of lock picks."

Cedena sighed. "That explains it."

Rachel headed for the door. "Good night. And here's hoping they find our things in Springer."

"Good night, Rachel."

~*~*~

Later that night, voices in the hallway woke Cedena. She threw back her covers and opened the door. Miss Upton and several of the other girls were gathered there. Cedena and Vivian joined them.

Miss Upton's gaze took in the entire group. "I'm pleased to say that all of the missing items were found in Sally's possession and will be returned after they have served as evidence of her crime in court."

"Will Sally go to jail?" Rachel asked.

Miss Upton sighed. "A jury of her peers will decide that, but it doesn't look good for her. Good night, girls."

CHAPTER 45

The following Sunday at breakfast, Rachel sat down across from Cedena and Vivian. "Did you hear? There was a jail break last night."

Cedena shifted her focus from her oatmeal to Rachel. "Who got out? Not the train robbers, I hope."

Rachel shook her head. "No, your favorite friend and mine, Sally Pederson."

"Is that right?" After Sally had been apprehended in Springer for stealing from the other girls, she had been returned to Las Vegas and placed behind bars.

Vivian sipped her orange juice and set it aside. "How did Sally get out? Not that I'm surprised. Anyone with a set of lock picks could probably open a jail cell."

Rachel shrugged. "Whether it was lock picks or Will Adams that got her out is up to question. For certain, she was not willing to go to trial for her crime. And word is out that Adams got his reward money yesterday for killing Bloody Burt and was told to leave the county by sundown. He could have laid low until dark and taken Sally with him." Rachel stirred her oatmeal and gazed up again at Cedena and Vivian. "So if

Will Adams got his reward money, your friends Orin and Paul must have gotten theirs, too."

Cedena exchanged glances with Vivian and then focused again on Rachel. "We haven't heard."

"But you'll see them today, won't you? What are they going to do with their money?" It seemed Rachel was becoming as nosey as Sally had been.

Vivian glared at Rachel. "Don't you know better than to go askin' such questions?" She tucked a spoonful of oatmeal into her mouth and Rachel followed suit.

Later that morning, Orin and Paul escorted Cedena and Vivian to church, and then they all took box lunches and Mexican blankets down to the river for a picnic. Cedena and Vivian had agreed not to ask about the reward money but to let the fellows break the news when they were ready. Once the sandwiches and cookies were gone and nothing was left but lemonade, Cedena began to wonder if the subject would ever come up. Then Paul raised his glass.

"I propose a toast to the Young Ranch! Our reward money came in yesterday and we've started a search for land!"

Vivian's smile stretched wide as the river. "That's wonderful news!"

"Congratulations to both of you!" Cedena touched her glass to the others.

Orin pulled a folded paper from his vest pocket. "I sketched this drawing of an idea we have for a ranch house. We'd like to know what you girls think of it." He spread it out on the blanket.

Paul pointed to the drawing, a front view of two single-story homes linked in between. "Since we'll both be working the ranch, we thought that two separate houses connected by a roofed patio might be a good design. There will be outhouses in the back and a well in front."

Cedena studied the illustration. "I really like the verandas running the full length of each house."

Vivian nodded. "The shade will be important in summer. It's only May, but already the weather is much hotter than I'm used to this time of year. I can only imagine that it will be scorching hot during June, July, and August."

Orin leaned back. "Mr. Rosenthal says we'll probably be sleeping on the verandas during the hottest weather so we ought to face them to catch the breeze."

Paul's gaze shifted from the drawing to Vivian and then Cedena. "Do you ladies have any suggestions for improvement on this plan?"

Vivian shook her head. "I think it's perfect." She focused on Cedena. "What do you think?"

"I agree. The plan is practical but also attractive."

"Great!" Paul rose. "Vivian, may I take you on a stroll along the river?"

"Absolutely!"

Paul pulled her to her feet and they wandered off.

Orin folded the drawing and handed it to Cedena. "You keep this."

"But won't you need it?"

Orin shook his head. "I've got another just like it in my room. I want you to have that one to dream about."

"But Orin, Vivian and I will be heading to Kansas City for a month at the end of this week, and when we come back, we'll be under contract through the twenty-fourth of December."

Orin reached for Cedena's hand and held it between both of his. "I'm going to miss you something fierce when you're gone. But while you're away, and for those six months after you come back, Paul and I will be working hard to construct that ranch house and buy stock animals. We want to be able to provide for the women we love."

"Oh, Orin . . . ." Cedena's heart raced. The warmth of his touch spread to her very core.

Orin raised her hand to his lips and brushed a kiss across her knuckles. Then his blue eyes, so gentle yet intense, held her gaze. "I'd ask you right now to marry me, but I want you to think it over while you're away. I want you to be sure. Promise me you'll think about what I've said while you're gone."

She raised her hand to his face and stroked his cheek. "I'll think of nothing else."

CHAPTER 46

Sunday morning, June 24, 1894

Cedena sent up a silent prayer of thanks that the train carrying her and Vivian back to New Mexico Territory from a month-long vacation in Kansas City was running on schedule. They would reach Las Vegas this morning at half-past seven. She thanked God, too, that their trip had been free of train robbers, weather delays, or mechanical difficulties that sometimes plagued the western rails. Now, if only Orin and Paul would be there to meet them, the trip would come to a perfect end, but Cedena held little hope of that.

The month's leave had seemed more like a year. Never had Cedena imagined she would miss anyone or any place as much as she had missed Orin and New Mexico Territory. She had missed her work as a Harvey Girl, too. It made her feel useful, productive, and independent. Living with Aunt Nancy and Uncle James again had intensified her appreciation for self-sufficiency, not that she didn't love seeing them and helping out the best she could with their household and business struggles, but it had been far less enjoyable than the rather carefree days at the Fair before the depression had taken hold.

Uncle James looked as if he had aged five years in the last six months, and Aunt Nancy perpetually wore a new set of dark circles beneath her eyes.

Aunt Nancy's efforts to arrange Cedena's reconciliation with Mother had failed, too. Aunt Nancy had even sent a wire urging her sister to invite Cedena home. The response came days later in a letter from Mother. She told Aunt Nancy, "I have no daughter." The news broke Cedena's heart all over again.

At least Father and David had written to Cedena in Kansas City as she had instructed them to do in her May letter to them. They had been faithful to correspond once a month since the February letter from Father in Cripple Creek. Each time she heard from them, she thanked God that they were both well and willing to stay in touch.

Aside from Mother's spurning, Cedena's Kansas City visit had produced another difficult situation. Seeing Matthew and Alice again had been awkward, to say the least. It was hard to tell whether Matthew was really as devoted to his wife of three months as he appeared to be. Could his doting on her in front of Cedena have been a way of trying to convince both Cedena and himself that his affections were now wholly and firmly devoted to Alice?

Cedena pushed thoughts of Matthew and Alice from her mind, opened her book, took out the last letter from Orin, and read it again.

My dearest Cedena,

How I miss your eyes that sparkle like sapphires in the New Mexico sunshine. I miss, too, holding your hand in mine and sitting beneath the never-ending azure sky, gazing at the distant peaks of gray ascending toward heaven. It is then that I know I have found heaven on earth, just to be in New Mexico Territory with you by my side. My heart is sore and growing more so the longer you are away, for words cannot describe how your sweetness and grace fill up my heart when you are near.

I hope you have been looking at the drawing of the ranch house and dreaming of our future. Paul and I have been hard at work on it along with Pedro. The adobe walls are under construction. After they are finished, floors and roofs will be done. As to the details of finishing these homes, they will be decided by you and Vivian upon your return. We are currently erecting a barn and fencing for a sheepfold. Depending on the progress we make, we may be able to meet your train, but I cannot promise it, or even say it is likely. The ranch is six miles from town, and we must continue working and supervising the crew until the need for supplies forces us to take a day off and return to Las Vegas.

Until I see you again, know that my days and nights are filled with longing for you.

Your most ardent admirer,
Orin

As the train pulled into the Las Vegas depot, Cedena tucked the letter back inside her book. She gazed out her window, but she saw no sign of Orin or Paul. When she stepped onto the platform, she looked up and down the way. Still, the Young brothers were nowhere to be seen.

Vivian came alongside Cedena. "I guess our soon-to-be ranchers are hard at work on their spread. Let's take our handbags up to our room and then get breakfast. We can even go to church afterward, if you're up to it."

"Sure. I need a good reason for having put on my best dress this morning." Cedena tried to put disappointment behind her, but it wouldn't be easy until tomorrow, at work, when she'd be too busy to think about anything but serving her customers.

CHAPTER 47

Thursday, June 28, 1894

"Can you believe it?" Orin asked Paul as he drove their farm wagon onto Railroad Street and approached the Las Vegas Depot.

"I'll be hanged. Looks like there's a rail workers strike."

Orin pulled his wide-brimmed felt hat farther down to shade his eyes from the morning sun. "And the eastbound California Express is dead in the tracks while picketers surround the depot."

"Pull up as close to the restaurant as you can, over there." Paul pointed to narrow space among several wagons and carriages that congested the street. "We've got to find out if the girls are all right."

When the wagon came to a halt, Paul jumped down and headed for the picket line.

Orin had to move double-time to catch up. "What if the picketers won't let us through?"

Paul flashed a determined look at Orin. "Then we'll fight our way through. I've got to see if Vivian is safe!"

Seconds later, Paul came face to face with a union worker carrying a sign that read, "No Raise, No Rail Traffic."

The burly fellow planted his feet in the dust and lowered his sign. "Where do you think y'r goin'?"

"I'm going to check on my girl. She works in there." Paul pointed to the depot restaurant.

The picketer shook his head. "Nobody crosses this line."

Orin stepped beside Paul. "Come on. Let's go."

"I'm not leaving till I see Vivian!" Paul pushed forward.

The burly fellow dropped his sign and jabbed his fist into Paul's nose, then followed with a cross punch to his left cheek.

In the same instant, a shot rang out.

Paul fell to the ground like a sack of potatoes.

Orin's heart stopped. He dropped to his knees beside his motionless brother. "He's dead! Somebody shot him!" He looked up at the striker.

The burly fellow stood with his hands on his hips and gazed down at Orin as picketers gathered around. "He ain't dead. Nobody shot him. He's just out cold. Jinx, here, fired into the air. It's a warning to the others in case of trouble. Now get that sorry fool out of here and don't come back!"

Orin dragged Paul away from the picket line. Blood trickled from his nose. Orin shook Paul's shoulders. "Brother, wake up!"

Paul groaned. His eyes blinked open.

Orin handed Paul his handkerchief. "Better wipe your nose. It's bleeding bad."

Paul staunched the flow, touched his palm to his left cheek, and groaned again. "Feels like somebody smashed a cast iron pan into my face."

"Doesn't pay to challenge a railway union striker. Come on. We've got to clean you up and get to the mill to pick up some lumber."

"What about Vivian and Cedena? Aren't you worried about them?"

"Absolutely not! With those picketers guarding the depot, nobody's going to get through to bring harm to the Harvey Girls."

CHAPTER 48

Ten days later, Sunday morning, July 8

Cedena woke from a very sound sleep. The bright sun slanted through the window. It had to be late. Very late. She gazed at the clock on her bedside table. Almost ten.

In the bed next to Cedena's, Vivian sat propped against her pillows reading one of her dime romance novels. She glanced at Cedena. "Awake finally, are you?"

"I'm so tired I think I could sleep for a week straight. Aren't you tired?"

"Exhausted, but I woke up about an hour ago and couldn't get back to sleep. Thinking about Paul, I guess; wondering when I'll see him again."

"Should be soon, now that the train has finally moved on. I hope I never experience another situation like that." Two-hundred-fifty passengers had been stranded at the depot, for-bidden by picketers to go into town to buy food. The restaurant had fed every one of them three times a day at first. Harvey Girls had served from dawn until dusk without breaks. When supplies ran low, they served two meals a day. The chefs got permission from the Santa Fe Railroad to rummage through the freight cars on the train to find what they could and make the best of it. Eventually, nearly all the available food had been consumed.

As if that weren't bad enough, a new conflict had arisen. Protesters threatened to run the Pullman porters out of town at gunpoint. Yesterday, soldiers came to town, and last night the train had finally pulled out of the Las Vegas station. If only the restaurant could close for a few days and give everyone some time to recover. But that wasn't the way the Santa Fe or Harvey Company operated. At least Cedena and Vivian had today to themselves.

A quiet knock sounded on their door and Vivian opened it. "Miss Upton, come in."

She stepped across the threshold, her brow furrowed and her gaze shifting from Vivian to Cedena.

"Ladies, I have a problem only the two of you can solve for me."

Cedena bit her tongue. She was in no mood to solve anyone's problem, in no mood to do anything except spend the day in quiet rest.

Vivian sat on the edge of her bed. "What's that, Miss Upton?"

"It seems two gentlemen by the last name of Young have driven their wagon into town and parked it in front of the dormitory. They have sought permission to take the two of you to the ranch they are building, and they have promised to return you before dark. I just don't know what to say to them. Are you willing to go, or should I send them away?" Miss Upton grinned.

"Don't you *dare* send them away!" Vivian flew from her bed to the wardrobe.

Cedena whipped her covers aside. "Tell them we'll be down in a few minutes."

With a nod, Miss Upton headed for the door, then paused and turned to them. "Should I ask the kitchen to put some biscuits and jam into a box for your breakfast, and to prepare four lunches and plenty of drinking water for your trip?"

"Yes, please!" Cedena and Vivian answered in unison.

"Tell your friends to pull their wagon up to the kitchen door behind the restaurant before you all leave town."

A few minutes later, Cedena's heart ran ahead of her feet as she descended the stairs behind Vivian and stepped outside. Orin and Paul sat on the bench in front of the dormitory. They rose the moment they saw Cedena and Vivian.

An instant later, Orin captured Cedena's hands in his and offered a look full of tenderness. "My, but you are a sight for sore eyes."

"And you as well, Orin." The warmth of his touch flowed swiftly from Cedena's hands and straight to her heart. She wished he would never let go.

Nearby, Paul and Vivian were sharing a similar moment.

Orin gave a nod toward a wagon full of lumber parked a few feet away. "We'd better get moving if we're to have you ladies home before it's too dark to see the road."

Vivian spoke up. "Don't forget to pull around to the kitchen to pick up our lunches."

While Vivian and Paul settled onto a bench in the back of the wagon, Orin grasped Cedena tightly about the waist and lifted her to the driver's seat, then climbed aboard beside her.

With a word of encouragement, a pair of handsome gray draft horses clopped into motion. A few minutes later, having made a stop at the kitchen, they were trotting down the road toward the ranch while Cedena and Vivian munched on jam-filled biscuits and drank fresh-squeezed orange juice. As they passed meadows dotted with bushes, grasses, cacti, and small trees Cedena could not name, Orin inquired about her time in Kansas City.

"My time away was too long and too sad. After I found out that Mother still wouldn't allow me to come for a visit, I was ready to head right back to New Mexico."

Orin glanced her way, his blue eyes sending an avalanche of sympathy. "I'm so sorry. Maybe things will change." He focused again on the rutted road. "What about Alice and Matthew? Are they really as happy as her letters would have me believe?"

"They seemed so when I saw them." Enough about her trip. She gazed across the broad flatland that ascended into mountains in the far distance. "Tell me what grows here. Is there anything in the desert that will keep your cattle alive? And what about water?"

"Our land is particularly well-suited for sheep so we're not going to have any steers just yet. There's a creek running through our spread that is spring-fed, so water is available year around. As for forage, there's a natural abundance of grasses that sheep like—western wheatgrass, redtop, mutton blue-grass, sheep fescue, and about five others. If those aren't enough, bottlebrush squirreltail grows there, too, although sheep aren't too fond of it."

Suddenly, Vivian screamed.

Cedena whipped her head around. "What's wrong?"

Vivian tucked her feet beneath her and pointed to the area under the bench she was on. "A scorpion!"

Orin brought the wagon to a halt.

Paul stood up. "Stay still, Vivian. If you scare him, he'll go back into hiding. I don't really want to encounter him again when we unload the lumber." Paul bent down and peered under the bench, then glanced up at Vivian and placed his finger against his lips. As he straightened, the scorpion crawled into plain sight. Paul stomped on it and ground it into the wagon bed with his boot heel.

A disagreeable odor rose on a gentle breeze.

Cedena turned to Orin. "What's that pungent smell?"

Orin offered a wry smile. "That's what you get when you kill a scorpion. The odor won't last long."

Thankfully, as Orin put the wagon in motion again, the smell seemed much milder. Conversation lulled, giving Cedena an opportunity simply to enjoy the sunshine. But the farther they rode, the greater her curiosity grew. Would Orin ever bring up the proposal he had postponed until her return from Kansas City?

CHAPTER 49

After two hours on the road, Orin made a turn into a driveway. The entrance had been attractively marked by L-shaped split rail fence sections on either side. Above the entrance, a sign spanned two tall posts that read "Young Ranch." Cedena caught a glimpse of a free-standing roof about an eighth of a mile ahead.

As the wagon drew closer, details came into focus. A well and watering trough stood out front. Behind it, the patio between the houses had been finished with a brick floor and a corrugated metal roof supported by hefty beams. That was the most complete part of the entire design. The houses that were to connect on either side were still far from done. In the yard, Pedro was hard at work making adobe and filling brick forms.

Orin and Paul helped Cedena and Vivian from the wagon. It seemed like everyone was talking at once.

"Here's the outline of one of the houses." Paul pointed the toe of his boot to one of four scribed lines on the ground to the left of the patio.

Orin gestured toward the open sky above. "The ceilings will be high, and the roof will be corrugated metal."

"How many windows will there be?" Vivian asked.

"And what size will they be?" Cedena wanted to know. "We'll need to make curtains for them."

Orin took Cedena's hands in his and grinned. "No need for curtains. The windows will have shutters inside made of salt-cedar twigs. Paul and I will see to it. Right, Paul?" He glanced at his brother.

Paul had his arm about Vivian's waist and gave her a squeeze. "Right! Now I have a question. Is anyone hungry? I'm ready for lunch on our beautiful patio."

The fellows helped carry the lunch supplies from the wagon to the patio and left the girls to do their work while they unhitched the horses, drew water from the well to fill the trough, and unloaded the lumber.

The shade beneath the patio roof was welcome relief from the sun's heat. Cedena worked with Vivian to lay out the blankets and food. As she did, she spoke in a voice just above a whisper.

"Has Paul asked you to marry him yet?"

Vivian sighed. "If he had, I'd be shouting it from the rooftop—or patio top, I mean. Has Orin asked you?"

"No. What are they waiting for?"

"Maybe they need a little nudge. I have an idea." Vivian placed two box lunches, one on top of the other, in front of her on the blanket, did the same for Cedena, and whispered her plan. Cedena nodded and grinned. Moments later, the fellows sat down beside them on the blankets.

When Paul reached for a lunch box, Vivian prevented him by taking his hand in hers. "Before you eat lunch, isn't there a question you wanted to ask me?"

Paul shrugged. "May I have my lunch, please?"

Cedena chuckled. "Wrong question. Vivian was referring to the subject of marriage."

Orin spoke up. "Paul, don't you dare say one word until you hear what I have to say."

Cedena's heart stopped. Orin sounded earnest. After all this time, he couldn't be opposed to Vivian, could he?

Orin got on his knees and took Cedena's hands in his. "Cedena, would you do me the highest honor of becoming my wife as soon as your contract is up with the Harvey Company?" His sapphire blue eyes searched hers with great tenderness.

A lump rose in Cedena's throat, making her unsure if she could speak. She swallowed hard. "I would be honored and blessed to become your wife. Would a Christmas Day wedding meet with your approval?"

"If it can be arranged with a clergyman or a justice of the peace, we'll marry on Christmas Day." He leaned forward and placed a brief kiss on her lips.

"Congratulations, you two! Now it's my turn." On his knees, Paul took Vivian's hand in both of his, gently kissed it, and then cradled it against his chest. "Vivian, you are the sun, moon, and stars to me. I can't take a single breath without thinking of you. Please make me the happiest man in New Mexico and say you'll marry me as soon as your contract is up."

With her free hand, Vivian stroked Paul's cheek. "Yes, yes, *yes*!" She leaned forward and planted a kiss on his lips.

Orin looked on and beamed. "Looks like Christmas Day will be a double wedding day, if you ladies are willing. Or two separate weddings—whatever you prefer."

"I'm for a double wedding if Cedena is." Vivian's gaze met Cedena's.

Cedena nodded vigorously. "Double wedding it is!"

"Do you think the Methodist Episcopal Church will be available on Christmas Day after the morning service?" Vivian asked.

"We'll find out." Cedena handed a lunch box to Orin. "Now let's eat."

Later that evening, Cedena wrote a letter to Father and David telling them about her wedding plans and inviting them to attend. "It would be wonderful to have family here on Christmas, and extra-special to have you give me away, Father. You need not worry about Mother. I am certain she wouldn't attend if her life depended on it." Cedena sealed the letter with a prayer that Father and David could get time off from the mine.

CHAPTER 50

Six weeks later, Sunday morning, August 19

Cedena woke with a start, her heart pounding and her palms sweaty. In her nightmare, Orin and Paul were at work building their ranch when a dust storm blew in, crashing walls of the unfinished house down on them and scattering adobe bricks across the desert. She blinked, her breath coming in short gasps.

On the bed across from Cedena, Vivian had lowered her dime novel and was staring at her. "You're awake now. Were you having a bad dream? I heard you mumbling in your sleep."

Cedena pushed back the sheet that had been covering her and sat on the edge of her bed. "I just had a horrible nightmare about Orin and Paul. Why haven't they visited us, or at least written a note? I know they're hard at work building their ranch, but it's been six weeks since we last saw them, and I'm worried sick."

"Me, too. I couldn't sleep very well, so I've been sitting here, reading since first light."

Cedena stood. "Let's drive out to the ranch today. We could get box lunches from the kitchen and rent a small rig at the livery."

Vivian's brows narrowed. "Do you think we could find our way?"

"I'm sure of it."

An hour later, Cedena was at the reins, steering a one-horse carriage out of town on the road the fellows had taken to their ranch the day they had made their marriage proposals. The roan mare, Lady, moved along at a nice trot.

Vivian began singing "Molly Malone." Cedena sang with her on the chorus after each verse. Song after song they sang as the road snaked up and down hills and curved around rocks. When they were about ninety minutes from town, the buggy hit a pothole with a loud *crack*. Lady bolted, veering crazily back and forth.

"Whoa, Lady! Whoa!" Cedena pulled back hard on the reins, struggling to slow down and steer to the side of the road. When Lady had come to a full stop and calmed down, Cedena handed the reins to Vivian and climbed out.

Her heart sank. The left front wheel was broken. She looked up at Vivian. "We're stuck here in the middle of no-where until someone comes along who can repair a broken wheel."

Vivian glanced skyward. "It's going to be blazing hot soon. Maybe we should walk the rest of the way."

"And leave the horse and rig here?"

Vivian shook her head. "We could unhitch the mare and take her with us. Maybe she'd even let us ride her bareback."

Cedena shook her head. "I won't be climbing on her back. You can, if you want."

Vivian's focus shifted to the road ahead. "Someone's coming around the curve, a wagon."

Cedena prayed it was Orin and Paul. Her hope quickly died as a man and woman came into view. Suddenly, recognition dawned. "It's Will Adams and Sally Pederson!"

Vivian sighed. "More trouble. She's wanted by Sheriff Watts, and Will's not even supposed to be in the county."

"This is *not* our lucky day." Despite what Cedena thought of Sally and Will, she forced a smile as their wagon came to a halt alongside the broken-down rig.

Sally jumped up, a smile splitting her face. "Cedena! Vivian! What are you two doing out here? Let me guess. You're on your way to the Young Ranch."

Cedena nodded. "Yes, but we ran into some trouble." Cedena pointed to the broken wheel.

Will jumped down from the wagon, a pair of six-shooters hanging from his hips, and inspected the cracked rim and broken spoke. "I can fix this." He rose and focused on Cedena and Vivian. "But only on the promise you ladies won't go tellin' the sheriff I'm still in the county. Fair enough?"

Cedena and Vivian exchanged glances and then nodded.

"I gotta go back to my place and get some tools. Climb into the bed of my wagon. My place isn't far. You can wait there with Sally while I take care of this."

With Cedena and Vivian and their box lunches aboard, Will tied the rented mare to the rear of the wagon and began driving back the way he had come. Several minutes later, he pulled off the road onto a barely distinguishable two-rut driveway that wound through pinyons and ended at a small log cabin hidden in the woods. To the left, angled toward the house, was a three-stall livestock shelter. It was open on the front side, partly enclosed by side and back walls, and covered by a roof made of branches. Two of the stalls were occupied by painted ponies.

"Here we are! Home, sweet home." Sally jumped down and helped Cedena and Vivian off the back of the wagon while Will unhitched the mare and tied her to a post.

Cedena and Vivian gathered their box lunches from the wagon and followed Sally to the cabin. She opened the door wide and placed a rock in front of it. Daylight and a warm breeze flooded into the dirt floor house, which was no more than sixteen-feet square.

Furnishings were sparse. A small table stood in the center. Two three-legged stools were stowed underneath. An unmade bed hung from the left wall. Small windows on the front and back walls let in additional fresh air and light. In the center of the table was a lantern, and provisions were piled up in the back right corner.

Sally picked up the lantern and hung it on the wall. "You can set your box lunches on the table. It must be nearly time to eat." She pulled out the stools and gestured for Cedena and Vivian to be seated.

Will came and stood in the open doorway, almost smiling as he focused on Cedena and Vivian. "You two ladies make yourselves at home." His gaze darkened as it shifted to Sally. He beckoned for her to follow him.

Sally nodded and turned to Cedena and Vivian. "Go ahead, you two, and start lunch without me. I'll be back in a minute." She lifted her skirt and swiftly headed out the door, not quite able to keep up with Will.

Cedena moved to a place just inside the door, peering out to see what Will wanted with Sally. He took her behind the livestock shelter, out of sight and beyond hearing. Cedena joined Vivian at the table, sat on a stool opposite her, and opened her box lunch.

Vivian set her wrapped sandwich on the rough-hewn tabletop and folded back the paper. "Pretty crude, this place. How can Sally stand it?"

"She must think it's better than jail." Cedena opened her sandwich and bit into the ham and mustard encased in thick white bread. She hadn't realized how hungry she was until the delectable flavors hit her tongue. As she chewed, she gazed out the rear window. A creek ran through the property a few yards away, its banks dotted by trees and bushes on either side. The view was actually quite serene.

A few bites later, angry voices, their words unclear, shattered the tranquility.

Cedena jumped up, tipping over her stool in her hurry to look out the front door. Sally and Will were in front of the livestock shelter. She was gripping Will's arm, her words now distinguishable.

"Don't, Will! Please!"

Will cast Sally aside with such force that she landed in a cloud of dust. By the time she had gotten up, Will had untied the mare, mounted her bareback, and was trotting down the driveway. The *clip-clop* of the horse's hoofs faded into the whoosh of the summer breeze in the pinyons. Sally dusted herself off and began unhitching the horse that had pulled the wagon.

Vivian joined Cedena. "What's going on?"

Cedena shook her head. "Something is very wrong here. Will just shoved Sally to the ground and took off on our rented mare. No saddle, no tools. How is he going to fix the broken buggy wheel without tools?"

Sally finished unhitching the draft horse from the wagon and led it behind the livestock shelter. Cedena moved to the rear window. Sally was giving the horse a drink from the creek.

Cedena returned to the table, and with Vivian's help, slid it nearer the window to keep an eye on Sally. By the time the horse had had its fill of water and Sally came through the front door, Cedena and Vivian had finished the first half of their sandwiches.

Cedena extended the remaining half of her sandwich to Sally. "Have some lunch."

Sally accepted the offer, plopped down on the bed, took a giant bite of the sandwich, and talked as she chewed. "Mmm . . . . I haven't tasted anything this good since . . . I left the Harvey service. They don't exactly serve Harvey House fare at the jail. Although Mrs. Rosenthal—she's the one who cooks for the prisoners—does a pretty good job with beef stew. Heavy on the potatoes, though." She took another oversized bite of sandwich, nearly demolishing it completely.

Vivian took out the oatmeal cookies, stood to face Sally, and held a cookie out to her. "Will isn't going to fix the broken wheel, is he?"

Sally reached for the cookie, but Vivian withdrew it.

"Is he?" Vivian repeated.

"Yes, he is!"

"Liar!" Vivian took a bite of the cookie and sat again on her stool.

Cedena rose and stared down at Sally. "Will rode out of here without any tools."

Sally's earnest gaze met Cedena's. "He's gone to get the tools, and then he'll fix the wheel. Honest!"

Vivian rose and stood beside Cedena. "Get them where?"

"At the wheelwright's down the road."

Vivian let out a hoot. "You actually think we'd believe that?"

"Will Adams isn't even supposed to be in this county," Cedena reminded Sally. "He's too smart to show himself to someone who'd surely turn him in to Sheriff Watts. Now tell us: What were you and Will arguing about just before he left? What was he planning to do that got you so upset? And why are you even hanging around with the likes of Will Adams? He treats you like the dirt he shoved you into just before he left."

"We want answers, not lies," Vivian warned.

Sally stood and started pacing. "Will has gone to Orin and Paul's ranch. He's going to try to get money from them in exchange for you two. I'm supposed to keep you here until he comes back with the money. Then Will and I are getting out of here."

Vivian confronted Sally, their faces inches apart. "How could you let him do that? If he hurts Paul, I'll never forgive you!"

Sally took a step back. "I couldn't stop him. Believe me, I tried!"

Cedena approached them and rested her hand gently on Sally's shoulder. "I believe you. What I don't understand is why you are wasting your time with the likes of Will Adams. You could do so much better."

Sally lowered her gaze. "I'm afraid of him."

Cedena withdrew her touch. "There's only one thing to do. We've got to get to the ranch as quickly as possible."

"But—"

"Come on. Let's get out of here."

CHAPTER 51

With Pedro building a barn several yards from the house, Orin was helping Paul build walls on his side of the ranch. He paused in his effort to load the wheelbarrow with adobe bricks and gazed at his side of the ranch. The walls weren't quite finished, but they were a lot farther along than on Paul's side. The wooden flooring was finished on Orin's side, too, with a secret opening beneath for storing valuables. The gold coins he and Paul hadn't spent yet on the ranch were hidden there. Orin hoped it wasn't too obvious. But how could it be? Besides being out of sight, even if someone knew where to remove the floorboards, all they would see was the loose dirt that covered the cash box.

Orin wiped the sweat from his forehead and returned to his task. As he hauled another wheelbarrow full of adobe bricks toward Paul, a lone rider on horseback trotted into the driveway and then slowed to a walk.

"Paul, we got company." Orin's pulse quickened.

Paul pushed back his Stetson. "I don't recognize the horse. Do you?"

Orin shook his head. As the rider slowly drew closer, recognition set in. "Will Adams. I thought he was long gone from these parts."

Will halted at the water trough, dismounted, and let his horse drink.

As Orin and Paul approached Will, he greeted them with a grin. "Bet you fellas didn't expect to see me here today. You're lookin' for your gals to come drivin' down the road, right?"

Orin exchanged glances with Paul and then focused again on Will. "Our gals are in town."

Will's grin widened. "No, they ain't. Ya mean you didn't know they were comin' to pay you a visit today?"

"What are you talking about?" Paul edged closer to Will.

"Your gals were on their way here in a buggy when they hit a hole and broke a wheel. My gal, Sally, and I came across 'em. I took the ladies to my hideout and told them to wait there while I fix the wheel. Then I came straight here to see you two. I figure those two ladies of yours oughta be worth whatever's left of that reward money you fellas got, if ya ever want to see them again."

Orin's heart stopped. "You kidnapped Cedena and Vivian and are holding them for ransom?"

Paul stepped forward. "You'll never get away with this!"

Will placed his hands on his pistols. "Don't come any closer. Don't make me draw my Colts. You know I'm not afraid to use them. Go and get me the money, and I'll take you to your girls."

Orin took a deep breath. "All right. But it will take a little time for me to dig up the money. Then, you'll have to take us to the girls before we pay you a single dime. Meanwhile, you and Paul wait on the patio, out of the sun."

Orin gestured for Paul and Will to follow him to the patio. Once there, Orin faced Will. "I'm curious. Why do you need *our* money? Not long ago, you got over a thousand dollars in reward money. What did you do with it?"

"Got in over my head with some card sharks." Will jabbed his finger into Orin's chest. "No tricks. Come back with the money. And don't you take too long, or you'll have to dig a grave for your brother, here."

Orin took a step back and turned to go, eager to get away from Will's foul odor. Will probably hadn't had a bath since the day he'd shot Bloody Burt. Poor Sally, living with the likes of him.

Behind the partially finished walls of his house, Orin lifted the loose floorboards and set them aside. He moved to his bedroll in the corner and found his pistol. Then he carefully peeked out again at Will and Paul. They were sitting side by side on the patio bench, and Will was actually laughing at something Paul had said.

Good. Orin needed time to figure a way out of this. It wasn't right to let a criminal deprive him and Paul of the money they needed for their future. Giving Will Adams their remaining cash would be the same as giving up plans for ranch houses, cattle, and marriage.

But Orin and Paul couldn't jeopardize the wellbeing of Cedena and Vivian, either. They were worth more than any amount of money. There had to be a way to deny Will Adams the money *and* provide for Cedena and Vivian's safety. Orin checked his pistol's cylinder. It was fully loaded. Was he going to have to shoot Will?

CHAPTER 52

Cedena held on for dear life, her arms wrapped about the painted pony's neck as it galloped toward the Young Ranch. Sally rode ahead of her, on the horse that had pulled Will's wagon. Behind Cedena, Vivian rode the other painted pony that had been kept in the shelter at Will's hideout. All three of them were riding astride, even though they were not wearing split skirts. It was much safer and faster, and saving time was crucial. So, with their skirts hiked up and blowing in the wind, the three were soon about an eighth of a mile from the ranch.

Sally slowed her horse to a walk and pulled off the road. She had warned Cedena and Vivian that they couldn't risk going down the driveway in plain sight; they must go in the back way. She had a plan to take Will by surprise, but she hadn't given any details.

"There won't be any danger to either of you," she had promised as she had mounted her horse, "but you must follow me closely and do exactly as I say when we get near the ranch." Cedena and Vivian had no choice but to trust her.

Cedena's heartbeat quickened as her pony followed Sally's horse through the desert, taking a path around juniper and cactus. Vivian remained close behind. When they were a few hundred feet from the ranch, Sally dismounted and signaled for the others to do the same. Carefully, she led her horse behind pinyons and junipers as she drew ever closer to the unfin-unfinished ranch houses and the patio in between. When they were about a hundred yards from the ranch houses in the cover of bushes and trees, Sally tethered her horse to a pinyon and whispered to Cedena and Vivian.

"Wait here. No talking."

Cedena watched Sally's movements as best she could, but the girl was soon obscured completely by foliage. Sweat trickled down Cedena's forehead. She dabbed it with her handkerchief and yearned for a glass of water, but they had left in such haste that they hadn't brought any along.

Minutes slipped by. Vivian fanned herself with her handkerchief. Her cheeks were quite pink from the heat and remained so despite her efforts to cool them.

When sufficient time had lapsed for Sally to reach the ranch, Cedena wrapped her pony's reins around a pinyon branch and started after her. Vivian did the same.

CHAPTER 53

"Orin? What's keepin' ya?" Will Adams called out from the patio.

"I'm coming." With his finger on the trigger of his pistol, he took a deep breath and walked out the open door, his gun pointed at Will's chest.

Will stood, hands going for his weapons.

"If you draw either of your guns, you're a dead man."

Will grinned sardonically. "Orin, you don't have the heart to shoot me."

"Try me."

Will's hands again started to move toward his guns.

Before Orin could pull his trigger, a shot rang out.

Will cried out in pain. His left hand clutched his right hand.

Sally emerged from behind the partial wall of Paul's house, a one-shot Derringer in her hand, and looked Will straight in the eye. "I couldn't let you do it."

Will glared at her, his expression one of excruciating pain. "Traitor!"

Orin kept his gun aimed at Will. "Paul, take his weapons."

Paul unbuckled Will's holster and stepped back.

As Orin lowered his gun, Cedena and Vivian emerged from behind Paul's house. Cedena ran to Orin as Vivian rushed to Paul.

Orin let his weapon fall to the ground and wrapped both arms tightly around Cedena.

She spoke into his ear. "We were so worried about you and Paul. Six weeks have gone by since we've seen you. Why didn't you at least send word that you were all right?"

Orin pulled back and gazed straight into Cedena's troubled amber eyes. "We *did* send word. You didn't get our notes?"

Cedena shook her head.

Orin pulled her into his embrace again. "I'm so sorry. Pedro was supposed to deliver them to you when he went to town a couple of weeks ago for supplies. I'll have a talk with him later. His English isn't good. He might not have understood. Right now, I think we'd better bind up Will's hand and take him to the doctor."

Cedena nodded. "What about Sally?"

Sally approached them. "Yes, what about me? You're gonna turn me in to the sheriff, aren't you?"

"Yes, I am." Orin pinned his gaze on her. "And I'm going to tell him how you saved me and my brother and Cedena and Vivian, so don't you fret."

"But I'm guilty of theft and of breaking out of jail."

Cedena placed her arm about Sally's shoulders. "I'll do my best to convince Sheriff Watts that you should be given leniency. It will all turn out all right. You can't run away from these troubles for the rest of your life, can you?"

Sally lowered her gaze and shook her head.

Vivian approached Sally. "Cedena's right. Own up to what you've done, bad *and* good, and then you can move on with a clean slate."

Sally gave a slight nod and cast a glance toward the desert. "The horse and ponies—we can't leave them tied out there." She took one step in that direction and then turned back. "I suppose I ought to tell you they were all stolen a couple of weeks back. Will took them from Rosenthal's spread."

"You little snitch!" Will started toward Sally. "I oughta—"

Paul drew one of Will's guns from his holster and pointed it at Will. "Stop right there or one of your own bullets will land in your foot. Sit down on the bench and don't move."

Will did as told.

Several minutes later, with Will's wounded hand wrapped, his wrists tied behind him, and his ankles tightly bound, Paul helped Orin lift Will into the back of their wagon.

"I'll get you two for this!" Will claimed as he struggled to find a comfortable sitting position. When Orin lifted Sally aboard, Will's threats expanded. "I'll get you, too, you little deserter. I ought to kill you for ruinin' my shootin' hand!" His rant continued, calling Sally several euphemisms for a fallen woman.

Orin mounted the wagon and stared down at Will. "I've heard enough from you for today." He removed his bandana from his neck and tied it around Will's mouth, silencing all but muffled protests.

With everyone aboard and livery horse and stolen animals tied to the back of the wagon, Orin started down the driveway.

~*~*~

Cedena sat with Sally on the rear-facing bench while Orin, Paul, and Vivian occupied the front bench. Before the wagon even reached the end of the driveway, Sally stood up.

"I can't do it! I can't go back there!"

Cedena grasped Sally firmly and forced her to sit again. "Now you listen here. You made mistakes in the past, but today you did the right thing. You *have* to go back and make things right with Sheriff Watts. Do you remember the words in the note you wrote to me? You said, 'I wish I could be good like you.' This is how to be good. Go to Sheriff Watts."

Sally slumped down and crossed her arms. Her lips drew a thin line and her legs constantly shifted their position. Every few minutes, she stood and stretched, causing Cedena concern that Sally might try to jump out of the moving wagon and run away, but during the two-hour ride, she made no move to escape.

Orin pulled to a stop in front of the sheriff's office and jail. When Will's feet had been untied, Orin and Paul escorted him inside. Close behind them, Cedena and Vivian ushered Sally through the door.

Sheriff Watts swung his boots off his desk and rose to his full six feet, his brows bulging as he focused on Will. "What the blazes are you doing in my county? I thought you were long gone from here."

Orin and Paul explained Will's attempt at kidnapping and extortion, told about the stolen horse and ponies, and asked for the doctor to be called to attend Will's wound.

The sheriff shook his head. "The doctor is miles from here tending a fellow who should have kept more distance between him and his bull. I'll see what I can do about that hand. I've patched up bullet wounds before. I oughta be able to do it again, even if Adams *is* a first-rate criminal. Put him in there." He indicated one of the two empty jail cells.

After the sheriff had locked Will in the cell, he turned to Sally. "As for you, young lady, you are in some mighty big trouble."

Cedena set her gaze on the lawman. "Sheriff, I know Sally has broken the law, but—"

Sheriff Watts' face reddened. "She sure as shootin' broke the law. She stole from the Harvey Girls, she broke out of jail, and who knows how many times she was an accomplice to crimes Adams committed?"

Orin stepped face to face with Watts. "Sheriff, Miss Pederson, here, is innocent until proven guilty. If you would do Miss Rossier the courtesy of listening to what she has to say, you'll have a better understanding of Miss Pederson's situation."

The sheriff took a deep breath, his focus on Cedena. "Go ahead, miss."

Cedena described the mistreatment of Sally at Will's hideout, her attempt to change Will's mind about kidnapping and extortion, and her success in saving four lives and returning three stolen animals. "Surely she deserves leniency in light of the mistreatment she endured and for her helpful actions today."

Sheriff Watts slid his gaze to Sally and sighed. "Only the judge can grant leniency, but I'll do what I can. Until your case is tried, you're staying right there." He pointed to the empty cell next to Will. "And if you cause even a speck of trouble, you can forget about leniency."

"Yes, sir."

The sheriff locked Sally behind bars and returned to face Orin. "Take those stolen animals down to Rosenthal. He'll be glad to see them." His gaze swept to Paul, Cedena, and Vivian. "All four of you could be called as witnesses for the Pederson and Adams trials, so don't leave the county. Understood?"

Cedena nodded, as did the others. As she walked out of Sheriff Watts's office, she silently prayed that Will and Sally would be treated fairly by judge and jury.

CHAPTER 54

Nine days later

Late in the afternoon, Cedena, Orin, Paul, and Vivian stepped out of the courthouse. Cedena gazed up into the clear blue sky, drew a deep breath of fresh air, and let it out slowly, releasing with it the worries that had accompanied her testimonies in Will and Sally's trials.

Orin grasped her hand and parked his gaze on her, lines stretching across his forehead. "Are you all right?"

"I'm just so thankful the trials are over!" Cedena started down the courthouse steps.

Orin's mouth drew upward. "I'm glad that son-of-a-gun Adams got himself a new home in the penitentiary."

"And I'm glad Sally won't spend any more time behind bars."

Vivian spoke up. "I wonder what she'll do now."

Paul shook his head. "Whatever it is, it looks like she won't be coming back to San Miguel County once she rides out of here on the train tomorrow morning."

Orin turned to Paul. "We'd better start for the ranch if we want to get there before dark."

Paul grinned. "Or we could go to dinner with Vivian and Cedena, stay overnight, and drive back tomorrow."

"I like that idea!" Vivian smiled broadly. "After all, Cedena and I have hardly seen you two all summer long. And you know what happened when too much time passed between visits."

Orin groaned. "Kidnapping, threats at gunpoint, and trials. All right, you two, we'll wait until tomorrow to drive home." As the two couples started down National Street toward Orin and Paul's wagon, a man with drooping shoulders approached them.

Cedena blinked twice. Was she seeing things? When the man was but a few feet away, her heart skipped a beat and her feet stopped dead. "David! I thought for a moment my eyes were playing tricks on me."

David quickly closed the distance between them, drew her into his arms, and held her against his chest, which quivered. After a long, tight hug, he released her and gazed straight into her eyes with his red-rimmed blue ones. "I have bad news. Father is dead, killed in a mine cave-in last week."

"No!" It couldn't be. She'd mourned his death once. Must she go through the loss again so soon, this time for real? Moisture blurred her vision.

David offered her his handkerchief. "I buried Father in Mt. Pisgah Cemetery, just outside Cripple Creek. It's a real nice resting place for him. I'll take you there sometime, if you want."

Cedena shook her head and dabbed at her tears. She didn't want to see Father's resting place. She wanted to see *him*. But it was too late. He was gone from her life for good this time.

Now, it was just her and David and a mother who pretended Cedena didn't exist and didn't know David was alive.

Orin extended his hand to David. "Sorry for your loss. I'm Orin Young, Cedena's fiancé. And these two are my brother, Paul, and his intended, Vivian Duncan."

"Pleased to meet you." David shook hands all around.

Cedena returned David's handkerchief. "We're about to go and get some dinner at the Harvey House. You'll join us, won't you?" She'd lost her appetite, but the others needed nourishment, and she wanted to spend as much time with Orin as possible before he and Paul left town for who knew how long.

"You sure it's all right?" David glanced at the others.

Vivian offered her winning smile. "All right? It's more than all right. Cedena's like a sister to me, so you're like a brother I hadn't met until now."

Orin pointed down the street. "Our wagon is that-a-way. Let's go. I'm hungry."

~*~*~

Over dinner, Cedena learned David had arrived that morning on the seven-thirty train.

"I thought I'd find you working here." He stabbed a piece of roast beef. "The head waitress told me you had already gone to the courthouse to testify in a trial."

Cedena broke apart a fresh dinner roll, the only thing she had an appetite for. "Sorry I missed you. I left a few minutes before the train was due."

David smiled for the first time. "I got good service from Rachel." He glanced across the dining room to the section where Rachel was assigned and beamed his smile her way.

Vivian giggled. "Uh, oh. Could another Harvey Girl be in danger of losing her job?"

Cedena shook her head. "She's got four more months on her contract, same as us."

Orin tucked into his mashed potatoes and then focused on David. "How long will you be in town?"

David shrugged.

"You're going back to the mine soon, aren't you?" Cedena spread butter on her roll.

"I'm not going back. No more mining for me." David reached for his water glass.

Paul paused on his way to a bite of turkey. "What do you plan to do?"

"Don't know. I've got my savings from the mine, and Father's, too." He turned to Cedena. "I'll split Father's savings with you. That's the other reason I came here. At least it's not all bad news."

Orin cut into a chicken thigh. "If you're looking for work, Paul and I could use another hand out at our ranch. It doesn't pay like mining, but it's not nearly as dangerous, either."

"And you work in the sunshine all day." Cedena bit into her roll.

David set down his glass. "I was planning to head to California."

Paul filled his fork with turkey dressing. "There's a spread for sale next to Orin's and mine, a couple of hours' drive from town. Come out and take a look before you leave. It could be a good investment for you, and you'd be ranching right next door to your sister after she marries Orin in December."

David grew thoughtful. "I suppose I could put off going west for a day or two."

Orin scooped up the last of his mashed potatoes. "Good! Where are you staying? Paul and I will pick you up tomorrow morning."

"I checked into the Farmer's Hotel on Moreno Street this afternoon."

"That's where we're staying! We'll be out front with our wagon at seven."

~*~*~

When Orin and Paul brought their wagon to the front of the hotel the next morning, David was waiting for them. He didn't say much during the drive to the ranch as Orin and Paul explained their plan to start by raising sheep and eventually adding steers. And David wasn't saying much now as he gazed across the expanse of desert adjacent to the Young Ranch.

Orin pointed in the distance. "There's a nice creek that runs through there. I'll unhitch the team, and then we can saddle up and ride out there so you can see what you'd be getting."

David gave a nod and began helping Orin while Paul unloaded supplies from the wagon. Half an hour later, as the morning began to heat up, Orin and David mounted the saddled horses and rode out, leaving Paul to work on the walls of his house with Pedro's help.

After a few minutes of cantering between pinyon and cacti, Orin halted at the side of the creek, dismounted, and let his horse drink. "This is clean mountain water; flows all year. You can graze sheep or steers here. I think you'll do fine in the ranching business on this land."

David climbed down, knelt by the creek, cupped his hands, and tasted the water. With a nod, he rose and sauntered past his horse to study the landscape. "I don't doubt what you say, but I don't think I'm ready to settle into the ranching life."

Orin's hopes fell. Cedena would be disappointed. "I understand. It's hard work. You've got to want it if you're going to succeed." He climbed into his saddle.

David did the same and followed him back to the Young Ranch.

CHAPTER 55

Three months later
November 28, 1894

The day before Thanksgiving, as Cedena headed for the dormitory after the lunch shift, one question lingered on her mind. What did she have to be thankful for? Certainly not the fact that she hadn't heard from David since he'd left for California at the end of August. Not a day had gone by in the past three months that she hadn't thought of him, worried about him, and prayed for him. Why couldn't he at least have sent her his new address?

With a heavy heart, Cedena headed up the stairs and into her room. Vivian was sitting on her bed reading as usual, but instead of ignoring her, she slapped her book shut and beamed a smile at her that was wider than the Sangre de Cristo Mountain Range.

"I have something for you that will make you *very* happy."

"What? A letter from David?"

"How did you know?" Vivian's face fell as she pulled an envelope from inside the back cover of her book and offered it to Cedena.

"It was just a lucky guess." Cedena sat on her bed, slit open the envelope, and unfolded the plain white paper.

November 21, 1894
Dear Cedena,

Forgive me for not writing sooner. I have been very busy fishing out of San Diego. I bought a boat and nets and make a good haul every time out. A commercial fisherman can make plenty of money here if he knows where the fish are running.

Please write to me in care of Mrs. Garcia on Fifth Street in San Diego and tell me your news. Have you heard from Mother?

Affectionately,
David

Cedena folded the letter and slipped it back into its envelope.

"Well?" Vivian stared at Cedena. "Is everything all right with your brother?"

Cedena nodded. "Yes. David is fishing out of San Diego and evidently is quite successful."

"That ought to make your day a little happier."

Cedena nodded and suppressed the urge to dance around the room. Instead, she got out pen and paper and sat down to write a response.

Dear David,

I am glad to hear your fishing business is doing well. I had been wondering about you and hoping to hear something.

Please come to my wedding. Remember, it is being held on Christmas Day. It would mean so much to me if you were here to give me away. There is absolutely *no* chance of Mother showing up. I have not heard a word from her directly, only what news Aunt Nancy and Uncle James share. Take care of yourself, and come here if at all possible.

Your loving sister,

Cedena

She sealed her letter in an envelope and headed for the post office.

CHAPTER 56

Sunday, December 23

The first thought on Cedena's mind when she awoke was that she and Vivian had only two more days under contract, and then they would be free to marry Orin and Paul on Christmas Day. It had been a long six months since their betrothal, but Orin and Paul had needed the time to make everything ready. And ready it was.

The brothers had brought Cedena and Vivian out to the ranch a week ago to see their finished homes. Each house was the same size with only one room—a great room that was a living area, dining area, and kitchen. A loft served as the sleeping area. When more rooms were needed, they would be built onto the ends of the great rooms. The plan was simple yet affordable.

The homes were *not* identical, though. Inside, each bore the preferences of its bride-to-be. Orin had constructed a bed, dining table with two chairs, and a love seat, all of pine with a natural finish as Cedena had preferred. Paul had painted Vivian's furniture her favorite color, yellow, and instead of a love seat, he had built two rocking chairs.

Cedena could hardly wait to start life as Mrs. Orin Young, rancher's wife. Vivian had expressed the same sentiments about her upcoming marriage to Paul. In fact, with so much work awaiting all four of them at the ranch, Cedena and Vivian had both turned down the rail passes they were entitled to at the end of their contract. Their honeymoons would take place on the ranch.

But before a marriage or honeymoon, Cedena must make certain all plans were in order for the Christmas Day nuptials at the Methodist Episcopal Church following the morning service. Too bad no one from her family would be here. She had accepted long ago that Mother was opposed. Her biggest disappointment was that she had heard nothing from David. She pushed those thoughts aside, got out of bed, and woke Vivian. By half-past ten, they were headed to church.

Cedena talked as they made their way along Blanchard Street. "Last week at the ranch, while you and Paul were off by yourselves for a minute, Orin asked me the strangest thing. He wanted to know if I would be upset if our marriage were performed by a Justice of the Peace rather than a clergyman."

Vivian's head snapped around. "You're kidding! Paul asked me the exact same thing! He said ministers get very busy this time of year and things change when you least expect it. He doesn't want anything to stand in the way of me becoming his wife on December twenty-fifth."

"That's exactly what Orin told *me*!"

"Why would they say those things?"

"I don't know. I had already intended to confirm our plans with Reverend Ingram this morning after the service. We'll just have to wait until then to find out if something unexpected will force us to change our arrangements."

The service included Cedena's favorite Christmas Carols—"Silent Night," "What Child Is This?," "I Heard the Bells on Christmas Day," and "Away in a Manger." On the way out the door, followed closely by Vivian, Cedena paused to shake Reverend Ingram's hand.

"You're still planning to perform our double wedding after church on Christmas Day, aren't you?"

The reverend clasped both his hands around Cedena's. "Don't you spend one minute fretting. The double wedding will be the memory of a lifetime that you brides deserve!" He released her and shook Vivian's hand, offering a confident smile.

Cedena drew a deep breath and headed down the steps with Vivian. "I guess we can put worries about the wedding aside and see to other preparations."

"I need to finish taking in the waist of the traveling suit you gave me to get married in." Vivian sighed. "I keep thinking it's going to look odd, me in a suit and you in your beautiful blue dress. I know we chose to wear clothes we already owned to save on expenses, but maybe I should have spent some of my tip money for a nice dress rather than sending it to Mother."

Cedena put her arm about Vivian's waist. "Don't give it another thought. The fellows appreciate our frugality, and if anyone doesn't like the way we look when we take our wedding vows, they are just plain wrong for finding fault."

After church, Cedena and Vivian ate dinner and then returned to the dormitory to work on packing their trunks. Cedena made certain her blue dress was clean and pressed; then she began going through her trunk to eliminate anything she no longer needed. When she came to a stack of old letters and saw Uncle James's handwriting on his last mailing a month ago, her heart broke again over the words he had written. No, her mother would not be coming to her wedding. She wouldn't hear of it. He was sorry he and Aunt Nancy could not get away to be with her on her wedding day. Financial troubles had sapped them of every extra penny.

Cedena lowered the lid and glanced over at Vivian, who was standing in front of the wardrobe mirror holding the suit skirt up to her waist. "That suit will look better on you than it did on me."

Vivian reached for a hanger. "Thanks, and thank you again for giving it to me." She hung the skirt in the closet and glanced at the clock on the bed stand. "It's already time for supper and I still have packing to do."

"I'll help you with it after we eat." Cedena headed out the door.

A few minutes after they returned from supper, a knock sounded on the door. Vivian opened it. "Miss Upton, come in."

The head waitress stepped inside and glanced around the room. "How are you two brides doing with your packing?"

Cedena patted the lid of her trunk. "All packed. I've only left out what I need for tomorrow and for Christmas Day."

Miss Upton turned to Vivian. "And you?"

"I have a few more things to pack in my trunk, and then I'll be ready, too."

"Wonderful! Now I have some news for you. Mr. Harvey has requested that the Montezuma be reopened for the holidays for him and his entourage. They will be at the Montezuma tomorrow afternoon—he and all his family and a dozen friends. Mr. Harvey has always taken a personal interest in his employees, and when he learned that tomorrow is the last day of your contracts and that both of you are to be married on Christmas Day, he asked especially for you to come to the Montezuma and serve the midday meal so he can personally wish you well."

Cedena's pulse raced. Everyone knew Mr. Harvey was a perfectionist and could fly off the handle if something didn't meet his high standards. But if he had asked for her and Vivian specifically, then they had to go. It was in the contract.

"When do we leave for Hot Springs?"

"And when will we be back?" Vivian wanted to know.

"You'll serve breakfast here as usual and then the three of us will take the nine-thirty train to Hot Springs. We can return on the afternoon run that arrives here at half-past four. See you tomorrow."

CHAPTER 57

On the train to Hot Springs, Cedena tried to calm her nerves by taking deep breaths. Getting married was going to be a cinch compared to serving Fred Harvey. What if she spilled something or got yelled at? Stories had been told that if he found a spot on a glass or a piece of silverware, he would yank the tablecloth right off the table and send everything flying to the floor. She never thought she'd wish she were spending the day in Las Vegas rather than at the Montezuma, the one place she wanted to see more than any other.

Too soon, the train came to a stop at the Hot Springs Depot. Miss Upton and Vivian led the way out of the passenger car with Cedena close behind. The weather was cloudy and nippy, and snowflakes drifted slowly to the ground as the three of them walked from the depot to the Montezuma. When they arrived at the front door, Miss Upton paused and turned to Cedena and Vivian.

"Are you ready to meet Mr. Harvey?"

Cedena was too scared to speak. Vivian must have been, too, for both gave a silent nod.

Miss Upton pulled the door open and then stepped aside, motioning them through.

A mild scent of Christmas spices mingled with fresh pine hung in the air as they stepped into a world of beautiful wood paneling and furniture. The reception desk was huge and ornate, made of carved oak with pillars at either end reaching to a vaulted ceiling. Around the pillars was pine roping accented with huge red bows. Pine swags, also tied with red bows, decorated the front of the desk. Behind it were a couple of hundred wooden mailboxes, all empty.

Against the wall beyond the reception desk rose a gigantic fireplace lit with a glowing log. In front of it was a grouping of plump russet leather chairs and a matching sofa. But it was the people standing by the fire and sitting on the furniture that took Cedena's breath away. There were Uncle James and Aunt Nancy. He was holding in his hands his old straw boater. The old green feather was still stuck in the black grosgrain hat band. And there was David, and beside him, Mother.

Orin, Paul, Alice, and Matthew were there, too. With them also was an older couple who bore so much resemblance to Orin and Paul they had to be the boys' parents. And there was an older woman who must have been Vivian's mother, for she practically flew into Vivian's arms.

Cedena's eyes blurred as she all but ran across the polished hardwood floor and into Uncle James's arms. "I can't believe you're here!" she managed between sobs.

He held her close, gave her an extra-hard squeeze, and then put her at arm's length. "Your mother needs a hug, too."

Mother stepped forward. Tears spilled down her cheeks. "Forgive me, Cedena. I reckon I never should have shut you out like I did. I love you."

Cedena wrapped her arms about Mother. David joined them, enfolding them both in a hug. For the first time in a long time, a sense of peace rose within Cedena.

When the hug ended, Mother's gaze met Cedena's. "Isn't it wonderful, how David's amnesia went away in time for your wedding?"

Cedena caught a warning look from David and bit her tongue. She'd ask him later what this amnesia story was all about.

Aunt Nancy and Uncle James joined them. Aunt Nancy's face beamed, despite the circles beneath her eyes. "If not for Orin, Paul, and David, your Uncle James, your mother, and I wouldn't be here. They made all the arrangements for our train tickets."

Uncle James smiled. "It didn't cost us a single penny!"

Aunt Nancy edged closer to Cedena. "You look wonderful! Diddle-de-dum! The Harvey life must agree with you."

At mention of the Harvey name, Cedena gasped. Where was Miss Upton? Where were Fred Harvey and his entourage?

Orin must have seen the panic on her face, for he hurried to her side. "Looking for someone? Fred Harvey, maybe? He's not here—won't be here for another two days. It was a ruse to get you and Vivian to come up on the train this morning. Mr. Harvey *did* order his personal staff to open the Montezuma two days ahead of time for our guests and our wedding tomorrow. We'll be married in front of the fireplace by the Justice of the Peace."

Paul, Vivian, and her mother had joined them by now and Paul continued the explanation. "Justice Carsten is coming up on the nine-thirty train tomorrow morning to perform our double wedding ceremony. The preacher couldn't make it because he has to deliver a Christmas Day message at his church back in Las Vegas. Hope you ladies don't mind."

Vivian and Cedena exchanged glances and then Vivian focused on Paul. "Mind? How could we mind?" She gave Paul a quick hug.

Cedena conjured up immediate concerns. "But what about our wedding clothes? All our belongings are back at the dormitory."

Miss Upton approached. "Don't worry about anything you left in your room. It will all be here on the next run. Your neighbors, Rachel, Georgina, and Franny, promised to see that everything got packed up and loaded, including my own wedding dress."

Mr. Vetsch seemed to come from out of nowhere. He placed his arm about Miss Upton's shoulders. "Miss Upton and I are getting married tomorrow, too. Our ceremony will take place after your double wedding."

Vivian's eyes widened. "I can't believe it! Three weddings on Christmas Day!"

"Congratulations!" Cedena beamed at Miss Upton and Mr. Vetsch while they exchanged loving smiles. "Now, tell me something. How did you keep so many secrets?" She turned to Orin. "And how could you have possibly paid the fare for our relatives to come all the way from up north?"

Orin beckoned to the couple Cedena assumed were his parents and they came to stand beside him. "Cedena, my mother, Ophelia, and my father, Isaac. Mother, Father, meet your soon-to-be daughter-in-law, Cedena."

Ophelia took Cedena's hand in her pudgy one and leaned in to kiss her cheek. "Welcome to the family, Cedena. I'm sure you'll be a wonderful wife to Orin from all he's told me about you."

Isaac grinned. "Pleased to meet you, Cedena. You must be one very special lady for Orin to convince me to come all the way down here and to bring his sister and brother-in-law, besides."

Orin's gaze shifted from his father to Cedena. "Father sold some property in Kenosha to buy the tickets."

Paul spoke up. "And Orin and I had some reward money we hadn't spent on the ranch. Besides that, Mr. Vetsch put pressure on Mr. Harvey to get everyone a reduced fare since neither of you brides accepted the rail passes you were entitled to at the end of your contract."

Cedena turned to Miss Upton. "Will Vivian and I be serving meals to our folks today?"

"No, no. Mr. Harvey's private staff will do the cooking and serving."

Matthew and Alice, who had remained aloof, now approached.

Alice took Cedena's hand in hers. "I'm so glad you're going to be my sister-in-law."

Matthew's gaze paused tenderly on Alice and then pivoted to Cedena. "And about six months from now, you'll be an aunt to our first child."

Cedena smiled. "Congratulations, Alice! I'm sure you'll be an excellent mother." She glanced up at Matthew. "As for the child's father, I expect you'll probably spoil your child rotten!"

Matthew shook his head vigorously. "I'm leaving that to the child's grandparents and honorary grandparents, your aunt and uncle."

A liveried gentleman appeared carrying a tray of punch cups filled with amber liquid. "Wassail, anyone? It's Mr. Harvey's favorite temperance recipe."

Miss Upton made a sweeping gesture. "Let's all enjoy some beverage and conversation by the fire."

CHAPTER 58

"I now pronounce you husband and wife. Gentlemen, you may kiss your brides."

Orin tenderly pressed his lips to Cedena's. The contact, though brief, sent warmth to her very core. It was all she could do to keep from pulling him into another, longer kiss.

Relatives gathered around Orin, Cedena, Paul, and Vivian, shaking the fellows' hands, kissing the brides' cheeks, and offering well-wishes and teasing remarks. In the midst of it all, Cedena caught sight of an older, suited gentleman rounding the corner of the registry desk and stepping confidently up to the gathering.

"Excuse me. Which of you are Mrs. Orin Young and Mrs. Paul Young?" His deep-set blue eyes searched the faces.

"I'm Mrs. Orin Young, and she is Mrs. Paul Young." Cedena pointed to Vivian. "But who are you?"

"I'm Mr. Fred Harvey."

Cedena gasped. Her cheeks burned. The much-feared head of the Harvey Company was standing mere inches away. But he wasn't due here until tomorrow. What had brought him to the Montezuma today?

Mr. Harvey offered a modest smile. "I don't mean to interrupt your celebration. I simply wanted to deliver these." He pulled two sealed ecru envelopes from his vest pocket and handed one to Cedena and the other to Vivian. "I take a real interest in my employees, so since I was in the area, I couldn't resist the opportunity to stop by personally and wish you a very happy and blessed future, and provide coupons for dinner the next time you're in Las Vegas. Merry Christmas, everyone!" With a slight nod, he pivoted on his heel and strode away.

Thank yous and Christmas greetings trailed after him in response.

Cedena turned to Orin. "Sir, would you please take me to the Young Ranch?"

He grinned. "With pleasure!"

~*~*~

On the long drive out to the ranch, Cedena slipped her left hand out of her fur muff to admire the wedding ring Orin had placed on her finger. It was a wide band of yellow gold set with New Mexico turquoise. How thoughtful of him to remember her fascination with turquoise in the Territorial Building at the Fair.

Much later, Orin pulled to a stop in front of the ranch, got out of the wagon, and lifted Cedena down as Paul helped Vivian out of the back.

At the door, Orin lifted Cedena into his arms, carried her across the threshold, and set her gently on her feet. The cabin was cold, but Orin's arm about her chased the chill away as he led her to a window and swung open the salt-cedar shutter.

"Do you see that mountain way off in the distance?"

Cedena nodded.

"Even that tall peak is not big enough to hold all the love I have for you."

Cedena turned to him and wrapped her arms about his neck. "Oh, Orin. Between us, we have mountains of love!" She placed her lips over his, determined to scale those mountains one lingering kiss at a time.

THE END

AUTHOR'S NOTES

Historical fiction sometimes makes the reader wonder where the history leaves off and the fiction begins. I'll try to define the difference in this story.

The World's Columbian Exposition of 1893 was a true, spectacular event that took place in Chicago. Many pharmaceutical businesses had a presence there, but Paxton Pharmaceuticals is fictional.

The buildings, displays, and Midway Plaisance were portrayed accurately, as were the storm that damaged the tethered balloon and the stranding of fairgoers on the pier after the Independence Day fireworks. As to who untangled the balloon after the storm, that was totally made up.

The Harvey Girls were portrayed as accurately as possible, but little information was available regarding the Raton and Las Vegas Harvey Eating Houses in 1893-1894. It is true that a Harvey Girl in Las Vegas fell into a pit and sustained minor injuries. It is also true that the American Railway Union held a train hostage in Las Vegas for several days at the end of June 1894, and the Harvey Girls fed 250 passengers during that time.

It is true that a Harvey Girl stole from her fellow employees, but the location and circumstances were completely different from those in this story, which were a figment of the author's imagination.

The Montezuma, which had been operated by Fred Harvey for the Atchison, Topeka, and Santa Fe Railroad, closed in

September of 1893 due to the severe financial crisis. Following September 1893, the Montezuma was open seasonally from May to September. There is no historical information concerning Fred Harvey reopening the Montezuma for himself and his family in December of 1894, but it made for a good story.

As for Las Vegas, New Mexico, and its Harvey Eating House, some liberties have been taken. For certain, a small lunchroom existed in Las Vegas in 1883 prior to the famous La Casteñeda that replaced it in 1899. I have given that small lunchroom a dining room for story purposes.

ABOUT DONNA WINTERS

Donna Winters grew up in Upstate New York, moved to Michigan in 1971, and then to New Mexico in 2015. She began penning novels in 1982 while working full time for an electronics company in Grand Rapids, Michigan.

She resigned her full-time job in 1984 following a contract offer for her first book, *For the Love of Roses*. Since then, she has written several novels for various publishers, including Thomas Nelson Publishers, Zondervan Publishing House, Guideposts, and Bigwater Publishing LLC. Her nonfiction writing has been published by Chalfont House.

Her husband, Fred, a retired American History teacher, shares her enthusiasm for history. Together, they visit historical sites, restored villages, and museums, purchasing books and reference materials and taking photos.

Mountains of Love is Donna's first novel to include settings in the Southwest.

MORE DONNA WINTERS TITLES

If you enjoyed *Mountains of Love*, be sure to check out Donna Winters' other titles. You can find them at:

GreatLakesRomances.com

Historical Fiction:

- ❖ *Mackinac* (Mackinac Trilogy Book 1)
- ❖ *The Captain and the Widow* (Mackinac Trilogy Book 2)
- ❖ *Sweethearts of Sleeping Bear Bay* (Mackinac Trilogy Book 3)
- ❖ *Charlotte of South Manitou Island* (Lighthouse Trilogy Book 1)
- ❖ *Aurora of North Manitou Island* (Lighthouse Trilogy Book 2)
- ❖ *Bridget of Cat's Head Point* (Lighthouse Trilogy Book 3)
- ❖ *Queen City Candy Shoppe* (Queen City Duology Book 1)
- ❖ *Trail Ride by the Yadkin River* (Queen City Duology Book 2)
- ❖ *A Time to Love* (Fayette Trilogy Book 1)
- ❖ *A Time to Laugh* (Fayette Trilogy Book 2)
- ❖ *A Time to Leave* (Fayette Trilogy Book 3)
- ❖ *Unlikely Duet* (Butterfly Duology Book 1)

- ❖ *Butterfly Come Home* (Butterfly Duology Book 2)
- ❖ *Elizabeth of Saginaw Bay* (Standalone title)
- ❖ *Jenny of L'Anse Bay* (Standalone title)
- ❖ *Isabelle's Inning* (Standalone title)
- ❖ *Bluebird of Brockport—A Novel of the Erie Canal* (Standalone title)

Contemporary Fiction

- ❖ *For the Love of Roses* (Standalone title)
- ❖ *Saving Mossy Point—in the Fifty-First State of Superior* (Standalone title)

Nonfiction:

- ❖ *Adventures with Vinnie*
- ❖ *Picturing Fayette*

If you enjoyed *Mountains of Love*, please consider posting a review on Amazon, Goodreads, or your favorite book review site. Thank you!

Find all of Donna Winters' titles at:

GreatLakesRomances.com